Innocents in London

Sheila Rainey

all Best Wishes

Sheila Rainey

Heddon
Publishing

Second edition published in 2022 by Heddon Publishing.

Paperback ISBN 978-1-913166-58-8
Ebook ISBN 978-1-913166-59-5

Cover design by Simon Hatchard-Parr

www.heddonpublishing.com
www.facebook.com/heddonpublishing
@PublishHeddon

About the Author

A music lover, Sheila Rainey has worked with major orchestras and conductors, including the Philharmonia, English Chamber Orchestra, and the BBC Academy, attending them at all concerts in the UK and abroad. While with BBC Publications she prepared printed programmes for concerts, commissioning and editing programme notes. A lifelong lover of literature, in her spare time she contributed articles and stories for house and local magazines.

A road accident in 1981 resulted in serious leg injuries and an inability to work for several months. She then obtained work as receptionist in naturalist Gilbert White's Museum in Selborn. During the winter months, she catalogued the Holt White archives, among which were the series of letters from Gilbert White's niece Mary to her brother Thomas Holt White, as described in the Preface. She prepared a transcription of the letters for an M.Phil. degree, awarded in 1990.

Sheila moved to Eastbury, near Lambourn, carrying out freelance work for a Newbury publisher, Countryside Books, editing, proofreading and indexing. Failing sight forced her to relinquish this work. It was in Eastbury that she started her Shefford series of detective novels. After moving to Froxfield, she continued writing the Shefford novels, and it was here that *Innocents in London* was born. Sheila now lives in Kathleen Chambers House, a care home for the blind and partially-sighted. Despite sight problems, she continued during the Covid lockdowns to revise *Innocents in London*, the Shefford series, and to write *Alec in Blunderland - Alice's Adventures in Wonderland* as viewed by a grumpy complaining old man. She hopes to celebrate her 97th birthday in August, and intends to continue writing so long as wits and sight permit.

To the memory of my parents,
sister Jean, and brother James

Preface

On behalf of The Society for Superseding the Necessity of Climbing Boys [child chimney sweeps], in September 1803 The Gentleman's Magazine published an account of a four year old boy sold for eight guineas by a beggar-woman to a Yorkshire chimney sweep. Untrained, the child was taken by an older boy to sweep a chimney and left unsupervised. He fell, suffering severe bruising. His plight came to the attention of the aristocratic Strickland family of Boynton Hall. Impressed by his refined looks and speech they took him into their home. He showed an astonishing familiarity with the customs of upper class life. Though too young to know his name and address he informed the Stricklands his mother was dead, his father abroad and that he had been cared for by an uncle and aunt. The beggar-woman had taken him while he played in his garden. The Stricklands believed he had been either abducted or betrayed by unscrupulous relatives. They hoped the account would help trace his family.

Among the letters of the naturalist Gilbert White's niece Mary White to her brother is one dated 1819 which gives the sequel. Mary learned from relatives of the Stricklands that when no one claimed the boy he was named John Pendart and 'brought up to the sea service', by that time 'employed in the Mercantile way'. As was the custom then, John may have been as young as eleven or twelve when sent to sea; a seaman's life in the early nineteenth century during the Napoleonic wars was not the ideal career for a seemingly aristocratic boy. What if despite treachery John had been restored to his family? I have attempted to show how this may have happened after John's escape from the sweep and his many adventures alone in London; also those of his father as he searches London for him.

Though based on a factual event, the action transferred from Yorkshire to the London of 1803, all characters are fictitious, with the exception of Dr James Black, with whom Edward Maltravers becomes acquainted on the journey from the Cape of Good Hope to England. His character is based on that of another Gilbert White relative, his nephew Dr John White who from 1801 to 1803 practised as a surgeon with the East India Company in Fort St George, Madras and briefly at the EIC sanatorium for senior officials in Penang. His Journal, which I have transcribed and is now with the Hampshire Record Office, Winchester, describes in outspoken terms conditions in the EIC, medical inefficiency, and his opinion of the British officials governing Indian territory annexed by the EIC, the infancy of the British Raj. After various travels John White returned to England, where he had a practice in London.

ONE

Seasonal mist added ethereal beauty to the Maltravers estate gardens. Trees and shrubs glowed softly in the hazy morning sun. Dew bejewelled lawns and flower beds richly coloured with autumn blooms. The Hall, dating to Tudor times and added to by generations of Maltravers stood in dignified splendour, beyond its walls the Thames flowed shimmering silver through the Surrey countryside as yet undefiled by the industrialism wreaking havoc on England's green and, for those not living in poverty, still pleasant land. The year was 1803, the monarch ailing was George the Third. All beauty outside the Hall, inside the seeds of treachery and betrayal were soon to germinate.

In the breakfast room Robert Maltravers slumped over the table staring morosely into his coffee cup, his plate of kidneys and lamb cutlets untouched. Dissipation flawed once handsome features, now haggard after another late and unsuccessful night at the gaming tables. Seated opposite him his wife Sophie listlessly peeled a quail's egg, her face admirers described as beautiful made less so by the disconsolate twist of her sensual mouth. Her grey morning gown was tightly laced, raising to prominence partially exposed breasts which no longer had charms for Robert and even less so for the butler Phillips as he entered the room with a salver containing a letter. He averted disdainful eyes as he presented the salver to Robert who peevishly snatched the letter, dismissing the butler with an abrupt wave of a hand. Recalling the courteous thanks he would have received from his master - Edward Maltravers, not his boorish brother – Phillips slightly inclined his head, as he left the room exchanging rueful grimaces with the attendant maid who stood silently by the breakfast counter ready to replenish plates or refill coffee cups when imperiously summoned.

"Anything of interest or another bill?" enquired Sophie as Robert broke the seal and unfolded the letter. He grunted; shrugging her shoulders she peeled another egg, becoming alert as with an exultant oath Robert sat upright in his chair.

"Well?" she demanded.

With a brusque jerk of his head Robert dismissed the maid, then as the door closed replied, his voice hoarse with excitement:

"Edward is dead!"

No regret, jubilation only for the loss of his brother. He continued with more animation than Sophie had ever known in him. "The Indiaman Prospero bringing him home from Madras sank off the Cape with the loss of crew and passengers." He tossed the letter to Sophie. She read it, then silence descended as they considered the consequences for themselves, with Sophie the first to voice their thoughts.

"Presumably John inherits everything?"

Robert scowled. "After our last financial embarrassment Edward made it brutally clear he had settled our debts for the last time, that should he predecease me I need expect nothing from his will." Furiously he banged a fist on the table, causing the dishes to clatter. "Everything to a five year old brat! Healthy too, God rot him."

"But we are his only relatives, now legally his guardians." The look that accompanied the seemingly innocuous words gave them a meaning obvious even to Robert's torpid brain.

"True, if he ...dies, as Edward's only kin we automatically inherit." Abruptly he pushed back his chair. "Morning room, we cannot talk here, the servants will be shortly in to clear away the breakfast things."

He led the way, no giving precedence to a female for Robert. Not yet thirty his once slim figure had thickened from an excess of food and alcohol, his only exercise riding with the hounds and game shooting. Several years his junior Sophie still retained the beauty that trapped philandering Robert into marriage, refusing her favours until safely his wife. A hard beauty, that of a woman determined on her own way regardless of others, Robert had seemed a splendid catch, the younger son of wealthy landed gentry. His capture was an achievement for one of six daughters of a Fleet Street publisher with five sons to settle in careers. That Robert was a notorious wastrel and rake was of little consequence; having lovers of her own Sophie ignored his many infidelities. His whores were welcome to his grunting lunges, intent only on his own satisfaction. But she had not anticipated how quickly he would dissipate his considerable inheritance from his father, bringing them to the verge of bankruptcy.

Then salvation; a temporary escape from the Kensington lodgings to which Robert's profligacy had reduced them, escape from dunning tradesmen to the spacious comfort of Maltravers Hall with its free board. With his Company of Light Dragoons Edward Maltravers had been sent to India to assist Arthur Wellesley in his wars against the Mahratta and as there were no other relatives Edward reluctantly appointed Robert and Sophie as temporary guardians of his pregnant wife Harriet and small son. Letters to and from India were long delayed so news of Harriet's death in childbirth would not have reached Edward, returning home wounded after Wellesley's victorious Assaye battle against Scindia's massive armies. He had embarked on *Prospero* at Madras, now the report of his death left his five year old son at the mercy of weak dissolute Robert and unscrupulous Sophie.

In the morning room they quietly debated the fate of their small ward.

"If anything happens to him we will be suspected," Sophie reminded Robert.

"I know that!" he snarled. Then more calmly: "There must be a way." Petulantly he brooded, scowling at the coal fire glowing in the Adams fireplace. His suggestion came tentatively, anticipating Sophie's derision. "What if we go away for a few days, visit your brother Charles in Lambeth, leave the brat in the charge of that gin-tippling nurse, arrange a fatality... er... the river, have someone lure him there, easy to tip him in."

Sophie clapped her hands. "Bravo! And how shall we arrange that, pray?" The expected scornful response.

He shrugged, hoping her more devious brain would supply a credible plan. His Lady Macbeth. Before she could speak a loud clattering and piercing shriek came from the breakfast room.

"What the devil?" exclaimed Robert. Sophie rang a bell, the housekeeper Mrs Grant hurried in, forestalling Sophie's remonstrance.

"Sorry ma'am, sir, the chimney sweeper's boy took a tumble into the hearth. Poor little fellow is quite stunned."

Dismissing the climbing boy's mishap with an impatient wave of her hand Sophie snapped: "Disgraceful disturbance. Send the master sweeper here." She knew not why but a faint recollection had come to her.

A hunched and wizened man appeared at the door, nervously twirling a grimy cap between gnarled hands, an ingratiating grin disclosing stained broken teeth.

"Samuel Billings begging yer pardon me lord, me lidy. Boy too big fer the flue, eight year old but needs a really little 'un. Got stuck, 'ad ter be pulled art, fell into 'earth. I'll give 'im a good belting fer disturbing yer peace."

Sophie waved aside the child's beating. "Why not use a smaller boy?"

"Not easy ter come by these dies, me lidy. Agin the law, forbidden ter use climbing boys under eight, me lidy." The sweep added with a pathos that sat uneasily on his villainous features: "An what with new-fangled narrer twisty flues now folk use coal more than wood the law comes 'ard on us poor sweepers, me lidy."

There was no compassion for poor sweepers in Sophie's response. "But you do use smaller boys. Recently you swept my acquaintance Mrs Winston's chimneys. She told me you had used a very small child."

The sweep seemed unabashed by this exposure of his law-breaking. "True me lidy, bought off of a poor family but little fellers do not last long. A coupla falls..." He checked himself. "I beg yer not to tell of it, me lidy. Agin the law but what can a poor man do? Must mike a living, family ter support. Gotta feed an' clothe me apprentices like the law ..."

"Your problems are no concern of ours," irritably interrupted Robert. "Find some other method of sweeping chimneys..." He broke off as Sophie signalled him to silence.

"How young should the boys be for narrow flues?" she asked the sweeper.

"Oh, four or five year, six depending on size. No use younger, gotta be able ter walk an climb proper, me lidy."

Sophie looked directly at Robert, willing his torpid brain to follow her train of thought. It did, he nodded.

"Close the door, man," he ordered. "We may be of mutual assistance."

· · ·

The sun was setting behind gently misted trees, a large red globe. A waking owl tentatively hooted in anticipation of its evening's activities. One hand on the hoop he had patted along the close cropped lawn the child stared in fascination, small heart stirred by the beauty surrounding him. The sharply querulous voice of his nurse jolted him out of his reverie. He sighed. She was always cross, not like dear Bessie who Aunt Sophie had sent away. They had both wept, Uncle Robert told him to be a man, what would his soldier father think of him? He had been only four when Mama and his new brother were taken to Heaven in a carriage slowly drawn by four black horses with feathers on their heads, men walking beside it. Bessie held him tight as they watched from a window and wept. Uncle Robert and Aunt Sophie went with the carriage so could not scold him. Then they had sent Bessie away and horrid Nurse Hunt came.

Everything was different now, he longed for Papa with all his heart. The last time he came home he swung Jackie up in his arms and kissed him, then galloped across the lawn with Jackie on his shoulders shouting "God for Harry, England and Saint George!" and Mama laughed. There was nobody now to love and kiss him.

"Bad Master John," scolded Nurse Hunt, her black clad angular figure rustling over to him, her narrow beaky face screwed up in ill temper. "How many times must I tell you to return to the house. Your tea is ready in the nursery, then your uncle and aunt wish to see you in the drawing room. Hurry now or I shall have to punish you."

He silently followed her. She spoke unfairly; she who had told him to play outside now chided him for doing so. Perhaps the little bottle she kept in her apron pocket and drank from when she thought no one was looking made her forget. He had no need of her. On his fifth birthday he informed Aunt Sophie that Papa promised that when he attained five years he could dispense with a nurse for his own room and personal attendant. Aunt said no, he must wait until his father returned. Now many weeks past his fifth birthday he still endured the nursery and horrid unkind Nurse Hunt, ugly and old, not like pretty Bessie who was never unkind.

In the nursery the youngest maid Tildy was setting out his meal of buttered bread, cake and milk while Nurse Hunt roughly scrubbed his face and hands with a wet cloth and dragged a brush through his soft fair hair that curled to his shoulders. When Papa had him breeched on his third birthday he told Mama his hair should be cut but Mama said "please, not yet, he has such pretty hair." Papa kissed her and said "Very well, but on his fifth birthday we shall turn our Jackie from a child into a boy." But Papa had not come home on his birthday, had not even sent a letter.

"Now hurry with your tea Master John," said Nurse Hunt, pushing him into a chair at the table. "You must not keep your aunt and uncle waiting."

"Why do they wish to see me?" asked John. "Have they a letter from my Papa?"

Nurse Hunt cuffed his head. "Ask no questions and you will hear no lies."

This was a favourite saying of Nurse Hunt that always puzzled John. Why should she tell lies? Papa and Mama said it was very bad to tell lies. He knew that if he argued he risked a rap on his hands with the cane. Before she came no one ever struck him, but Nurse Hunt liked doing so even when he did nothing wrong.

Robert and Sophie had dined and now awaited their nephew in the drawing room where Sophie presided over the teacups. After the lengthy meal Robert was somnolent. Having indulged less freely in wine Sophie stayed alert. Just as well well, though there should be no difficulty deceiving a small child John was intelligent beyond his years so she must be wary. She smiled to herself as she noticed how Robert avoided looking at the fireplace. Despicable weakness, she would have to provide the strength.

A week had passed since their meeting with the master sweep Sam Billings, days of frantic preparations for their London visit. Brother Charles proved reluctant to offer hospitality, he detested Robert even more than he did his sister, but letters promising reciprocal visits to Richmond overcame mutual dislike.

They had not disclosed the report of Edward's death, so removing any motive for disposing of his heir. The letter would be produced on their return from London with appropriate expressions of grief and loss. And such distress on learning of John's disappearance. Where could he be? Every effort must be made to trace the darling child.

"Do you admire my foresight in sending away the nursemaid?" Sophie asked Robert. "She adored John, would not let him out of her sight. We have a splendid scapegoat in the Hunt creature, the entire household can vouch for her gin tippling, her drunken naps while the child wanders where he pleases. Gross neglect of her duty."

Jerking out of his own drunken doze Robert said thickly: "The master sweeper...er...Tillings?"

Sophie sharply interrupted, hoping to raise him from his apathy. He must have what wits he possessed about him during the coming interview. "Billings. What of him? He is fully primed with the story he has to tell."

Robert was now weakly querulous. "But can he be trusted? He could betray us."

Sophie tutted impatiently. "And himself? That he took twelve guineas to abduct a five year old child and turn him into a climbing boy? As he would say, "agin the law" of which he appears terrified."

"But when the child dies in a tumble the law will take a stern view of his using a boy so young."

A languidly dismissive hand waved away craven fear. "Even if Billings does not secretly dispose of him, there are too many fatalities among working children, unwanted by parents, workhouse orphans. Who cares about their fate? He cannot be traced to us. The corpse of a malnourished filthy climbing boy identified as the missing Maltravers heir? A fantastical notion!"

Robert nodded, as Sophie said, a fantastical notion. She had planned everything so efficiently....He started as the door was lightly rapped. Now for the first stage in his becoming the wealthy master of Maltravers Hall and estate. Though convinced of success that light rap momentarily unnerved him, Fate demanding entrance.

John had been escorted to the drawing room by the thirteen year old maid Tildy. She had worked at the Hall for two years, the eldest daughter of an estate labourer she found the Hall paradise after the cramped cottage with its seemingly never ending squalling infants and the drudgery caring for them and her ever-pregnant mother. She loved Captain Edward, fervently wishing he would return and evict Mr Robert and his wife who never had a civil word for anyone. She adored little Jackie more than her own siblings. In a clean white apron and cap she held his hand in an elder sister fashion, knocked at the drawing room door and when bid "Come" opened it, bobbed a curtsey, announced "Master John, sir, madam", and after a sly friendly squeeze of John's hand left him with the usurpers.

After a gravely courteous bow John stood facing his uncle and aunt, silently waiting to know why they wished to see him, praying it would be about a letter from Papa. Robert appraised the boy. Somewhat above the average height for his age, slight of build, promising his father's tall spare figure. Involuntarily Robert glanced towards the fireplace, shuddered and looked away. He could not meet John's eyes, young as the child was Robert saw the father in the steady gaze. Edward and Robert were the only survivors of six children. The over-indulged youngest, Robert had been in awe of Edward, two years his senior. He imagined condemnation in the son's innocent eyes.

Sophie was fully aware of Robert's unease. Infirm of purpose!

"Sit down John," she instructed. He perched on a chaise longue, his legs dangling, hands on knees. "Will you have a little cake?"

"Thank you Aunt but I have already eaten." John had no wish to prolong the visit, disliking these relatives indulging themselves freely in his father's hospitality and who mostly ignored him though they were his guardians.

From Aunt Sophie an indifferent: "As you please." Then briskly: "Now, we asked you here to inform you that we are going away for two weeks or more. You will be in the charge of Nurse Hunt and must promise to obey her, to behave in a manner befitting the son of a gentleman. Do you promise?"

John bit his underlip to suppress an indignant reply. He did not need to be told to act like the son of a gentleman. But always show respect to your elders, however little they merited it. He steeled himself to answer politely yet firmly. "Yes Aunt, I promise." Unable to restrain himself further he asked eagerly: "Please Aunt, may I ask if there has been a letter from my father?"

Robert answered, though guardedly. "No, nothing. You must remember how long it takes for letters to come from India."

"Yes indeed sir, but my father wrote often to my mother, sometimes twice a week. Since she...left us only two letters. And sir, a few days ago I saw the man who brings letters with one that seemed to come a long way. I thought it might be from my father."

Robert tensed. He asked sharply: "You saw the letter's direction?" The letter giving news of Edward's death was addressed to Mrs Edward Maltravers.

Though puzzled by the question John answered with due courtesy.

"No sir, I can write words as I did on my mother's last letter to my father but I cannot yet read joined up words."

Robert relaxed. "The letter was from a friend who is travelling abroad..."

Sophie interrupted. "That will do John, it is no concern of yours. You are too inquisitive for a child, a very unpleasing trait." Having no children of her own and determined never to have any, Sophie was unaware that a child's curiosity was a very natural trait. "I shall speak to Nurse Hunt, she must correct that fault. No more for now, I will summon the maid to take you back to the nursery." She pulled a bell cord then, on Tildy's arrival, said: "On our return I will arrange for a tutor, you require more discipline." There would be no tutor but as well to have a witness to her expressed intention, allaying any suspicion of complicity in John's abduction. "As we leave early tomorrow we shall not see you until our return..." or ever, she hoped. "...so, remember your promise to be an obedient boy. Good-evening John."

Bending low she lightly touched his forehead with her lips. Aware of its lack of affection John bore it stoically, holding his breath to avoid breathing in her lavishly applied perfume.

Robert flinched. The kiss of betrayal? Again the vision of Edward as the child bowed his farewell before joining the maid and leaving the room.

Sophie nodded her satisfaction. "No difficulty there, the first stage in our journey to prosperity." Then acidly: "Not that you were of much assistance."

Robert wanted to protest; experience taught him to refrain.

"You as always were superb, my love." No love discernible in his shifty untrustworthy eyes. Nor in the contemptuous glance bestowed on him by his Lady Macbeth.

Two

The days following his guardians' departure were dreary for John. To make his abduction easier Sophie gave instructions that he no longer should be allowed social contact with the servants or estate children, a contact that had been encouraged by his parents. Edward had enjoyed an easy relationship with all who worked for him, believing that to distance himself from those loyally serving his family was despicable arrogance. A fortunate accident of birth did not make the wealthy superior to the less fortunate working long hours to make a meagre living. They should be aided, not scorned.

Edward's plans included good housing for estate workers. He had already provided a school for their children, evening classes for those from large families who had to work, bribed to attend by a penny, milk and bun. Following the example of Robert Raikes' schooling for the working children of Gloucester the school was not solely for Sunday bible lessons. What use, Edward answered his critics, to teach children their catechism and commandments when they could not read or write? Give them a good basic education that would guide them to better lives than their illiterate parents. His peers regarded Edward as a muddle-headed Radical.

Why meddle with the destined estates, high and lowly. Educating the lower orders would lead to discontent. Not so, Edward argued. Discontent with their deprived estate, their hunger, dire poverty led to mob violence, rebellion, and had led to the wanton destruction of the Gordon Riots, the bloody revolution in France.

Strongly opposed to Edward's ideals, Robert and Sophie had no intention of wasting money on improvements for labourers believing their own improvements were a priority.

John had not understood much of beloved Papa's thinking, but treasured the words in his heart. Now he was denied contact with those he considered friends. His main grief was forbidden access to the stables where his pony Dobbin was housed. He loved chatting to the grooms who made much of him, recalling the days of his infancy when baby Jackie was handed up to Papa astride his favourite horse, Major, for a gentle trot round the park, Mama pleading "Oh do take care Edward." Papa laughing with Jackie nestling safely against him, crowing his delight.

Now the pony was brought to the front of the Hall by stable lad Will Cooper, forbidden to speak to John save for necessary instructions. On the second morning of the new regime the ride again took place in silence. In the park they dismounted, John from Dobbin, Will from an elderly mare, to tighten the pony's girth. Overwhelmed by grief at his erstwhile friend's silence John burst into passionate weeping.

"Why do you not speak to me? Why does everyone hate me? What have I done?"

At fourteen Will was used to comforting small siblings. Quickly glancing round to make sure he was unobserved, he crouched beside John and hugged him.

"Hush now Jackie. No one hates you but 'tis your aunt and uncle see. They bid us keep our distance or lose our places. Really, 'tis none of our doing." Then as John's sobs subsided: "Tell you what, I shall keep silent till we be clear of the Hall then we can have our usual chatter, will that please you?"

John wiped his eyes with the large kerchief Will offered him. "Very much indeed, but Will, why do my aunt and uncle stop my friends talking to me? They are away so would not know if anyone did disobey that unjust instruction."

Though Will was also mystified by the edict he attempted to explain. "Ah but there is that nurse of yourn, and the new footman Parker your uncle hired to keep a look out, spying on us more like. None of us know why, 'tis a very rum do."

"Papa will make things better when he comes home." John held out his hand. "Shake on our friendship, be my brother Will."

"Gladly Jackie," said Will, firmly grasping the small hand. "Anything I can ever do for you I shall, my word on it." Months later that pledge would be honoured.

The new footman, Jem Parker, had not been employed merely to spy on fellow servants, but more importantly to supervise John's abduction. Formerly in the employ of Robert's acquaintance Sir William Mardon and dismissed for theft, he escaped prosecution and a death sentence through the indolent good nature of Sir William who deplored the harshness of the legal system which sentenced culprits to swing even for minor crimes. Recognising in Parker a fellow unscrupulous rogue Robert hired him, a large bribe and the threat of exposure as a thief securing his tarnished loyalty.

The master sweep Sam Billings would be in the Richmond area a week after the Robert Maltravers' departure. The abduction was planned for late morning, after the child returned from his ride. Somehow he had to be persuaded to play in the area of the park most accessible to the gates, outside which Billings' woman would be waiting, the lodge keeper called away on some pretext. Parker, a handsome scoundrel, soon ingratiated himself with the ill-favoured Nurse Hunt, flattered by his attentions and welcoming the gin he liberally supplied. She was not overly attentive to her small charge who wandered as he pleased while she dozed. As Sophie had predicted, the perfect scapegoat.

After his morning ride John habitually spent the rest of the morning in the nursery at his learning, supervised by Nurse Hunt. While his mother lived this was a great pleasure to him, she would read from the little books for children made popular by John Newberry of St Paul's Churchyard whose publications Mama had read when no older than John. Soon, Papa said, he would study in earnest with proper tutors. No thought yet of a school. Edward had bitter memories of his own schooldays, the so-called academy for the sons of gentlemen to which he was sent at the age of five: the floggings for the least misdemeanour, scant food, the coldness of unheated dormitories, classrooms, the abuse by older boys – and masters. After his eldest brother died with other boys of a virulent fever the academy closed and Edward was taught at home by tutors. Jackie also would be taught at home by good masters, then guided by Papa in his estate duties. Edward had a low opinion of universities, most students attending the minimum terms necessary for their intended professions and many students studied just enough to scrape through to a degree, the rest of their stay devoted to less admirable diversions.

Since Mama left him, John's learning had been far from pleasurable as Nurse Hunt read badly and he made no progress in writing; he could do so better than his teacher. Eager to learn and receiving no guidance he often left the nursery while Nurse Hunt slept, wandering in the grounds unchaperoned, free of restraint.

On that morning Parker ensured that Nurse Hunt was more than usually inattentive by adding a few drops of laudanum to the flask of gin he secretly passed her. After nodding in her chair she finally slumped into a drugged sleep, open-mouthed, snoring and John happily made his escape. A sunny early November day, he would take his hoop for a spin. Fretting with impatience Parker had lurked outside the nursery, sighing with relief as John made his escape. He smiled obsequiously.

"You have finished your studies Master John, and now intend taking the air?"

John did not like Parker, his smile or his questioning.

"I shall," he replied haughtily. "Why do you ask?"

Parker's crafty smile would have raised an older person's suspicion. "I thought you would wish to know of the new pen the head gardener has erected for the pet rabbits and their young. It is near the lodge gates."

John, unused to deceit, believed him. He loved animals. "Oh I must see them! Why has he put the pen there? I shall ask Dan at the lodge to show me." He inclined his head. "Thank you Parker."

It was a long walk to the lodge and he should not go unsupervised but there was no one now to accompany him. He couldn't find any sign of a pen or rabbits, nor was Dan at the lodge - perhaps he was away on an errand. As he stood undecided a woman came through the gates looking looked very unkempt and not the sort of person Dan would have admitted.

"Are you visiting someone at the Hall Madam?" John asked in a courteous grown up manner.

He was answered with a toothless smile. "Why yes if you please, young master. Be your name John?"

Surprised, with an effort John retained his courteous manner. "It is; you wish to speak with me?"

She bent over him, speaking confidingly. She smelt horrid, John restrained himself from wrinkling his nose. "I have a message from your papa."

John's heart leapt for joy. "Papa!" His eyes bright with unshed tears he impulsively placed a hand on the woman's bony arm. "Oh pray where is he?"

Another gust of foul smelling breath was exhaled. "At the Bell Inn where I work, he wishes me to take you there."

Joy was now tinged with doubt. "But...why does he not come here?"

A quick improvising, she had not been adequately primed.

"He has not the time. He arrived by coach from... foreign parts and awaits the midday London coach. He greatly longs to see you afore he do leave. We must hurry or you will miss him."

Though bewildered, John was so overwhelmed with joy he did not stop to consider his answer. At the age of five he knew nothing of deceit, of treachery. He ran to the gates, the woman following.

"I have a gig and pony round the corner," she called to him. Well out of sight of the house.

John turned the corner into the deserted road, not seeing the man standing in the shadow of the trees but he was briefly aware of pain as the blow to his head stunned him.

"Careful Sam," croaked the sweep's woman. "Do not kill him afore you have use of him."

"It were only a tap." Billings lifted the child onto the cart, covering him with sacks. "When 'e comes to, a dose of laudanum should keep 'im quiet until we reach Saint Giles. Keep yer eyes on 'im, if yer doze off yer will feel the whip."

Lashing the horse he set it off at a gallop. His third infant climbing boy, destined to share the fate of the other two?

John was not missed for almost two hours. With the exception of footman Parker the servants assumed he was in the care of Nurse Hunt. She slept on until roused by the maid Tildy bringing the midday meals. It was an easy time for the kitchen and dining room staff now the Robert Maltravers were visiting relatives. When Edward was at home, busy with estate duties he dined in the evening, three courses only. With no duties Robert and Sophie had a protracted afternoon meal of five courses starting at three o'clock until five when tea was served. Even more protracted when Robert and Sophie, making the most of free board at Edward's expense had guests, the males usually as bibulous as Robert. Now only simple meals were prepared with care for dear Jackie, more grudgingly for the nurse.

With difficulty Tildy aroused Mrs Hunt – a courtesy title, Tildy believed no man would have married such a hag unless she had a fortune. When at last she groaned and opened bleary eyes Tildy asked: "Where is Master John?"

"At his books, leastwise he was not long since." Having lost all sense of time Nurse Hunt vaguely looked round the nursery, the ache in her head making her even more evil-tempered. "Wicked child, he has gone outside to play. A good thrashing is what he deserves."

"Indeed he does not!" Tildy bravely answered. "His ma and pa never struck him and nor should you. A dear little fellow like Jackie?"

A pert reply that roused Mrs Hunt from her stupor. "Master John to you, Miss Impudence. He is entrusted to my charge, not yours."

Fury drove Tildy to more impudence. "And you let him wander off on his own? You should not be entrusted with a puppy dog. I shall go and find him."

Before the outraged nurse could respond Tildy ran into the grounds. The drunken old hag should be dismissed, would be when Captain Edward returned. No sign of Jackie. Now afraid she summoned other servants to help in the search. Had he left the grounds? Please God, not to the river! Dan at the lodge was questioned. No, he had not seen John leave. Then shamefacedly he confessed that he had been duped into leaving the lodge on a false errand. A woman claiming to come from the inn told him that Captain Maltravers had arrived there to await the London coach and wished to speak to him. Though mystified Dan, not the brightest of men, did not ask himself why Captain Edward had arrived without prior notice or calling at the Hall, a mere mile from the inn, to ensure all was well. Blindly obedient Dan accompanied the woman to walk the mile. When she stopped to tighten her shoe fastening he walked on and saw no sign of her when he looked back. At the inn there was no sign of the Captain, the host denying any knowledge of his arrival, no coaches had stopped there since early morning so Dan returned to the Hall, believing himself the victim of a stupid senseless hoax.

With other searchers Tildy and Will realised it was no hoax but a ruse to ensure Dan's absence during Jackie's abduction. A groom was sent into Richmond to alert the town crier and the constables. What else could they do wondered the anguished servants. Another groom was sent to Kew, the home of Edward's estate steward Horace Danvers who sent a man post haste to South Lambeth to summon the Robert Maltravers. In Edward's absence they were John's guardians, they must return immediately to initiate enquiries. Danvers had no illusions as to how distraught they would be at the news. An honourable man, he could not have suspected their delight on learning of the successful abduction. Although also having no illusions as to the Robert Maltravers' grief the genuinely distraught servants had as yet no suspicions of their involvement. Realisation of incredible treachery was still to come.

Recovering consciousness John became aware of the jolting cart, the evil-smelling sacks covering him. With a terrified cry he threw them off, sat up and looked wildly around. Sitting opposite him was the beggar woman who had lured him from the park, beyond her the back of a man lashing a horse to greater speed. The road was deserted; nothing to be seen but trees shedding their autumn colours, hedgerows, fields and more fields.

"Where are you taking me?" he cried. Then with a feeble attempt at authority: "Take me home at once."

The woman called to the man: "Halt you Sam. The boy has woke."

With an oath Billings violently jerked the horse to a standstill.

It gave a sharp neigh of pain, then obediently stood, head lowered. It had suffered too many lashings to rebel. Billings climbed over into the cart and seized John round the shoulders, roughly shaking him.

"Stow that row or 'ave yer neck broke. Come, drink this."

Pulling a flask of wine laced with laudanum from his pocket he tried to force it into John's mouth.

"No!" he squealed, turning aside his head. Grabbing his long hair Billings jerked back the boy's head, thrusting the neck of the bottle into his mouth so that with chokes and splutters he had to swallow the contents, the woman holding his flailing arms. He was thrown back under the sacks where he lay, sobbing his terror until the laudanum took effect and he sank into drugged oblivion.

"That settled 'im," muttered Billings, climbing back onto his seat and lashing the horse into a snorting gallop.

"Pray you haven't settled the brat for good," muttered the woman, with a twinge of pity staring at the small huddled form. "Might be as well for him if you have."

Sam Billings was indifferent as to whether the child lived or died. He had his twelve guineas and there were plenty of small waifs wandering London's streets for the lifting and better suited to the job. This one was soft, less than two weeks' use. Big job tomorrow, new-fangled narrow flues and, after that, pretty boy could end up in the river with the other brats. If he survived Billings knew of places where gentlemen paid handsome for pretty boys. He wouldn't last long that way neither.

THREE

John Maltravers woke to terror. Where was this? He lay on rough sacking, his head ached, his mouth was dry. He sat up, looking around the damply cold squalid room dimly lit by candles that threw menacing shadowy forms on the walls. An overpowering stench made him want to vomit but he had not eaten since early morning. Was this Hell? Nurse Hunt said that if he was bad he would go there. But people burned in everlasting fire and he shivered with cold. Was this where they waited in turn to be thrown into the flames? What had he done wrong? Slipped away from the nursery to the park alone which was naughty but not wicked. He often had done so while Nurse snored.

He glanced down. Where were his clothes, why was he wearing this rough itchy shirt, grey shabby trousers, no shoes or hose? And his hair! He put a hand up to his roughly cropped head. Mama so loved his hair though Papa wanted him to become a boy. Now he surely had, but such a ragamuffin Papa would not know him.

He now became aware that beside him sat a boy a few years older than himself, grimy of face, sore-looking eyes rimmed with black dust.

"Who are you?" asked John. "What is this place?"

The boy regarded him, sore eyes squinting with the effort of focussing. His voice was hoarse, expressionless. "Me nime is Tad. We live 'ere, least, yer does nah, yer the new prentis"

John answered with an attempt at defiance, his voice tremulous. "I do not live here. How came I to this horrid place? What is a prentis?"

A puzzled frown creased the prematurely wizened small face as Tad strove to answer. A weird one this little feller, greener than grass. "Yer works fer the chimbley sweeper ter larn the tride. Dunno 'ow yer come, spec yer pa sold yer ter Sam like what mine done me arter ma died when I were six year old."

Now fear engulfed John. "Sold? Papa would not sell me, he is away in the army but will soon find me when he comes back."

Tad laughed scornfully, his teeth yellow, his cracked lips black. "Lor, ant yer the green un. Nobody ant gonna find yer 'ere."

John was silent. Papa would not have sold him...but...the woman knew his name, told him Papa was waiting at the inn on his way to London. How had she known, who told her? Not the servants, they were his friends. The new servant Parker told him of the rabbits and that was not true. Treachery was an unknown concept to John, he struggled to understand. He asked Tad: "Where is this place?"

Another puzzled stare. "London a course."

London! Where the woman said Papa was to go. So he could find him! The woman may have lied. But somehow he knew Papa would come.

His eyes had adapted to the dimness of the very large room, the light further diminished by the rags stuffed in broken windows. Looking round he saw people in poor clothes, sitting huddled together in what seemed to be family groups, others were restlessly pacing the floor of the large room. Ragged curtains hanging from beams afforded scant privacy. Some people sat on mattresses, others on worn blankets. Each had a small heap of possessions, were eating meagre meals or staring hungrily at those who were.

"Who are those people?" he asked Tad.

"Why, they lives 'ere, like what we do."

John became aware of a pressing urgency. Used to privacy on such occasions his face flushed with embarrassment as he whispered to Tad:

"I need to...to relieve myself. Where is the...place?"

Tad stared. "Eh? Do what? Oh, yer mean piss?" He waved a hand to a far corner of the room. "Over there. Mind no one grabs yer."

John looked across to a large pail, the source of the stench. But his need was urgent. Warily he made his way to it, weaving between the groups of people. The pail was almost full of urine and faeces. Quietly sobbing his horror he used it, thankful he had no need to squat. As he returned to his corner a hunched legless man perched on a wooden board with wheels lashed out at him with a stick, another man tried to grab him, snarling "Come 'ere bitch's whelp." Evading him John threw himself onto the sacks, pent up anguish giving way to a violent storm of weeping.

Tad at first watched in silence. Nothing in his eight years had taught him pity, none shown to him. He had survived two years with Billings, a vicious taskmaster who himself had survived a childhood and youth of unremitting hardship. Tad's early childhood had been spent in a hovel with his family, the eldest of an ever increasing brood until his mother died giving birth to stillborn twins, her sixth pregnancy in as many years. From his fourth year he had earned a few weekly pence carrying out odd jobs on a farm a mile distant, assisting his labourer father by crow-scaring, root crop pulling, clubbing rats as they fled from the harvesters. On his mother's death his father, not daring to do so while she lived, sold his six year old son to Billings for three guineas and his five year old daughter to a mill owner. The girl died while cleaning lint from under looms, mangled by the machinery. So Tad had little cause to feel pity for the small newcomer. But experience had not yet hardened a heart nature intended to be gentle.

"Come nah cully," he said. "No use squalling, soon git used ter it." Words he knew to be false, this was a soft one, last two weeks at most. Tad already had witnessed the corpses of two little uns stuffed into sacks to hide evidence of illegal use, then by night dumped into the river to be fished out by watermen, well used to dredging up corpses. Mostly suicides or victims of footpads but also unwanted infants or ill-used children.

John controlled his sobs, sitting up and again glancing round.

"What do these people do?" he asked.

"Night workers mostly. The cove what grabbed yer collects shit a piss, empties jakes." He indicated the pail. "Tikes that away fer a start, sells it ter farmers fer spreading. The cove on wheels lost 'is legs in a thresher when a nipper, not up ter snuff 'ere," tapping his head. "Begs fer 'is bread." He pointed to a woman in a grimy low-cut gown giving prominence to slack breasts, her face marked with sores. Beside her a small girl who might have been seven or eight, though her face devoid of childhood, expressionless. She was wrapped in a soiled grey woollen shawl, from which protruded stick like arms and legs covered in bruises. "The lidy-bird is cheap meat, lifts skirts on street corners, doling art to coves doses of the pox; dark so them as desperate fer it can't see proper what she's like. If coves wants 'em young she gives Effie, belts 'er if she displeases. Like Billings does us." Tad pulled up his shirt, showing John a grimy back where every rib showed, covered in half-healed weals. "Come a tumble darn a chimbley coupla weeks back. Not my fault, flue were too narrer."

John stared in horror, not knowing the chimney was at Maltravers Hall. The nursery was too remote from the breakfast room for him to have known of the sweeps' visit. He had not understood Tad's descriptions of their neighbours' occupations, innocent of sexual knowledge or the disposal of night soil. But he wanted to weep again, this time for Tad's suffering.

"That is very wicked, when my Papa comes I shall ask him to take you away also, he will see that you are well cared for. You shall be my friend."

Unused to sympathy Tad stared at him. This was a rum un. He drew a sharp breath as a great boy entered the room and slouched towards them.

"Tis Barney," Tad muttered to John. "Billings' boy. Mind 'ow yer speak, land yer one if yer raises 'is bristles."

Barney dumped a tray between them. "Yer supper," he said in a loudly harsh young voice. "Eat up then git yer 'eads darn." He leered at John. You an all Jacko, early start so be sure yer ready or else." He thrust a fist at John's nose. Heeding Tad's advice John silently nodded. Aiming a kick at him Barney slouched off.

John stared in dismay at the meal, two hunks of bread smeared with a fatty substance, two mugs of a light brown liquid.

"What is it?" he asked Tad. "Is this all we have?"

"Yeah, our vittles. Bread an ale. Some cove told me the law says master sweepers gotta feed us proper, give us clothing an Sunday learning but does Billings? Does 'e fun!" He hesitated. No affection had entered his life, he had none for others, but Jacko spoke fair, had called him friend. From his jacket pocket he took a cloth wrapped packet, unwrapping it to disclose a large slab of gingerbread. "Got it from a market barrer." Breaking it in half he passed a portion to John. "Git that darn yer quick afore anyone nabs it." Only dimly aware of the extent of Tad's sacrifice John thanked him, quickly devouring it before turning to the bread. The fat was rancid, he spluttered on the unaccustomed ale.

"That is horrid, can we not have milk?"

Tad laughed. "Cats lap? Best not try asking Barney fer that."

"What does Barney do?"

"Reckons pa will mike 'im master sweeper, keeps us in trim. Too big fer chimbleys so does some thieving in the rookeries. A dip mostly."

John stared. "A dip? He goes into water?"

"Pocket picking, dummy! Lord, ain't yer green. Billings ant above 'elping 'imself ter stuff from where we sweeps." Tad realised that when he got too big for sweeping Billings would either set him adrift to fend for himself or send him with Barney on thieving. He mentally shrugged, resigned to his fate. "Come on, Jacko lad. Gotta git some kip."

They lay on the sacks, drawing one to cover them, scattering cockroaches but not lice. A cold November night, John shivered, then drew close to Tad who placed an arm round him. Like two small animals the children nestled together for mutual comfort, the gently reared heir to a wealthy estate and the unloved brutally treated labourer's boy. They slept, oblivious to the voices around them, the oaths, the groans, the scuttling of rats and mice emerging to scavenge for unprotected food.

His bewildered brain as yet unable to grasp the full horror of his situation John could only accept he was to sweep chimneys, visualising this as pushing a brush up flues. His sleep would have been less sound had he known the true work of a climbing boy. Edging with elbows and knees through soot encrusted flues, half blinded, choked by falling soot. On the morrow the hell of John's childish imagination would become stark reality when he experienced the daily perils of a climbing boy.

Four

John woke early, briefly keeping his eyes tightly shut in the hope that on opening them he would find the events of the previous day were a bad dream. He could not long deceive himself that he was in his clean little nursery bed, he was aware of the roughness of the sack covering him, the stench, the muttering, groans and restless tossing of his neighbours. The thought of what lay ahead that day filled him with sick dread. Recalling he had not said his prayers as Mama taught him he struggled free of the sacking and knelt, folded his hands and with closed eyes softly whispered his appeal to Jesus, who Mama assured him loved children, to see him safely through the perils of that day. And to bless dearest Papa and tell him where to find his Jackie.

Comforted, he opened his eyes and looked round the room, lit only by guttering candles. No one was awake though by their restless movements not sleeping peacefully. Even Tad beside him whimpered and muttered incoherently. John softly added his name to be blessed by Jesus who loved and cared for all children. As yet there was no seed of doubt in John's innocently trusting heart.

Profiting by his experience of the previous evening he gently weaved through the prostrate forms to the now empty pail, relieving himself. He felt unbearably itchy, never before had he slept in his day clothes. He pulled up his shirt, looking in horror at the specks of blood where lice had feasted on his tender flesh. With a stifled cry he stripped, violently shaking shirt and trousers free of the pests, then reluctantly re-dressed, he had no other clothes. For the first time in his life he undressed and dressed himself, a forced step towards independence. He longed to clean himself, but where?

From outside the building a clock struck the sixth hour. The room's inhabitants were already stirring, preparing for the grim struggle to earn their daily bread, not to be had by prayer. John knew with sick certainty that soon Barney would come for him. He must escape. Creeping towards the door he stretched up to the handle. Before he could reach it the door was thrust open, knocking him off his feet. Barney glared down at him.

"What the devil are yer up ter?"

John stood, head tilted, limpid blue eyes meeting dull expressionless brown.

"I wished to find somewhere to cleanse myself." Not a complete lie, nor the complete truth.

A harshly mocking laugh. "Yer gonna be a lot muckier afore too long chuck, then yer goes under the yard pump, get yer washed darn." He pushed John back to his corner where Tad now sat up, eyes wide with fear. Returning to the entrance Barney collected a jug and bowls he had put down to open the door.

"Yer vittles." He poured a thin broth into the bowls, thrusting them at the boys with hunks of bread. "Git a move on, soon as pa gits the cart ready we sets orf."

He stood over the boys as they hastily ate, John following Tad's example and dipping the stale bread into the broth. When he gulped down the last mouthful Barney bent and pulled him to his feet by his shirt collar, pushing him to the door.

"On yer way Jacko." To Tad. "Yer ant tiking it easy neither, job fer yer when we gits Jacko started."

Still grasping John's collar and jerking his head for Tad to follow Barney pushed him out of the building into a large yard where by the light of a lantern Billings was fastening the submissive horse to a cart laden with brushes and sacks.

"In yer go," said Barney, picking up John by his shirt and throwing him into the cart, then no less gently assisting Tad to clamber aboard before joining the boys.

"All aboard Pa," he shouted. In his usual surly morning mood after a night's drunken carousing Billings merely grunted as he lashed the horse into action.

The morning was dark, cold, made damp by a thick mist that hid from view the streets through which they travelled, the cart occupants dimly lit by the lantern on Billings' seat. John shivered uncontrollably until Barney fished from under the sacks a jacket, throwing it at him. Not from benevolence, Barney a stranger to such an emotion, but the boy had to be in a fit state to work. John pulled it on, his size, little knowing it had belonged to his equally small predecessor, indeed deceased after cracking his skull open in a fall from a chimney. The coat had not not been cleaned, still bearing ominous brown stains.

After more than an hour's jolting ride, silent apart from Billing's violent curses whenever the horse slowed its pace, the cart clattered over cobbles, Billings violently wrenching the horse to a standstill. Through the now thinning mist John saw they had stopped outside a grand house in a street of similar buildings.

"Darn wiv yer Jacko," said Barney, grabbing John and dumping him onto the cobbles. To his father. "I'll join yer when I gits this un started."

"Mind the brat gits well up afore yer leaves" growled Billings. To John. "No monkey tricks or yer gits a flogging till yer skin 'angs in strips, savvy?" With that encouraging assurance he again thrashed the horse into action to a house in a neighbouring street.

Barney hustled John to a side entrance, pulling the bell cord. A maid admitted them, raising eyebrows at Barney's diminutive companion.

"Could not be much littler than that," she observed. "In the reception room, fire smoking for days past."

"Soon settle that me duck," Barney assured her with a lascivious leer.

"Keep your ogles on your work, mooncalf," she pertly answered, leading the way to the large reception room. Attempting to control sick shivery panic John thought it elegant but less so than Papa's. He shut his eyes tight, praying that when he opened them he would find himself at home. The maid's voice shattered that hope.

"Take care you do not make a sooty mess," she warned Barney.

Unstrapping his shoulder pack Barney showed her the rolled cloths it contained.

"Nary a speck ter worry yer sweet 'ead."

Tossing that head the maid left the room. A lumpish youth not worth a banter. At sixteen Kitty had higher aspirations. Already there had been overtures from Master Joseph but she had refused his invitation into the airing cupboard. Kitchen maid Lisa had been dismissed when the bump in her belly could no longer be concealed. Master Joseph? At home from his grand school about the right time. Lisa hadn't said, wouldn't have been believed anyway.

Barney ordered John to help spread the cloths over the carpet surrounding the fireplace, another in the hearth. As John waited, almost paralysed with fear, Barney pushed a scraper into his hand and tucked a small hard brush into his shirt. Before John realised what was happening Barney seized him round the waist and carried him to the chimney, thrusting him into it.

"No, oh please no!" shrilled John, struggling to free himself.

"Stow that row," snarled Barney, thumping his back. Standing in the hearth he boosted John further up the chimney, then climbed as far as he could to thrust him through the narrow flue, giving him belated instructions. " Git climbing, 'ang on ter 'olds, use yer elbers an knees ter climb. Scrape away the soot. If yer tries ter git darn afore yer done I will light a fire an Pa will beat yer senseless."

His duty done Barney struggled out of the chimney. Too big now but Pa would set him up with his own trade and boys. Barney was sadly mistaken, Pa had no intention of allowing him to become a rival. Now an expert dip, time had come to introduce him to house breaking. Master sweeper Billings had good knowledge of the best cribs to crack.

Blissfully unaware of these plans Barney shook himself free of soot, briefly waited to ensure Jacko did not try to climb down, then left the house to join his father and Tad on another sweep, after which they would come back for Jacko. The thought that some training in chimney sweeping should have been given before thrusting a small child into a narrow flue did not enter his desensitised brain. He had worked for his father from the advanced age of six. Eight years had blotted out the memory of that first fearful climb.

Heart pounding with terror John desperately clung to a slight projection. Believing Barney would light a fire if he climbed down he edged up further, closing his eyes as soot blinded him, mouth firmly closed, struggling for breath through clogged nostrils. Tightly enveloped, a prisoner in the silent suffocating blackness. Nothing in his worst dreams had prepared him for this hell. Only one person to whom he could appeal.

"Papa," he silently screamed. "Help me Papa or I shall die."

Somehow, from somewhere he felt the courage to survive. Wedging himself with bent knees against the flue he attempted to use the scraper but his hands were too small, it slipped from his grasp, dimly he heard it clatter on the hearth. As he struggled in the narrow space to pull the brush from his shirt a fall of soot enveloped him. He tried to raise his hands to protect his face, one foot slipped, then the other. Panic stricken he reached for the projection, tearing his soft hands, now too slippery with blood to hang on. His strength failing he could not save himself from sliding down the black hell, with a despairing wail crashing into the hearth, striking his head. Then oblivion.

Hearing the scream as she prepared the morning room for her ladyship and Mrs Claremont, now at breakfast, the maid Kitty ran to the reception room. No sign of the older boy and at first she mistook the small black heap in the hearth for a pile of soot. Nervously edging closer she recognised the sweep's boy. Surely dead! She ran to the kitchen, breathlessly gabbling to the housekeeper:

"Oh Mrs Hobday, the climbing boy is dead in the hearth and the sweeper taken himself off. What must we do?"

Mrs Hobday, a tall woman with pleasant features and a calm temperament ideal for dealing with hysterical maids said sharply: "Now stop getting yourself in a state Kitty. Climbing boys are used to falls, the truth may be he is merely stunned. Come, show me."

Kitty led the way, feebly protesting this climbing boy a small child. Used to her fanciful ways Mrs Hobday ignored her, then as she surveyed the pathetic small bundle realised that for once Kitty did not exaggerate. As they stared in dismay John gave a babyish whimpered "Mama!" and slightly stirred.

Despite her efficient ways Mrs Hobday had a compassionate heart.

"Little more than an infant. What wickedness is this?" A pause for decision, swiftly made. "Kitty, quickly fetch Lawson, tell him to bring a board to take the unfortunate little creature to the kitchen, see what can be done for him."

Kitty ran to obey. A few minutes later the head gardener came with a lad and makeshift stretcher to convey John to the kitchen, placing the board on the long table. Under Mrs Hobday's instructions the scullery and kitchen maids stripped John of his torn blood-stained shirt and trousers, washing the small bruised body with hot water from the kettles and laundry soap. From his cottage the gardener collected his youngest child's outgrown nightshift to clothe him. As his torn hands were bandaged John recovered his senses. He stared at the faces bending over him, for one delirious moment of joy believing himself in the kitchen of his home among his friends. But...he knew none of the faces. He put a hand to his head where the bump that had stunned him throbbed painfully. He gazed up at Mrs Hobday, his voice no more than a whisper.

"Please ma'am, what is this place?"

Mrs Hobday had expected a roughly spoken child. This one spoke with grave courtesy. A finely featured boy despite his pain-drawn countenance.

She answered more fully than she would a street urchin. "You are at the home of Sir Edwin and Lady Georgina Forester in Blackheath. You fell while sweeping a chimney."

"A chimney..." John slowly recalled the horror of that black hell. "Oh yes, Barney pushed me there. The sweeper will flog me until my skin falls off, he beat Tad for falling." He struggled to sit up, reaching out his bandaged hand to clasp Mrs Hobday's arm. "Please ma'am, I pray you do not let him send me up again. I would surely die."

Though moved by the child's appeal Mrs Hobday was at a loss. The decision was not hers. The problem solved as the butler entered the kitchen.

"Lady Georgina wishes to know what is happening. I informed her of the child's fall, she is curious to see him in the morning room." He looked down at John, clad only in a night-shift. "He will have to come as he is, at least he is clean."

"And well-spoken," said Mrs Hobday. "No urchin, that is for

sure." Lifting John onto the floor she said gently: "Go with Mr Webb, child. Her ladyship will decide what is to be done with you." She placed a hand on his head. "God go with you."

Still dazed, on shaky legs John followed the butler to the morning room.

"The climbing boy, your ladyship," intoned Mr Webb, then left the room.

A woman of middle years, to John a formidable grey personage, grey hair, stern grey features, a grey long gown fastened at her neck with the only colour about her, a red ruby brooch. John knew it was ruby, Mama had one similar. He thought that her tight collar the reason she held her head high. She sat erect on a straight backed tapestry covered chair such as they had at his home. Near her on a chaise longue a young woman in widow's weeds, fine sensitive features marred by sadness. As he had been taught to greet adults John bowed.

"Good morning your ladyship," then to the younger woman "Madam."

Lady Georgina – she refused to be called Lady Edwin, she was her own person - nodded in response, staring at the boy. As had Mrs Hobday she recognised this was no parish cast off or labourer's rejected brat. Angelic in his white shift, standing erect, no deference. His clear blue eyes steadily meeting her dark non-committal appraisal. She saw intelligence there, integrity? In one so young?

"What is your name, child?" Her voice as chilly as her countenance.

Though dismayed by the coldness of her tone John strove to answer steadily "John, your ladyship."

More sharply: "John who?"

He bit his lip. He had never been called anything but John, Jackie to his parents.

"I am only known as John, ma'am," he faltered.

"You must have a surname. Who is your father?"

"His name is Edward, some say Captain Edward." Then with evident pride: "He is fighting abroad to make our country great." More tremulously: "My Mama ...mother ...was taken to heaven with my new brother some months ago."

A slight lessening of her ladyship's curtness. "Who takes care of you? How came you to be with a chimney sweeper?"

John told her how his uncle and aunt were caring for him in his father's absence but they were away on a visit. While he played in the park – was it only yesterday? – a woman told him his father wished to see him at the nearby inn. He remembered no more until he woke in a room with many poor people and he was dressed in foul clothes next to Tad, a climbing boy who told him he would be a prentis and sweep chimneys. Today the sweeper and his son brought him to her ladyship's house and put him into a chimney.

There had been no softening of her ladyship's grim features during his recital. Aware of the younger lady's sympathy he looked away from that stern face, noticing her daughter had tears in her eyes. Eyes he thought the most beautiful he had ever known, even Mama's.

She turned to her mother. "Oh, such wickedness! The child stolen from his home and so ill-treated." She had noticed John's weariness. Though still standing straight she saw how he trembled with the effort. "Here John, you are still unwell. Sit beside me."

John hesitated, glancing at Lady Georgina for permission. She nodded, he perched on the chaise longue, nervously tense as the inquisition continued. It began gently. Caroline Claremont asked softly: "What is your age John?"

"I became five years on the fifth of September... oh I do not know the date today but I think several weeks ago." Responding to her compassionate regard he confided: "My Papa promised that then I should have my own room but my aunt told me I must await his return. Cook made me a special cake and..."

Tiring of these confidences Lady Georgina asked abruptly:

"Where do you live?"

Reluctantly he turned to her. "In a big house with large gardens and a park and farms and...."

She tutted impatiently. "But the address, child. Surely you know that? Come, you must say the truth."

The ordeals and terrors of the past hours, his longing for home and the shame of having his words doubted proved too much to endure. Covering his face with his bandaged hands John sobbed bitterly, shaking with grief.

Lady Georgina again tutted. "Come John, behave like a..." she paused. Stern as she was how could she expect this scrap to behave like a man? She did not know how to comfort, that she left to her daughter.

Caroline's heart was attuned to grief and pity. Six months previously her sailor husband who, despite her mother's disapproval, she married for love was killed in battle, the shock so great she miscarried their first child. Now again living at the home she so thankfully left two years ago she knew too well her mother's inability to understand and sympathise with the grief of others. Even the loss of three children had been accepted with resignation. Such was the way of life. The eldest of the survivors Caroline had no liking for her siblings, as cold-hearted as their mother. Her father she loved and respected but he was so often away, she wondered if always of necessity, no love between husband and wife though surely at one time? As with Charles and herself? Now Papa at the Assizes, how greatly he was needed in this situation.

Putting an arm round the weeping child she murmured. "Please do not distress yourself, John. My mother asks her questions so that we may trace your family." To her mother, "he is such an innocent, with no experience of the world about him. But there should be no difficulty in tracing his family, there must already be a hue and cry for him."

John's sobs subsided. The lady's arm as comforting as Mama's had been. Drying his eyes on the handkerchief she put into his hand he confided: "Uncle Robert and Aunt Sophie are away but the servants will be searching for me. They are my friends."

He was interrupted by a knock at the door, the butler.

"The master sweeper is here your ladyship. He wishes to collect his apprentice."

"No!" cried John, clinging to Caroline, anguished eyes imploring mercy. "No please, he threatened to flog me as he did Tad when he fell. I will be your servant, anything but pray do not let him take me."

"Hush." said Caroline. "My mother will deal with Mr Billings." By the grimness of Lady Georgina's expression Mr Billings would not enjoy her dealing.

"Bring the man here," she instructed. "I wish to speak with him."

After tugging a black greasy forelock Sam Billings stood before Lady Georgina, grinning nervously. On first entering the room he had glared malevolence at John. As the boy gave a small cry of fear Caroline held him closer to her.

"Now, my man," began his inquisitor. "You claim this child is your apprentice?"

An obsequious leer. "'e is, craving yer ladyship's indulgence."

"You have of course his indentures? You have had permission of two..."

A hasty: "I only acquired the boy yesterday, no time ter mike it legal yer lidyship."

"You...acquired him? From whom, pray?"

Glibly, without hesitation: "From a beggar woman ma'am. She sold 'im me fer six guineas, wishing 'im ter be settled in a tride."

"And where did this unseemly transaction take place?"

Sam Billings had been well primed with his tale." At an inn

near me lodgings. The boy was strapped ter 'er back, asleep ma'am or dosed with laudanum ter keep 'im quiet."

Although astonished at this false tale John said nothing. He had only the haziest memory of waking in the cart with the woman and his forced drugging by Billings. He knew the sweep told wicked lies but had not the words to refute them. He could only shake his head, noticed only by Caroline.

"So," continued Lady Georgina. "You purchased a young child intending to apprentice him to your trade. You acted against the law. No boy under eight can be apprenticed, this child is barely five years of age..."

Sam Billings affected astonishment, hastily improvising. His instructors had failed to prepare him for a query as to the legality of his purchase. "Me lidy, I 'ad no notion 'e was that young. 'is ma said as 'ow 'e was undersized fer 'is age on account of some wasting disease."

An imperious wave of her ladyship's hand. "Pshaw! Do not try to bamboozle me with such moonshine! Now, we are certain this child was abducted, where from?"

Billings crossed himself. "As the good Lord is my witness ma'am I know nuffink of no abduction. I pied eight guineas fer 'im in all good faith."

Derision now, her ladyship tearing the sweep's tale to shreds. "Six guineas on your first account. It says much for the Lord's mercy you are not struck dead for falsehood, not to say blasphemy. The child is no beggar woman's brat, he remains here while we attempt to trace his family."

Billings stared at her in dismay. If it came out he had been paid by Robert Maltravers to forcibly abduct the boy it would be all over for him. He rightly guessed that Maltravers would deny all knowledge of the transaction, away at the time of the abduction. The woman who had lured John from his home had been Billings' accomplice. Folk would take Maltravers' word, not a sweep's.

As he groped for words Lady Georgina continued: "If you have any complaint about your loss I shall refer it to my husband. Sir Edwin Forester is a High Court judge, he will know how to deal with you."

Desperately Billings babbled: "I got no complaint yer lidyship..."

The imperious hand waved away any hopes he had of an escape from retribution. "But I have. You made this household an accomplice in your unlawful use of an underage apprentice. You sorely treated him, thrusting a small inexperienced child into a chimney and leaving him, uncaring as to whether he fell and was injured or killed. I shall ensure Sir Edwin instigates enquiries into your trade. Now go, but be assured you will hear further from us."

Defeated, Billings silently shambled from the room, not before casting another look of virulent hatred at John.

"Mama!" exclaimed Caroline. "You were magnificent!"

"Thank you my dear," drily replied her mother. "I detested the wretch, and his audacity in thinking to fool me with his tara-diddle. Sheer impudence!"

Fearing her mother's detestation for the sweep might not translate into compassion for John Caroline asked tentatively: "And John?"

Lady Georgina looked over to where John sat, eyes wide with apprehension. Not known for indecision, without due consideration which she would later regret, she pronounced: "We shall advertise for his family. In the meantime he stays here, the nursery is unoccupied since Rebecca and George outgrew it. I will allocate a maid to see to his needs." To John. "You are to be a good boy and not abuse our hospitality."

Though overwhelmed with relief to be spared Billings' cruelty John was subdued by Lady Georgina's cold words. In a voice he strove to keep from trembling he answered:

"You have my word, ma'am, I am deeply grateful for your

kindness."

"I shall provide for him," said Caroline, also grieved by her mother's severity. To John: "A maid will take you to the nursery where you need to rest after your ordeal. She will bring a meal when you wake. And," looking at his nightshift, "This afternoon I shall shop for more suitable clothing. Will that please you, John?"

John's vulnerable heart ached with love for her. "Oh yes ma'am, yes indeed!" Then with taught formality: "I am vastly obliged to you ma'am."

After the maid took him to the nursery Lady Georgina reproached her daughter.

"You make too much of him. Remember we know nothing of his background, his name or where he lives. True, he is a refined and intelligent child but I believe it is the custom in some families to allow the children of upper servants to be educated with their own. He speaks of servants as his friends."

Used as she was to her mother's lack of compassion and grateful for her grudging permission for John to be given shelter, Caroline could not refrain from protesting: "But Mama he is no servant's child. He speaks of a soldier father, of an uncle and aunt, of his poor dead mother..."

A testy interruption. Mama did not approve of her judgements being questioned. "Yes, yes, but until we know more about him I would prefer that he is kept apart from your sister and brothers. I also wish that you use caution in your dealings with him. He must not be allowed to take advantage of your misplaced kindness."

"Mama, that is unjust!" But Caroline knew from her mother's tightened mouth that it was useless to argue. Despite Mama's disapproval she would show every kindness to the little boy. What mattered it if he were a servant's child? She would do everything in her power to ensure his welfare. As she would her own little son had he survived.

FIVE

S am Billings had to plan for his own welfare. After viciously drubbing Barney, with a clout at innocent Tad for good measure, he lashed the equally guiltless horse into a cart-swaying gallop away from Forester House, vowing vengeance on the Maltravers brat, the cause of his downfall.

Downfall it was, he could no longer trade as chimney sweeper, that hellcat would ensure no one among her wide acquaintance employed him. Nor could his business survive the investigation she threatened. No choice but to expand his other trade – thieving, profiting from his knowledge of the desirable contents of grand houses. Forester House for certain but not while suspicion might fall on him. If the brat was still there he would make sure he never blabbed again.

To avoid being traced he must leave his lodgings. With his woman and children he occupied a room in a near derelict house in St Giles, forcibly ejecting the feeble half-starved family residing there and installing his apprentices on the much inhabited ground floor. Now he had no more need of them, set Tad adrift to fend for himself, he knew too much about Billings' dealings. Plenty of other houses in the rookeries where the Billings could settle among neighbours with their own reasons not to be inquisitive. Barney as his accomplice in thieving, the younger boy used for shoving through small windows, fifteen year old daughter Jess was already plying her own trade. Peg could do the same, nothing to occupy her now there were no children to buy or snatch as apprentices. Maybe it was for the best, he'd had thirty years as a sweep since the age of six, time for a change.

The Robert Maltravers' complacency at the success of their scheme was abruptly shattered by the advertisement for news of John's identity, not only in The Times but also in the more widely read Public Advertiser. All had gone so well. On their return from South Lambeth the pretence of finding among their letters the appalling news of Edward's death, their public grief made more desolate by dear John's disappearance. Doubtless he had wandered out of the grounds during the lodge keeper's fool's errand, the little innocent taken by a passing ruffian for some vile purpose. An all too common occurrence. Scapegoat Nurse Hunt was summarily dismissed for her neglect.

Robert and Sophie had been convinced that John was dead. Such a gently nurtured child could not long survive the ungentle hands of Sam Billings. The report of his rescue, the failure of their carefully laid scheme, had Robert wishing he could lay ungentle hands on the bungling fool of a sweeper. His tentative suggestion that they could reclaim the child from the advertiser, finding other ways to dispose of him was rejected with scorn by Sophie. The boy could testify he had been abducted by false words about his father wishing to see him, how could the abductors have known about the family other than by information from within. Did Robert imagine the sweep when traced would remain silent about their involvement? Robert suitably abashed, their problem still unsolved, how were they to untangle themselves from the web they had spun?

Sophie soon recovered from dismay, her more agile brain reasoning that only the name John appeared in the advertisement. The child did not know his surname or address. He had been rescued from a chimney sweeper, believed either sold to or abducted by him from a good home. A sadly common occurrence.

Robert was still uneasy. "But those who know of John's disappearance will surely suspect," he argued as they sat in the morning room with the newspapers.

"How many people?" asked Sophie. "This household yes, but we can ensure they do not see the papers, that is, those who can read. Burn them." Removing the advertisement pages she viciously thrust them into the fire. "There, see how they blaze. If only the little wretch had gone the same way."

Robert was still doubtful. "But the estate steward Horace er... Danvers is well able to read, he may make enquiries. And Edward's lawyers."

Sophie gave this more serious consideration, staring into the fire where the advertisements had crumbled to ashes. Her brow cleared, she nodded self-approvingly.

"Of course, so simple. Should they raise the matter we shall inform them we have made enquiries of the advertiser who gives no name but reached only via the newspapers, and are informed the child has been claimed by his family. We can spread the same story to all enquirers." She gave an impatient sigh. "Our real problem is that John seemingly resides with the advertiser, while he lives you cannot inherit. We must contact that wretch Billings for the address, the housekeeper will know where he is to be found. Let me think of an excuse to contact him..." A brief pause, then that self-satisfied smile Robert hated. "Yes, the chimney of the upper parlour needs attention. There my dear," she concluded complacently. "Have I not considered everything?"

"You have, my love," replied the still bemused Robert. "Everything." For his peace of mind he earnestly hoped so.

. . .

Not everything. Sophie greatly underestimated the loyalty, devotion and intelligence of the despised servants, genuinely grieving the loss of Captain Edward and their darling Jackie, bitterly resenting the loathed intruders.

Butler Walter Phillips, a tall lean man, impassive featured and of erect bearing as befitted his exalted position was deeply troubled, sharing his bewilderment with the housekeeper Mrs Grant. Relations between them were of an intimacy they imagined discreet but the source of sniggering comment among the younger servants. A harmless liaison, Phillips a bachelor, Mrs Grant a widow. They had awaited Captain Edward's return for permission to regularise the relationship, permission they knew would be warmly granted. Now they must await the permission of the new master of Maltravers Hall, if this happened to be Robert then with other servants they would seek more congenial places.

In the butler's pantry Phillips gave voice to his troubled thoughts.

"The letter conveying the appalling news of the Captain's death. I am convinced it was the same letter I passed to Mr Robert a week before his visit to South Lambeth."

"But how can that be, Walter?" asked Mrs Grant, a plump motherly woman, her pleasant countenance equally troubled. "Mr Robert found it among his letters on his return, he summoned us all so that he could read it to us in a sorrowful voice that deceived none of us. We were the ones that truly wept our grief."

"Indeed Charity, but I noticed the letter was definitely directed to Mrs Edward, so was the one I gave him some two weeks previous, and furthermore, as you know I have charge of letters the man brings and during their absence none bore that direction. Still grieving the loss of our dear lady I would have surely noticed."

Charity shook her head as if to clear her thoughts. "What can it mean, Walter? Why should he pretend to receive it on his return?"

"That is what greatly troubles me, Charity. I fear there is some wrong doing in this, but am at a loss to know what, and how I should proceed."

Charity recalled a matter that had bewildered her. "I also have a puzzle. Mrs Robert asked me to contact the chimney sweeper as soon as maybe, saying the upper parlour chimney needs attention. I informed her that he comes about every two months to this area and messages are left for him at the Bell Inn. But Walter, the chimney is in no need of attention, he saw to it on his last visit."

Phillips recalled the visit, the day the climbing boy had fallen and...yes, the day he handed Mr Robert that letter. It was too great a mental leap to suspect treachery but the doubt lodged in his intelligent brain. They looked sorrowfully at each other, unable to comprehend the evil now rampant in the once honourable Maltravers Hall.

The maid Tildy Pender had sobbed inconsolably at the news of Captain Edward's death and Jackie's disappearance. As a frightened eleven year old she had come to Maltravers Hall as scullery maid, finding a warmly pleasant home, courteously welcomed by Captain Edward with whom she fell in love, so tall and handsome, always kind. And Mrs Edward, gentle faced, fragile as a spring flower. Little Jackie, then a happy laughing three year old, adored by his parents. No banishment then to the nursery, with brief appearances in the parlour to receive a few condescending words from the Robert Maltravers. No, his parents revelled in his company, the Captain sweeping him into his arms for their exchange of kisses, the games they played while Mrs Edward laughed her pleasure. A loving little boy, when Tildy brought his meals Jackie would run to her, arms outstretched for a hug.

Such a difference when the Robert Maltravers arrived. Mrs Edward sickly with her confinement and mostly in her bed, meekly deferring to Mrs Robert's domineering ways, Jackie was not allowed to visit her, a boisterous four year old too wearing in her delicate condition. After her death, Jackie had been confined to the nursery, allowed only his morning rides and afternoon play periods in the gardens. He was forbidden contact with estate children and the comfort of his friends, haughtily dismissed by Mrs Robert as servants to be kept in their places.

Stable boy Will Cooper tried to comfort her though no less distraught. Tears were unmanly but he grieved inwardly. Guilt also, Jackie had called him brother, they had shaken hands on it, yet Will had not been able to protect him.

His arm round Tildy's shoulders as they sat on a bench in the park – out of view of the Hall – he spoke low in his husky not boy not yet man's voice.

"Blessed if I can fathom it. Jackie never wandered so far on his own, little feller such as he. And on the day the lodge keeper goes off on a false errand. What make you of it Tildy?"

Tildy dried her eyes on her apron. Cook would scold her something cruel if she knew the kitchen maid – promoted from scullery maid when Meg took off with a common foot soldier – idled in the park in her apron chatting to a stable lad. As yet only on friendly terms, she was a good girl and intended to stay that way though fond of quite handsome Will. Anyhow, Cook herself was taking it easy in her favourite chair toasting her feet at the kitchen fire. She considered Will's words.

"'Tis strange that the woman knew of the Captain. Ned told as how she accompanied him to the inn but a short way, then he lost sight and sound of her. What if she went back to the lodge to lure our Jackie away? If she told him the same tale he would willingly go with her to meet his dear papa."

Will considered her words, then recalled the lodge-keeper's tale. "But Ned saw hide nor hair of any one passing him as he walked to the inn and back. You say the truth Tildy, how came it she knew of the Captain? Only one of us could have told her, Mr Robert being away."

"None of us would do such mischief!" indignantly replied Tildy. She paused. "Oh, save for footman Parker, nasty spying wretch. And yes," she rattled off excitedly. "I did see him pacing outside the nursery the morning Jackie disappeared but did think it was Nurse Hunt he was sniffing after." She shook her head. "But what would it gain him to pass on family matters to a beggarly woman?" She jumped up. "Lor, there's the chapel clock striking eleven. Must get back."

"So must I," said Will. Then angrily, "But I tell you this Tildy, I shall not rest content till I find out what devil took Jackie. I shall get him back, just you see."

Tildy gazed at him with shining eyes. "You are a true man Will." Then coyly: "You may kiss me if you wish."

Will very much wished. Embracing her he planted an inexpert kiss on her lips before they scurried off to their tasks.

Robert and Sophie Maltravers were too absorbed in their own problems to be aware of the servants' seething discontent and suspicion. Their need of money became desperate. Although household expenses were met by the estate steward they were dangerously low on private money for clothes, entertainment and Robert's gambling, his creditors increasingly clamorous despite his assurances of great expectations. He fretted to approach Edward's lawyers, Sophie urged caution. Wait until the search for John proved fruitless, his death accepted as a certainty. Their attempts to contact sweeper Billings had been unavailing. In answer to enquiries at the Bell Inn the host informed them that Billings had given up the trade and his whereabouts unknown. So died their hopes of tracing John's rescuer. Their tale of contacting the advertiser only to discover the child sadly was not their John and claimed by his family was believed, why should it be doubted? Were they not honourable people? Relatives of the much lamented gallant Captain Edward? They were far from being honourable but who could suspect such treachery?

Robert's impatience could no longer be denied. A particularly disastrous night at the tables and an inability to meet his debts resulted in exclusion from his club. Without informing Sophie, the following afternoon he rode into Richmond to call on Edward's lawyers Harlow and Stanford. He received a frosty greeting from the senior partner Lancelot Harlow. Partner Stanford, a pug dog, drowsed through the winter day in a basket near the small office fire. Harlow was a small neat man affecting the costume of some twenty years past, long frock coat, patterned waistcoat, ruffed shirt, knee breeches and silk hose, buckled shoes, a powdered wig that had lost its popularity after the younger Pitt's tax on hair powder. He sat at his desk, regarding with disapproval the arrogant young man lounging opposite him, an elegantly-booted foot across a knee.

"You wish to consult us sir?" he asked in a chill precise voice. Partner Stanford snored, twitching in his sleep.

"Obviously," drawled Robert. "As you are aware my brother Edward is sadly deceased and his only son missing some two months and unhappily must also be presumed deceased." A false rueful smile. "Sad but as my brother's only kin may I know how long I must wait before receiving my inheritance? I realise these matters take an accursed tedious time so a substantial sum in advance would be acceptable".

Mr Harlow blinked his astonishment at such uncouthness, unseemly haste. Though happily aware of Edward Maltravers' wishes he took from a shelf a packet tied with ribbon. Untying it with slow deliberation he withdrew a document which he pretended to peruse with several muttered comments, ignoring Robert's exasperated exclamations.

"The last will and testament of Captain Edward Fitzjohn Maltravers," he finally pronounced with a wintry pleasure in exploding this insufferable smirker's hopes. "He stipulates that should his offspring not survive to inherit, his entire estate is to go to his wife's brother Josiah Templeton, close friend, sober and trustworthy..." the words emphasised, "... who would manage the estate efficiently, respecting those serving it and furthering Captain Maltravers' concept of good housing and schooling. Mr Templeton to ensure an allowance of two thousand a year, comfortable quarters at Maltravers Hall and every consideration shown to his widow should she survive him. There are also bequests to Captain Maltravers' steward and servants."

Robert had listened in sick disbelief. "Damn it, what of me?"

"Your brother leaves you nothing apart from the generous annuity you receive," replied Mr Harlow with scarce concealed satisfaction. "He states you were informed that having received many considerable sums to pay off your debts you need expect nothing from his will." Harlow longed to repeat Edward's confiding that Robert was not to be trusted with the estate and would bring bankruptcy and disgrace to Maltravers Hall, to the name of Maltravers.

After foul oaths that had Mr Harlow raising shocked eyebrows and a drowsy growl from his partner, Robert shouted: "Be damned sure I shall contest the accursed will through the courts. Who is this wretch Templeton? Never heard of him."

Having recovered his professional aplomb Mr Harlow spoke in his normal precise tone as though Maltravers' coarse outburst had not taken place. "At present he is resident in the West Indies, he owns a plantation run by freed slaves who have a colony there. I am awaiting possible news of John before acquainting Mr Templeton with the news." Again Mr Harlow refrained from adding that had Templeton resided in England he would have been appointed guardian of Edward's wife and son, Robert was the choice born of desperation and Edward had not anticipated so long an absence. With deliberation Harlow replaced the document in the packet and tied the ribbon. "That sir is all the information I am able to give you. Obviously I shall keep you informed of future developments. Good day to you sir."

"You have not heard the last of this," snarled Robert as he flung out of the office.

"Nor has the deplorable Mr Robert," Harlow informed his sleeping partner. Stanford snuffled his agreement.

In a fury Robert rode back to Maltravers Hall, using his whip to goad the horse into a breakneck gallop. Already the winter daylight was fading, trees and hedgerows spectral silhouettes. A post chaise and four rattled past him towards Richmond, he could discern no passenger. Had it taken a visitor to the Hall? No one he or Sophie had invited.

Reaching the Hall he dismounted, flinging the reins to the stable lad, not deigning to look at him so unaware of the boy's joyful face and shining eyes. Striding angrily round to the front of the house he approached the entrance...then halted abruptly, the blood draining from his face, knees threatening to buckle. At the top of the steps, silhouetted against the candle-lit hall stood a tall uniformed figure, to Robert's terrified eyes an avenging spirit.

"My God," he mumbled through bloodless lips. "It cannot be."

The man ran down the steps to confront him, face contorted with agonised grief.

"You damned fiend," hoarsely whispered Edward Maltravers. "Where is my son?"

Six

Robert Maltravers' exultation at his brother's death had been somewhat premature. Six weeks before he received the letter, Captain Edward Maltravers boarded the East Indiaman *Pelican* at the Cape of Good Hope, healed of wounds received at Assaye. In the heat of battle Sergeant Tom Hart had pulled him from under his stricken horse, at the risk of his own life half-carrying his Captain to the medical tent where Edward received superficial treatment. There had been so many other horrific injuries during that bloody battle. Accompanied by Tom Hart, with other casualties he was taken by wagon to Madras for treatment at Fort St George hospital, enduring several days' agonised journey during which two of his companions died. After more days of conflicting medical attention by doctors disagreeing on the right treatment he shakily rose from his bed, shouting furiously as they argued.

"No more using my body as a battlefield for your poisons. Cupping, leeches, arsenic, mercury, bark, steel... What next? Eyes of newts and toes of frogs? Birth strangled babe? No more, I am returning to England..."

"You cannot," interrupted the chief torturer. "You must stay until cured."

Maltravers continued his diatribe, his voice hoarse with pain and fatigue. "Cured, when you were still treating those wounded at Seringapatam years after the battle? No, the Prospero sails tomorrow, I shall be on her. Sergeant Hart," he called to where his faithful attendant waited for the doctors to complete their consultation. "My clothes please. Here's my purse; book our passages on the Prospero, take care the thieving captain does not overcharge."

"Willingly sir," replied Tom Hart, equally angered at his captain's treatment. "Leave before these boobies kill you. And I know how to deal with ships captains," adding to himself, even though I cannot always deal with a stubborn Dragoon captain, the good Lord bless his brave heart.

So they left Fort St George, the doctors disclaiming with relief all further responsibility for the troublesome ingrate captain.

At the Cape the *Prospero* docked for fresh provisions. By then Edward's leg injury had become infected, he sweated profusely with fever. Refusing the ministrations of the ship's medical men who advised amputation, Edward demanded to be taken off the ship for treatment. By the Treaty of Amiens that year the Cape of Good Hope had been returned by the British to the Batavian Republic, the colony again in Dutch hands. Permission was sought and granted for Edward's treatment there, attended by Sergeant Tom Hart. Almost delirious with pain Edward refused to be taken to the hospital where British surgeons still practised, he would sooner be left to die. While in Madras he had been informed of an East India Company doctor who, hearing of cures obtained by Indian doctors, experimented with herbal and plant remedies. When dismissed by the outraged Medical Board he settled at the Cape, purchasing land on which he grew medicinal plants and herbs, fruit trees, at his small private hospital tending all who came, regardless of nationality. "Eccentric fellow," Edward was warned. "Treats everyone as equals, wears native dress. But report has it he effects miraculous cures."

"I want herb... doctor," he muttered through dry lips to Sergeant Hart. "Ask bearers to take me to... Mark...who? Halliday? Yes...Halliday."

Sergeant Tom had doubts. "Are you sure of him, Captain? Sounds more like our own cunning men with their mumbo jumbo quack cures, toad eaters and the like."

Made irritable by pain and fever Edward snarled: "Do as I say!" Then, all energy spent: "Butchers at hospital... have my leg off...kill me in ... days. Must die... whole man."

His will prevailed, he was carried by litter to Mark Halliday who having had word of the injured man's insistence on seeing him welcomed Edward and his Sergeant with smiling tranquillity, starting the treatment immediately Edward had been bathed.

Sergeant Hart suspiciously regarded the lean bearded long haired man in an outlandish white robe girded at the waist, sandals on bare feet. Did he imagine himself the Lord Jesus? Blasphemy! He watched with horror as Halliday covered a cloth with a thick green paste, placing it on Captain Edward's festering wound.

"It will draw out the infection," he told Edward. He placed a cool slender hand on Edward's fevered moist forehead, compassionate dark eyes seeming to penetrate his soul. "You must fast for thirty-six hours to rid your body of poisons. Drink only juice of freshly pressed fruit and vegetables."

"The compress is very soothing "murmured Edward. "Having no appetite fasting will not trouble me."

"No," said Tom, now less suspicious of Halliday. "The past days the captain has not eaten enough to keep a sparrow alive, but he is always sparing in his diet."

"Good," approved Halliday. "That will greatly aid his recovery. Too many of our compatriots here and in India greatly overindulge and suffer for it." He eyed the Sergeant's sturdy frame. "A little abstinence would do you no harm sir."

Not a regime good trencherman Tom was likely to adopt. Halliday left him to tend the Captain while he saw to other patients. A herbal sleeping draught sent Edward into his most restful sleep in months, his fever abating. The dressing to be changed twice daily, faithfully attended to by Tom Hart.

After three days Edward was back to his clear thinking self, his wound cleanly healing. With normality came a sense of urgency.

"I must return to England immediately," he told Sergeant Tom. "During my illness I had distressing visions of great harm in my family." He did not confide to Tom the appalling conviction he had of Jackie screaming out to him for help and his prayer to the God in whom he had lost faith to help his beloved child as he was powerless to do so. There had been a loving bond between him and Jackie since he first held the squalling new-born in his arms, the healthy survivor after Harriet's two miscarriages. Had that bond snapped? Tom's practical words shook him out of his musings.

"You had a high fever. Ranting at times like a lunatic in Bedlam. Not that I've been there," he added hastily. "But so I've heard tell. Not surprising you were troubled by strange dreams."

"Possibly, but there has been no news for so many months. I realise letters would not reach me while in action, with constant moves and I have been unable to write, but I am still uneasy." He sighed impatiently. "I am weary of bloodshed. I became a soldier to protect my country, not to assist a plunder hungry Company take possession of territories not rightfully theirs. A trading company allowed to build an empire by bribery and corruption! Nor do I wish to boost the vainglory of Richard and Arthur Wellesley."

"Ah but Captain," argued Sergeant Hart. "Think how we benefit a benighted heathen country where rulers fight among themselves with no thought for their people, remember they voluntarily cede lands for military aid in their many squabbles. British rule will unite them. And the Company gives employment to native soldiers..."

"To fight their own people." Mark Halliday had entered the room. "Commanded by British officers, often with insensitive arrogance. The Sepoys, many of high caste have a culture older and finer than those they serve."

Sergeant Tom was silent. Having had many similar arguments with the Captain he now felt beleaguered. With a reassuring smile for Tom, Halliday said to Edward:

"You should be fit to travel in a few days. The Pelican is docked here for provisions, she leaves on Thursday. Are you so bent on leaving here? Stay until completely restored to health."

"Aye," agreed the Sergeant who had revelled in the comparative peace and plenty of the Cape. "A very acceptable prescription, doctor."

"What!" exclaimed Edward. "Leave my wife and little Jackie, my new child, the people on my estate at the mercy of..." He broke off, family loyalty prevailing. "I have already left them too long thanks to the Company's lust for new possessions, Arthur Wellesley's revelling in the people's adulation." Rising still somewhat shakily from his bedside chair he placed a hand on Halliday's shoulder . "I am eternally grateful to you, Mark, I owe you my life. But I am compelled to be on the Pelican when she sails."

Halliday spread out his hands. "So be it, though I shall miss your company, I seldom have the opportunity to converse with someone who shares my interests. You will write to inform me of your progress?"

Edward held out his hand. "Gladly, here's to friendship. Visit us when you can be spared here. Talk to our learned medical men, instil your knowledge into their addled pates. Some may listen."

As they warmly shook hands Sergeant Tom hid a smile. The Captain and his airy notions! A diet of vegetables and fruit, no red meat, herbal medicines? Moonshine, the doctor's methods would never be accepted in England.

Three days later Captain Maltravers and Sergeant Hart boarded the *Pelican* for the journey home, little knowing what awaited them. Nor did unprincipled brother Robert and even more unscrupulous Sophie.

The voyage from the Cape encountered no hazards. The *Pelican* sturdily rode out all winter storms, beneficial in that no enemy ships ventured to engage the fully armed Indiaman. Edward Maltravers chafed with impatience while Sergeant Tom Hart revelled in the company, particularly the female element. Passengers included soldiers, families returning to England, ailing Anglo-Indians hoping to regain health after suffering the climate and self-inflicted ailments. Also East India Company officials on leave, some of high position in India, unaware that their own compatriots would not afford them the deference to which they had become accustomed.

Edward was among those chosen to share the captain's table, a nightly ordeal enduring inane chatter. On one such evening he listened with tight-lipped contempt to a brainless fashionably gowned woman, powdered hair piled high, flashing with jewellery as if the workaday ship were an aristocratic soiree. Nothing particularly grand about her, a tax collector's wife, her rich attire giving some credence to tales of how much, or little, of the collected tax was received by the Company. In her shrill voice she told of one dreadful experience.

"I was taking the air in our grounds, a native servant keeping his distance behind me when a snake rose up before me, deadly poisonous I was later told. The servant pulled me away before it could strike." Murmurs of horror from her listeners. "Well, of course I was grateful but so appalling to be handled by a black servant! We had to dismiss him, naturally." Murmurs of agreement.

Edward's indignation could not be restrained. "Dismissed for saving your life madam?"

The woman had rather taken to the handsome captain, now she bristled at the implied criticism.

"Indeed no, but such familiarity is not to be tolerated. A black man!" She gave an exaggerated shudder, other ladies squealed their revulsion, fanning themselves as if to ward off the vapours.

No more black than you are white madam, thought Edward. Aloud he said:

"It is to be hoped the poor fellow learned his lesson and if he managed to secure another place he would leave memsahibs to their fate sooner than risk his livelihood." A comment not well received by the company who thought Edward an uncommon odd fellow. He was somewhat entertained by the experience of another woman, small and dowdy compared with the collector's wife. As one of a party on a hunt using a tamed tiger to kill antelope she was seated in the cart with the blindfolded tethered creature. Blindfold removed it was set loose among the herd to make its kill, then recaptured, blindfolded and returned to the cart.

"So terrifying," she squeaked. "The creature growling, its tail lashing inches from my face." With an unbecoming wrinkle of her snub nose: "And such an...an odour!"

Edward grinned unfeelingly. After that experience she would find fox hunting very unexciting; risk free riding with a score of companions after a small terrified creature, the killing done by a pack of baying hounds. For a country squire Edward realised he was indeed a very odd fellow.

He often sat next to an ex-Company surgeon whose ideas were nearer his own, though James Black was perpetually discontented. On many subjects they agreed, the inefficiency of Company rule, its greed for new territory, the bellicose Wellesley brothers, the appalling state of medical care. Black's wife had died of dysentery after much suffering, not aided by conflicting treatment by her doctors. This Edward could well understand, citing his own experiences. That evening Black talked at tedious length on the inefficiency of collectors, uncaring that he was in hearing distance of the collector and his lady. Ridiculous of the Company to appoint newly arrived employees as collectors to replace the native Zemindars - collectors – who knew the country, how weather affected the crops and consequently how much tax to collect... Wearying of Black's calculations Edward escaped on the plea of exhaustion, still convalescing from his injury, exaggerating his limp as he left to join Sergeant Hart on the deck. Black an interesting intelligent man of wide learning but too dogmatic, so sure of the rightness of his opinions, dismissing those of others. Edward longed to be free of them all: Anglo-Indian hauteur, collectors, tiger hunts, Zemindars. He looked for a tranquil life among his own people, his family, the fresh green of English countryside.

Tom Hart had adapted well to his environment, not caring he was excluded from the quality at the *Pelican* captain's table. Captain Edward seemed weary of it. Tom found himself a great favourite with the ladies of lesser rank, especially disillusioned women who with the Company's encouragement had gone to India seeking husbands, unkindly dubbed the fishing fleet. Those unsuccessful in making a catch were forced to keep themselves as best they could until the Company, concerned for their moral welfare, assisted their passage home. Tom Hart was regarded as a possible catch, he slipped through their nets by pleading he already had a wife. Untrue, as a soldier from boyhood, ever on the move, he took his pleasure where offered. A personable fellow he had no shortage of offers.

When the Captain appeared on deck that evening Tom was consoling a sergeant's widow who bitterly complained of her sleeping arrangements, a hammock slung over bilge water on the cannon deck. As the poor ailing Captain's attendant Tom shared his quarters, though in truth Edward, almost restored to health, sturdily refused any mollycoddling. Pressing the lady's hand to express his sympathy Tom abandoned her to join the Captain. A plague on her hammock, the lady was charming and willing but the risk of the hammock collapsing into bilge water was not so alluring.

Edward was in a more than usual thoughtful mood. "I am mortally weary of this mode of life," he confided. "When we reach England I shall resign my commission, devote myself to managing the estate, I have so many ideas for improvement. And to care for my wife and children, little Jackie is in need of a father's guidance and I have been a neglectful husband to Harriet." More brooding, Tom waited, sorry at heart at the thought of losing the Captain. Staring across the calm waters gleaming silver under the starlit sky Edward continued: "See here Tom, will you give up soldiering? I need someone I can trust to help with the estate. Not a personal attendant, I am well able to ten to my own needs, I have never employed a valet. But as a trusty friend I can think of none better than yourself."

Tom Hart's turn to brood. After the carnage of Seringapatam and Assaye, he too had enough of slaughter. At fourteen he had joined the army, running off from his apprenticeship to a London brewer who after too freely sampling his wares entertained himself by flogging his boys or carnally using the more appealing, Tom not among them. Twenty-five years of soldiering, he had done enough for king and country. Time to settle. And the Captain needed someone to bridle his fantastical notions, an innocent, unworldly despite his learning and experience. Personal attendant? He needed a nursemaid.

Awaiting his reply Edward said: "You would not lose by it, you have my word. Come Tom, your answer?"

"Your word is more than good enough for me, Captain. A straighter man never lived." He held out a hand. "Your man, sir."

· · ·

Reaching Dover the *Pelican* docked at six on a bleakly cold February morning. Those passengers unprepared for the change of climate shivering in their Indian muslins and fine cloth, envying Edward Maltravers and Sergeant Tom Hart their warm greatcoats and mufflers. In eager haste Edward hired a post chaise and four to convey Tom and himself to Maltravers Hall, promising double fare for a swift journey. To lighten the load he arranged for their boxes to follow by delivery wagon. He had not the opportunity to send word of his coming, he knew of the *Prospero's* fate but not that his name was listed among those lost, a Company clerk's inefficiency not recording his removal at the Cape. Nor had letters reached him with news of Harriet's death. So nothing to cloud the happy anticipation with which he travelled through the much loved, much missed English countryside, excited as a child pointing out to Tom Hart the towns and villages through which they travelled. A brief halt at an inn for a hurried meal and change of horses, then off again, reaching Maltravers Hall by late afternoon.

Throwing his purse to Tom Hart to pay for the journey Edward ran up the steps and pulled the entrance bell cord. A footman appeared, one he did not know. Staring at the dishevelled traveller the man said disdainfully: "Mr and Mrs Robert Maltravers are out. What is your business with them?"

Astounded at such discourtesy Edward pushed past the man. "My business, whoever you are, is as master of Maltravers Hall. I trust you do not welcome all visitors in that boorish fashion. Where is Mr Phillips?"

As he strode through the hall Phillips appeared, alerted by the raised voices. At the sight of Edward he abruptly halted, wide eyed, mouth open.

"What the devil, Phillips?" demanded Edward. "You look as if you observed a ghost. And why did this man attempt to deny me entrance to my own home?"

Recovering from his astonishment Phillips' normally grave

expression gave way to a great beam of delight. Never had Edward seen more than a brief smile from his austere butler.

"Captain Edward!" Phillips seized his hand, another unknown gesture. "Oh Captain, we believed you dead! This is...I cannot express my delight."

Edward warmly shook his hand. "Dead? Far from it." Then the answer to the puzzle. "You believed I had gone down with the Prospero? I was taken off when we reached the Cape, infected wound and fever."

Mrs Grant had come into the hall, hearing the last words. Running to Edward she embraced him, tears of joy glistening on her face.

"Oh dear sir, you are restored to us. God be praised!"

Deeply moved by this display of affection Edward was briefly silent. Tom Hart had come into the hall, a witness to the Captain's rapturous welcome. He nodded his approval. Such devotion on the part of the servants boded well for his new position as the Captain's right hand man. The maid Tildy was another witness, with a little scream of delight she ran to spread the happy news to other servants, including stable boy Will.

After his rapturous welcome Edward glanced towards the stairs. No sign of Harriet coming to welcome him, of Jackie. A surge of sick premonition.

"Where is Mrs Maltravers, is she not well? And Jackie?"

Phillips and Mrs Grant glanced at each other, shock replacing delight.

"Oh sir," whispered Charity Grant. "Do you not know, did you not receive the letters?"

"Know what?" hoarsely demanded Edward. "I have received no letters these six months or more. My many moves, the voyages...For pity's sake, what news?"

Again the glances between the servants. Who was to break the news? A woman's place, Phillips' expression seemed to say.

Guessing the truth Tom Hart took his position by the Captain's side.

"Come sir, I fear bad news. Will you not be seated?"

Edward resisted Tom's attempt to steer him towards a hall chair. He stood erect, soldier-like as Mrs Grant gently broke the appalling news. Mrs Edward dying in childbirth, his new son also dead. And dearest Jackie... disappeared some three months ago, believed abducted by a beggar woman. Mr Robert and his wife had been absent, staying with relatives at the time. Tom Hart did not miss the glance Mrs Grant and the butler exchanged, nor did he suppose had the captain.

Edward now slumped into the chair, head bowed as he absorbed the news. A stricken man, his life fallen apart. The servants were silent, sharing his grief, Tom with a hand on his shoulder.

A few moments only, summoning all his inner strength Edward raised his head, white faced, features haggard with anguish. In a scarcely recognisable voice he asked:

"My brother and his wife, where are they?"

"Mr Robert rode off some two hours ago," replied Phillips. "Mrs Robert has taken the carriage to make calls before she and Mr Robert dine....Ah, that sounds like Mr Robert's horse."

Without a word Edward strode to the door and flung it open. He stood, heart filled with scarcely endurable grief, anguish, waiting for Robert. As he approached the entrance Edward ran down the steps to confront him, in his fury blind to his brother's shocked expression.

"You damned fiend," he hoarsely whispered. "Where is my son?"

Seven

John Maltravers still lived with the Forester family, begrudgingly by some members. Apart from his beloved Mrs Caroline he found favour with Sir Edwin Forester, impressed by the child's solemn courtesy, his intelligence. At first John was somewhat in awe of the judge. Sir Edwin was tall, of spare build, grave featured as befitted a high court judge, though his brown eyes spoke of a gentle nature. His shock of white hair added to his distinction. Neatly barbered, not tied back as this had become an outmoded fashion. No powder. John had expected to see him in robes and full wig as in the pictures he had seen in books. Not even a small wig and his attire no more fanciful than Papa's when out of uniform. What had Mama called him? Yes, neat but not gaudy. The judge was respected as a fair man though by some as over-inclined to leniency, sending only the worst male-factors to the gallows. By contrast his lady showed no mercy. Judge, jury and executioner in one imperious frame. Two months after John's rescue she held court in the morning room attended by Sir Edwin and daughter Caroline.

"We have been patient long enough," she decreed. "Despite our advertisement no one has claimed the boy…"

"But many people have written to say they have also lost children in that way," bravely interrupted Caroline. "They too have failed in their search."

Her comment impatiently waved away. "That is not our concern, Caroline. Kindly do not interrupt. No one has claimed John, if he were of a good family we should have heard by now. As I conjectured, he is probably the son of an upper servant, as is the custom in some misguided families educated with their children. Servants would not have access to newspapers, even if able to read. It is possible a parent sold him to the beggar woman, thence to the chimney sweeper. We should no longer have him in the house, he must go to the foundling hospital..."

"Mama!" Caroline exclaimed in horror, her father uttering an appalled "No!" "Pardon my frankness but that is so unjust! I am convinced that John is of gentle birth. I have already promised to provide for him and would do so until he is of an age to be settled in a profession or respectable trade. He cannot go to a foundling home to be bullied and ill-used, in too few years apprenticed to a villainous master. We have advertised but once, I will pay for another appeal, the first may have been overlooked..."

Lady Georgina had tried to interrupt, now she did.

"Poppycock! The advertisement was well displayed, could not have been overlooked. No one wants the boy, maybe with good reason. How do we know what seeds of viciousness and corruption may develop as he grows."

Caroline gasped in disbelief, Sir Edwin delivered his own verdict.

"As Caroline says, you are unjust. I speak from experience, there is no evil in that good obedient child. You have banished him to the nursery, he can have no bad influence on our children..." Quite the reverse, he told himself, our wretched brats are ill-disciplined, unmannerly. My fault for frequent absences. "...but treat him well. We can consider a suitable trade or profession when he is more grown – say have him trained to the sea service or the army, he tells us his father is a soldier, a captain."

Lady Georgina had remained silent, pursed lips proclaiming her displeasure. But she recognised defeat.

"Very well, as my wishes count for nothing I have nothing further to say." She had, to Caroline: "You have taken responsibility for the boy, I hope you do not live to regret it. A waif of unknown parentage! He should be sent from this house but as my opinion is set at nought... I shall go to my room, I have a headache."

Aching head nevertheless held high she made her dignified way to the door, the judge hastening to open it for her grand exit. He heard the scurry of feet. Aha, his detestable offspring had been eavesdropping. Much good may it do them.

George and Rebecca Forester believed their spying had done them much good. More ammunition for their campaign against the hated intruder. True, John was virtually a prisoner in the nursery save for walks with Caroline Claremont. But though isolation had been intended to protect the Forester children from possible contamination, it did not prevent those children tormenting John whenever they could sneak unseen to the nursery, whilst John's attendant maid was employed on other duties and Rebecca free of her governess. George had a tutor, Mr Lester, who was engaged during the school holiday to instil some knowledge into his thick skull but Mr Lester had only two hour periods morning and afternoon to accomplish that hopeless task.

Twelve year old Rebecca was a willing accomplice. George, at thirteen a well grown bully, the terror of smaller boys at his school, also tried to enlist the aid of brother Joseph, at eighteen awaiting entry to Oriel College, Oxford, but he had too many other interests to participate in childish amusement. He was to study law, his father's position assuring his admission to the Inner

Temple whatever the results of the necessary terms at Oriel. As the Forester heir with wealth at his disposal on his father's demise, Joseph did not intend to exert himself when eventually called to the Bar. Why should he? There would be no need of money. Now he was learning the ways of a dashing young buck, perfecting his seduction skills on the female staff and lower-order Blackheath wenches. So what cared he for an infant incarcerated out of sight of his lofty self?

The other son of the family was of no account. Matthew, a sixteen year old simpleton damaged at birth by the maladroit use of forceps, was secreted in the country to spare the family the disgrace of an idiot son. So it fell to George and Rebecca to uphold the honour of Forester House.

Hostilities commenced shortly after George returned home for the extended Christmas holiday, he would not return to the academy until February. A lengthy spell of freedom for idle hands to find mischief. On that first occasion he and Rebecca waited until sister Caroline brought John back from his morning walk. He was perched on the window seat gazing across to the bleak leafless trees and bushes of the wintry heath, thinking of spring at his own home, green lawns and flower beds, playing games with Papa. Startled out of his reverie he gave a small cry as the door was thrust open and a large boy, to John a clean version of Barney Billings, and a rough girl ran in.

"Here you," shouted the boy. "I am Master George Forester, son of this house, and the lady is Miss Rebecca. Stand up when I address you."

John had already risen at their entrance, now he stared, astonished at such crudity. He slightly inclined his head in greeting, the boy deserved no more.

"Good day, my name is John..."

George contorted his already unprepossessing pimpled face. "We know who you are, John no name. You have no right in a gentleman's household, chimney sweeper's boy."

"Climbing boy!" shrilled Rebecca, sticking out her tongue. Then holding her nose: "Phew, how he stinks!"

Though shocked and bewildered at this boorish attack John stood erect. He spoke quietly but with dignity.

"I am no sweeper's boy. My father is a gentleman, Captain Edward, a soldier fighting for this country. You should not speak to me so rudely."

"A soldier!" jeered George "Did he lay with your harlot mother in a ditch?"

"Bastard son of a harlot!" Rebecca's governess would have swooned had she heard her charge utter such words. Rebecca was also a pupil of her brothers who delighted in making her language as foul as their own.

John did not understand the words but knew a gross insult had been intended. Face flushed, eyes bright with anger he confronted them, small fists clenched. The Maltravers household would have recognised a miniature replica of his father in a rare rage.

"My mother was a gentlewoman just as my father is a gentleman. If he heard you say such bad words he would be very angry. Apologise or..."

George loomed over him. John glared back, head high, defiant.

"Impudent harlot's spawn," snarled George. "Apologise? Kiss my arse! Take that for your insolence."

Seizing John by his hair he cuffed his head repeatedly until he felt giddy. He flailed out with his fists but his feeble blows made no impression on George's solid body. Rebecca pranced round him viciously pinching his arms, trilling "Harlot's spawn, harlot's spawn!" John endured. He would shed no tears before these... devil's spawn. He did not know what spawn was but it must be a bad word.

The torture came to an abrupt end when the maid's steps were heard on the back stairs. Rebecca ran giggling out to the main stairs. George hissed: "Say one word of this and I will come here tonight and set fire to your bed." With a final cuff he too ran from the room.

The maid entered the nursery with John's meal. She saw with concern his flushed face and dishevelled clothing. She liked the child, always polite, and no trouble to care for, unlike the fiendish George and Rebecca. Rudely spoken they amused themselves by untying her apron strings and throwing her cap out of the window into the mud, getting her into the housekeeper's bad books.

"Why, what is amiss with you John? And tears not far off neither."

Mindful of George's threat John blinked back the tears.

"It is nothing, Mary. I fell off the window seat and bumped my head."

Mary had some inkling of the truth, having heard the voices as she ascended the stairs. But what could she do, more than her place was worth to report those young devils, especially as her ladyship had for some reason taken against John.

"Lor now, what a child you are for tumbling." She wetted a cloth in the wash bowl and rinsed his face and hands. "Is that clean enough for your lordship?"

A feeble smile. "Thank you Mary. I am not a lordship, please call me Jackie as my friends do."

She bent to kiss him. "Bless you, Jackie it will be. Now eat your meal like a good little Jackie."

The tormenting had been repeated, not regularly as the pleasure for the Forester children would have soon palled. Infrequent as it was John lived in dread of another attack, of being set alight in his little bed, he believed George well capable of it. His was a lonely sad existence lightened only by his walks with Caroline. She also visited him when she could, bringing little books to help his reading. Unknown to her mother she paid Mr Lester to give John an hour a day tutoring, Lester finding him a more rewarding pupil than numskull George. The maid Mary would stay for a chat when not needed elsewhere. And so the long days passed. Then came the day George and Rebecca eavesdropped on the discussion of John's future. Such a gift! They ran to the nursery where John was carefully practising his letters.

"Here, bastard boy," George greeted him. "We have some very special news for you. No need to be at your books any longer." He waited for John's response. In vain, John kept his eyes lowered on his book, ready for the cuff he knew would come. It did, with the usual pinch from Rebecca.

"Take heed when I speak to you, ditch born of a drab." Dullard George had happily absorbed the more colourful language of Shakespeare and his peers.

John looked up, meeting George's eyes with a steady defiant stare.

"What is your news? Tell me then leave me in peace. Mrs Caroline will be here soon for our walk, she will not take kindly to your presence."

George was angered by this defiance. "You are too saucy, beggar's imp. You will not be so calm when we tell you that you are presently to be sent to sea."

"Yes," said Rebecca. "Mama said a foundling home where they will beat you every day, but Papa said you must go to sea as soon as maybe."

"To sea!" exclaimed John. "But I am a soldier's son."

"What a fine soldier you would make," jeered George. "No, you are to be sent to sea. They need small ones to get inside the cannons to clean them. If you get stuck they fire the cannon, blow you to the devil." George's imagination now took fresh flights. "And to climb the rigging in storms to repair it." Now a final most damaging thrust. One that George had secretly revelled in since he had concocted it. "Seamen are very short of women so they make carnal use of young boys."

"What does that mean?" whispered John, his face pale.

George grinned. "Upon my word, are not you the innocent!" Bending over John he whispered details of what to expect of women hungry sailors. Overhearing, Rebecca sniggered behind a hand, adding to her own knowledge, not to be repeated to her governess.

Wide-eyed with horror and disgust John cried: "You lie! That is bad, evil!"

"Call me a liar would you," snarled George. As he lifted a fist to aim a blow at John's head Caroline called from the hall.

"Bring your coat and cap John. Time for our walk."

Seizing them John ran from the room. George and Rebecca waited until he and Caroline left the house, Rebecca pouring ink over John's copy book, his carefully formed letters and numbers.

"That will spoil his walk, sneaking little toad," said George as they left the nursery.

John usually loved his walks with Caroline, the highlight of his lonely days. When the weather was inclement she would join him in the nursery, reading to him, admiring his writing. Very soon, he promised, he would write her a letter, how he wished he could write one to Papa. On their walks they would rest on a seat in the park to watch the fashionable people take their constitutionals.

"In the summer the ton parade in all their finery," Caroline told John. "Some quite fantastical, the posturing and prinking of the dandies vastly absurd. But very gay and colourful."

John looked at her dark clothing. "And you ma'am, do you dress more gay?"

"I have not yet completed my period of mourning." Never would her grief for the loss of Charles and their child be complete. "Even when it is I shall not join the ton, I am not enamoured of society folk." A prattling shallow crowd, she told herself. Her secret longing to purchase a cottage far removed from Forester House, her mother and siblings. To live quietly with John as her adopted child. What fury and outrage that would cause in her family, perhaps with the exception of her father. For certain her mother would disown her. Blissful thought! Her spirit freed from the shackles of her mother's domination. But nothing could be done until all attempts to trace John's father failed.

On the day George and Rebecca taunted John on his fate their walk was unusually subdued. No eager chatter from him on the sights they passed, no shared amusement at absurd fashions, his mind too full of dread at the thought of the perils he would shortly encounter. As they sat on their favourite park bench Caroline asked gently:

"Why so sad, dear little friend. What troubles you?"

John looked up at her, biting his lip to control tears. He so wanted to tell her but always George's threat haunted him.

"Nothing ma'am, I was thinking of what is to become of me. I have long been a guest in your house and fear I am now a burden."

Sadly true where my mother is concerned, thought Caroline. She took his hand and gently squeezed it.

"Why no John. You are no trouble to anyone."

John was not a devious child, at the age of five he had no experience in evasive speech and always spoke frankly, without guile. Now without divulging George's revelations he had to speak less than fair.

"If my papa does not come it may be that I shall...that it will be ...that I shall be put to some trade...um, perhaps the sea service?"

Briefly, Caroline was at a loss for words. It was as if the child had divined the discussion on his future by her parents and herself. How to reply? As he gazed at her with solemn trusting eyes she chose her words with caution.

"We shall of course hope to see you settled in life but..."
Before she could tell him no decision would be taken for another
eight or more years and then with his consent, even hinting at her
own secret wish, John leapt from the bench with a shrilled
"Papa!"

Looking up Caroline saw approaching a tall soldier splendidly
uniformed in a dark blue jacket with white braid, gleaming white
breeches, a red plumed dark hat. His head was turned as he
chatted to two fashionably dressed women. At John's cry he
turned to look at him. Whispering "Oh no!" John's countenance
clouded with disappointment. He returned to the bench, his head
lowered.

The soldier laughingly spoke to his companions: "Upon my
honour I have never before set eyes on the little fellow." He bent
over John, placing a hand under his chin to raise his head. "I
would not be unhappy to acknowledge such a handsome child."
He saluted Caroline. "Your servant, ma'am."

Though improper to address a man unless introduced Caroline did so.

"Your pardon sir, what is your uniform?"

"That of the Light Dragoons, ma'am."

John piped up: "Please sir, do you know my papa...my father?
His name is Captain Edward and he is of your uniform."

"Edward who, my chuck? There are many such."

As John silently shook his head Caroline said: "I fear that is all
the information we have sir. Thank you for your courteous
attention."

"My pleasure ma'am." The Dragoon again saluted before
joining his giggling companions.

John stared mournfully after them. "I should have known he
is not Papa. The braid on his jacket is white, Papa's is silver to
show he is an officer."

Caroline put her arm around him. "I grieve for your disappointment, dear John. But consider, we now know your papa is a captain in the Light Dragoons, information I shall include in my new advertisement." She clicked her tongue as she recalled that the original advertisement, placed by her mother, had no reference to a Captain Edward as the child's father. A bad oversight, one she would remedy in her own advertisement. Captain Edward of the Light Dragoons no less!

John was scarcely aware of her words. He knew nothing of regiments but to him the presence of the Dragoon must mean Papa too had returned home and surely seeking him. When he was sent to sea Papa might never find him. It must not happen, he would think his best thoughts what to do, how to escape.

Had Caroline completed her assurance that if his father could not be traced – perhaps dead? – she would ensure he remained with her family, or her, and that several years would elapse before a decision was made on his future, events would have taken a very different course.

EIGHT

Sam Billings still seethed with resentment at the memory of his encounter with acid-tongued Lady Hoity-Toity and the devil's whelp Jacko, the cause of his humiliation. He had only moderate success with thieving, on two occasions narrowly avoiding capture. For this he blamed not his own ineptitude but the clumsiness of his sons Barney and Zack, a scrawny nine-year-old ideal for wide chimneys, less so for small windows. Jacko would have been ideal but Billings dismissed the notion; once inside a house the brat would alert the occupants with his hollering. Sam determined to crack Forester House, nab the best stuff and carry off Jacko if only to throttle the varmint and dump him in the river, no more to blow the gaff on folk like him and Barney.

His planned assault was for the night of the same day George Forester tormented John on his future, at five the youngest ever naval recruit. Billings still had his sweep's cart and the long-suffering horse of no name other than oaths, its staring ribs bearing witness to Billings' experiment as to how little food the animal needed to survive.

With Barney and Zack he set off from their new St Giles lodging, another grudge against the Foresters and Jacko, the house more damp, more cockroach, flea and rat infested than their previous dwelling. They reached Blackheath as the church clock struck the midnight hour. Forester House was in darkness, its occupants well asleep by now, conjectured Billings. He concealed the cart and horse behind bushes on the part of the heath conveniently opposite Forester House, the horse desperately gnawing frozen grass and twigs. The conspirators hurried across the deserted road to the house, their dark clothing making them invisible in the black of a moonless night, the myriad stars invisible in the mist shrouded sky.

Barney had already cased the crib when accompanying John on that fateful chimney sweeping day. By the subdued light of Sam's dark lantern he led the way down the basement steps, below street level so their presence hidden from any zealous night watchman prowling the road. Silently he pointed to a small scullery window, a silence broken by the faint tinkle of glass as the window gave way to a cloth protected fist. Zack then pushed through, his malnourished frame still needing a brutal shove from his father. He stifled a yelp as he cut his hand. More muffled squawks as he scrambled to his feet after landing with a bruising thud on the scullery floor. By the light of the lantern passed to him by Barney he crept up the stairs to the front door, with both hands pulling back the heavy bolt. Using the large key conveniently left on a nail near the door he unlocked it, pulling down the handle to admit his father and brother. The door was left slightly ajar for a speedy exit.

"Two big rooms fulla good stuff," hissed Barney. "Over 'ere."

Swiftly they filled two sacks with silver plate, clocks, ornaments, porcelain, anything that looked of value. The sacks full Barney was all for leaving, quiet as they had been, sharp ears could have detected their movements.

"Come on Pa, we got enough."

"Shut yer fice," hissed Billings. "I wants Jacko. Dump the sacks 'ere while we looks fer 'im."

Knowing the penalty for disobeying, Barney accompanied his father while Zack stood near the door, poised for flight when they returned. He sucked his dirty hand still oozing the blood that had liberally bedaubed surfaces of the raided rooms.

Stealthily Sam and Barney ascended the stairs to the bedroom floor, inching open doors to peer in on sleeping occupants.

"Not nowhere 'ere." whispered Barney.

"I kin see that, he must of bin sent orf."

"Gotta young 'uns room on the next floor near the servants," said Barney.

Again stealth as they crept up another flight. Not quietly enough. John was awake, unable to sleep as he thought his best thoughts on what he should do. He heard the stealthy steps, George coming to set him on fire! Struggling free of his bed covers he ran to the window, hiding behind the heavy curtains. The door opened, by the light of Billings' lantern he saw not George but the hated sweep...and the equally loathed and feared Barney.

"Gotta be 'ere," whispered Barney, "Bed all mussed up."

They padded round the room. John not daring to breathe. Soon they would find him. As they opened a clothes closet to peer inside he ran to the door, his voice a piercing treble shriek.

"Help! Thieves! Robbers!"

Barney hurtled after him, putting out an arm to bar his way out of the room. John ducked under the arm, still screaming. Now servants crowded out of their rooms. On the floor below Sir Edwin came from his room, Caroline from hers.

"Run fer it!" shouted **B**illings. As they dashed from the room he tried to grab John, knocking him off his feet and down the stairs, his light suppleness saving him from injury. At the foot of the stairs he curled into a protective ball, Billings made another grab, halted by Barney's warning shout.

"Cove's gotta pistol!"

Glancing up Billings saw Sir Edwin cocking a pistol. Releasing John he raced after Barney to the door. Sir Edwin fired, too late, the thieves were already haring across the road to the cart. Tumbling into it Sam lashed the startled horse into action, rattling off in the direction of home and safety.

Eventually home but not safely. Two further mishaps for the Billings trio, in their panic they had forgotten the sacks of stolen goods and even worse, as they clattered through the city the horse, disproving Sam Billings' dietary experiment, collapsed in its shafts, mercifully released from a life of cruelty and starvation. If justice there were in the hereafter free to graze peacefully for eternity in lush Elysian fields.

The cart occupants were hurtled painfully onto the road. With foul oaths Sam Billings unhitched the cart. Angry shouts from windows of wakened residents were answered in kind by the enraged trio. Leaving the carcase lying in the road for scavengers, no further use even as dog meat, they limped to St Giles, Barney and Zack pulling the cart. Having arrived at their far from delectable dwelling Sam somewhat relieved his frustration by thrashing Barney and Zack, his only pleasure of that disastrous night.

When calm was restored at Forester House and residents more seemly clad in night robes John was made much of by those already kindly disposed towards him. Sir Edwin patted his head, a gallant little soldier. John did not believe himself gallant, his actions motivated by fear. Caroline hugged his still trembling body, the maid Mary led him back to his bed, kissing him and staying until he slept from exhaustion.

The following morning saw the inquest, chaired not by the judge but Lady Georgina. The servants were severely berated for leaving the front door key in such a conspicuous place. Used to undeserved reprimands they did not reveal that the key was left there on the instructions of Master Joseph so that he could use it when wishing to freely roam the night streets, amusing himself with women, gambling and other gentlemanly pursuits. Master Joseph being such a pet of her ladyship no servant dare reveal this, she might well doubt their word and the thought of his wrath descending on them not to be contemplated. Least said soonest mended.

Having dismissed the suitably contrite servants, Lady Georgina turned to her favourite target, John.

"It is obvious," she told Sir Edwin and Caroline, "the boy's presence in this house is a danger to us. The man Billings was determined to take him at the risk of his own freedom. Doubtless he will try again. John must be sent away."

Accustomed as Caroline was to her mother's outrageous verdicts, this one astonished her. "Mama, you cannot do that! Forgive my frank speech but last night John saved us the loss of our most treasured possessions. Is he to be so rewarded?"

Sir Edwin's sense of justice was equally affronted. So much so that he was driven to assert his authority.

"I agree with Caroline. We would be doing the child a great wrong to send him away – to where? He is little more than an infant, unable to fend for himself though mature in courage if not years."

Her voice high, imperious, Lady Georgina broke into the eulogy.

"I refuse to stay in the house while that child is in it – a viper in our bosom, I would spend sleepless nights fearing another intrusion."

Sir Edwin's long pent-up exasperation with his wife now found voice, raised above his lady's threatened hysteria.

"If the child is so unjustly dismissed I shall take up permanent residence in my Inner Temple chambers, I too shall refuse to stay in this house." A threat Sir Edwin dearly wished were possible, having even less love for his lady than she had for him.

"I also shall leave here," cried Caroline. To her dream cottage with her dream son.

"Leaving the house in the destructive hands of our deplorable children" drily commented Sir Edwin, now recovering his normal calm reason. "There is a solution. As your mother feels unsafe here I suggest we remove to our Chelsea house immediately ...er... that is when the housekeeper has had sufficient warning. The villainous Billings will not trace us there."

"But we are not due there yet," protested Lady Georgina, taken aback by her husband's determined show of authority. Even more his threat to take up permanent residence in his chambers. That would cause such a scandal!

"It will do no harm to take up our Chelsea residence earlier," pronounced Sir Edwin. "I shall send Patrick there to inform Mrs Bailey to make preparations to receive our household by...where are we now? Saturday. Then say Tuesday. That will give the servants here time to pack what is necessary. There, that is settled." In other words, as master of the house I have spoken.

Lady Georgina's mouth worked as though seeking objections. Finding none suitable she rose from her chair.

"As my wishes are again set at nought and that...foundling allowed to disrupt our lives I have no choice but to abide by your decision, Sir Edwin. Events of the past hours have given me a violent headache, I shall retire to my room. Good day to you."

With alacrity Sir Edwin leapt to his feet to open the door, bowing as without sparing him a glance she made her frosty exit, aching head imperiously high.

Caroline remarked to her father: "I fear my mama is seriously displeased, sir."

A rare smile transformed the judge's grave features. "I fear she is, my dear."

. . .

Great was the bustle and excitement as the family prepared to migrate to their London house.

On their last Blackheath walk Caroline prepared John for their move to Chelsea, little realising what fresh dread her words were to awaken in his heart.

"There is so much to be seen. Nearby is an elegant hospital for old soldiers, poor men with no resources, a home where they can live peacefully for the remainder of their days. Also near us a vastly interesting Physic Garden full of beautiful plants and herbs from all over the world."

"Are there plants from India?" asked John. "Papa wrote of the strange flowers and plants he has seen there."

"Why yes, also from Africa and America..."

"We fought the American people. Papa was not long born so could not fight, if he had we would have won."

Caroline laughed. "Such a loyal little son! Perhaps it is as well he could not fight. The Americans wished to be free from the government of our rulers."

After a pause for thought John responded with a gravity befitting a philosopher: "I think Papa would agree with you ma'am. He believes people should be free, he is very angry about slaves, it is wicked to keep people in ...bandage?"

Caroline smiled fondly down at the solemn little face. "Bondage, not free, the property of another person, working without pay."

John interrupted: "As Tad and myself? Tad said we had only our food and clothes."

"Well yes in a way," Caroline tried to explain. "But when an apprentice's time is out he is free to work for himself. A slave is never free. Your papa sounds a good honourable man, as are others who strive to end slavery." She stroked John's fair hair. "And you, my dearest John, are far too serious for a little fellow. I should dearly love to see you laugh and play, have fun like others of your age."

An attempt at a smile as he reassured her. "I always did while with Papa and allowed to play with other children and my friend Will would laugh and jest with me when we rode out with my pony Dobbin. I do so miss them." As Caroline squeezed his hand to show her sympathy he asked with an answering squeeze: "What else is there to see in Chelsea, ma'am?"

"A fine porcelain manufactory, you like beautiful objects John, I have seen your eyes light up at some of our precious ornaments." John nodded vigorously, recalling those in his own home. Caroline continued: "Oh, how you will enjoy the bun house. Every Easter crowds visit there to taste the delicious cakes and buns."

"I beg you will allow me to purchase one for you ma'am," implored John. "Sir Edwin was kind enough to present me a whole guinea."

Caroline gently patted his eager small face. "Such a wealthy gentleman! I gladly accept your offer kind sir. We shall eat our buns while seated alongside the river bank, the fashionable folk will envy me my handsome beau as we watch the yachts and pleasure craft. We may even take one to the docks." She broke off as all the animation died from John's face, his body tensed. "Why John, what ails you?"

"N...nothing, ma'am. It has come colder."

Caroline also shivered, an icy rain had begun to fall.

"Come John. Off home, I shall ask Mary to bring you a hot posset."

The walk back to Forester House was made in silence, Caroline troubled. What had caused John's sudden dejection?

Though longing to confide in her he dare not do so. When the move was first announced George and Rebecca had taken advantage of the bustle to launch another attack. George furious at the praise lavished on John after the attempted robbery. He had never received such praise from his father. Indeed, Sir Edwin detested his youngest son, wondered how he could have sired such an oaf. Not that he could imagine his dear lady betraying him with a lumpish country yokel. Indifferent to his father's disapproval George nevertheless resented his partiality for John, spite adding venom to his taunts.

"My mother has the greatest dislike of you, beggar's bastard. She wants you gone the soonest. When we are in Chelsea there will be more opportunities for having you placed on a ship. A fine time of year for sailors, you will be frozen solid before reaching the sea and will be tossed overboard as food for gulls and fish. No one will grieve for such ordure as you..."

"Indeed Mrs Caroline will do so!" Despite his determination to ignore George's taunts John could not refrain from defending his love for her.

"Caroline!" sneered Rebecca. "The great soft thing! No one takes any heed of her. She brought disgrace on the family by marrying a common sailor." Untrue, Charles Claremont had been a captain, the youngest son of a respected county family.

John's eyes flashed anger. "You lie! Mrs Caroline would bring disgrace to no one, she is a good kind lady."

"How would you know, drab's misbegotten brat?" jeered George. "Very soon you will be in your rightful place among the lowest scum of seafarers. Take that for your impudence!"

Their cuffings and pinchings were again terminated by the arrival of the maidservant Mary with John's meal.

His dread that the move to Chelsea must make easier his removal to a ship would have been lessened had he known the nearness of Blackheath to the river at Greenwich from where vessels frequently sailed. Caroline had considered taking him there to see them, his trust in her removing all fear, but her loss still so raw she could not bring herself to do so, thus leaving him the target of George's taunts.

Guided by his best thoughts John decided to delay any action until the move to London. The beggar woman had told him Papa was going there. She lied, but he knew Papa made frequent visits

to the city on business so it would be easier to find him. He had
no notion of the vast size of London, equating it with the village
near his home, a street of houses and cottages, butcher, dairy and
baker shops, a church and an inn. Papa had promised to take him
to London when he was older to see beautiful paintings and a wax
museum containing models of famous people.

The removal to Chelsea disabused him of the village fallacy.
He shared a carriage with Caroline and Sir Edwin, Lady Georgina
refusing to allow him in the family coach. He was both excited
and alarmed as they travelled through London streets. So vast!
Such buildings! So many people! How would he ever find Papa, or
be found by him?

The Chelsea house was less grand than Forester House. No
nursery, John was allocated a small room, still attended by Mary.
George and Rebecca traced him there, unnoticed in the general
bustle.

"Did you see the river as we crossed Battersea Bridge, sweeper's brat?" asked George. "Mama says that tomorrow you are to be
taken there and put on a craft to the docks…"

"Whatever are you doing here, Master George, Miss Rebecca?" Mary had come unnoticed into the room. "Your mama
wishes you to attend to the disposition of your possessions." Mary
suspected they had been teasing Jackie and pleased to put an end
to their nasty spite. She accompanied them out of the room, she
believed leaving John in peace.

John was far from peaceful. His mind in turmoil, he must act
now, make his escape or he would never again see Papa.

Taking up his copy book, a new one replacing the book
ruined by Rebecca but for which he was rebuked by his tutor, he
removed a page and with a newly sharpened quill carefully
printed his first letter.

I BEG TO THANK FOR ALL THINGS BUT DO NOT
WANT TO GO TO THE SEA AS JORGE SAYS I SHALL
TOMOROW I GO TO SEEK MY PAPA MY VERY MOST

BEST THANKS TO MISSIS CAROLINE NEVER WILL I
FORGET HER I AM SIR AND MADAMS YOR SERVANT
    JOHN

He placed the letter on the table, then realising he would need clothes to be clean when he found Papa, from the box left in the room took under linen, shirts and trousers, hose, a jacket. Papa would pay for what he had taken, for all that he had been given. He still had the guinea Sir Edwin had given him. That would buy plenty of food. Wrapping the clothes in a tablecloth he put on his coat, muffler and cap. He peered outside his door. Still much bustle, men were carrying heavy boxes to the bedrooms, they did not know him so took no notice as he slipped by them to the open ront door. None of the family, no servants to notice his departure. With a little sob of fear he crept down the steps to the pavement. The house stood on a corner. He turned into the next road and ran, awkwardly for the bundle was heavy. At the end of the road he stopped, breathless. He was in a busy street, carts, carriages, men on horseback. Passers-by jostled him. He stood still, wide eyed, mouth trembling but determined not to cry. What to do? Where to go? An innocent in London, a town where innocence seldom survived.

NINE

Never had John been in a street unaccompanied, without his hand held, being protected from jostling crowds. Small, frightened, vulnerable, surrounded by what seemed a forest of trousered booted legs, long gowns, walking canes. Propelled by chattering groups he walked on dragging his clothes bundle behind him. Instinctively he kept close to couples walking arm in arm, supposing them to be man and wife and that passers-by would take him for their child. No one heeded him, his good clothes blending in with the affluent area. A street urchin would have had them wary for their pockets or purses.

Hunger assailed him, he had not eaten since an early breakfast. Where could he eat? There were coffee shops but what an odd figure he would make among grown men, very learned and wise-looking. No women he could covertly attach himself to. Did ladies in London not drink coffee when out?

He came to an arcade with stalls displaying so many different goods, including food. He hesitated at a stall with pies, bread, cakes and buns. Sadly he recalled his last walk with Mrs Caroline when they discussed the delights of Chelsea and his promise to purchase her a bun. Papa said a gentleman always kept a promise.

When he found Papa they would visit her and take all manner of gifts.

He had a guinea but no idea of its value and had never made a purchase. The smell of the pies and increasing hunger overcame fear.

"Please sir," he asked the burly stallholder, "What are those pies?"

The boy's well-dressed appearance kept the stall-holder's tone civil. "The finest mutton pies yer ever tasted, me young lord." Not a boast John could confirm, he had never tasted a mutton pie.

"And the twisty buns, please?"

The stallholder held one out to him. "Ant yer never seen Chelsea buns? Baked this very morning."

Chelsea buns! John experienced a pang of pleasure mixed with sorrowful remorse. "Please sir, I wish to purchase two pies and two buns." That should last him all day.

"If yer pays fer them, eight pence me little lordship. First show me yer money." An overcharge, the stallholder assumed correctly the child could not decipher the price labels. John held out his guinea. The man stared, surely the well-spoken lad was no infant dip?

"How came yer by that, young sir?" he asked cautiously.

John's imaginative brain worked quickly. "My mama, sir. She awaits me in the hat shop." He had noticed a boutique in the arcade, staring in open-mouthed wonder at the fantastical confections. "She asks me to buy nice food to eat while sitting on seats by the river watching the boats sail by."

"Fine weather fer such a caper," remarked the man. But he was used to odd folk in that district. Putting the pies and buns in two bags he counted out the change, not daring to under-change for fear of a wrathful mama descending on him. He gave John a small bag to keep the money in. It was as well to encourage wealthy customers.

Elated by his first purchase John thanked him, running in the direction of the milliner's as the stall man might be watching him. He sat on the plinth of a central fountain to eat one pie and bun, saving the others for later. He put his hands under the fountain to clean them and rinse his face, then drank from the flow. Papa had warned him that not all water was safe to drink, perhaps he should have bought milk from a woman at a stall but she looked dirty and smoked a clay pipe. He had never seen a woman smoke.

His bundle grew irksome and the mire of the streets had altered its pristine whiteness. At another stall he saw bags and clothes cases. He selected a satchel with buckles and a long loop he could hang over his shoulders, also mittens as his hands were cold, paying two shillings, which the man took from the money John held out, again with the story of the mythical mama in the hat shop. Out of sight of the stall he transferred his clothes into the bag, disposing of the now filthy tablecloth behind a stall among an existing pile of litter. Now he felt like a soldier with a pack on his back.

He wandered through the market, full of wonder at the different goods for sale. His delight came to an end at a stall with cages of birds, even large cages with ducks, geese and swans. He looked sadly at a cage with small song birds, so crowded they could not flap their wings, weakly piping their distress. He remembered Mama reading him a poem by Mr William Blake, one of her favourite poets.

A robin redbreast in a cage

Puts all of Heaven in a rage.

A woman came to the stall and spoke to the man. Though it was not right to keep song birds in a cage John hoped she would rescue some as pets. He watched in horror as the man seized a number of larks, wrung their necks and threw them into the woman's basket. Another two lines of the poem came to him.

A skylark wounded in the wing

A cherubim does cease to sing

"What is a cherubim?" he had asked Mama.

She kissed him. "Baby angels. You, my dearest little boy."

The memory, the destruction of the lovely songsters made him sob out:

"That is wicked! You have put all of Heaven in a rage."

The stallholder jerked his head. "Off wiv yer, whelp."

Made brave by pity John stood his ground. "But it is wrong to kill song birds!"

The man laughed mockingly, turning to share the joke with other customers. "Why not? Yer eats other birds, fowl and the like. The lady is cook in a grand household, uses 'em for garnish. How about a nice swan fer roasting?" He laughed again as John ran off, sobbing.

A weeping child was not so unusual as to attract attention, most of the arcade customers ignored him. Except one, a fashionably dressed woman. The wife of a wealthy Lloyds broker Mrs Arthur Blunt was addicted to good works, having little else to occupy her long idle days. Bending low over John she held his shoulders, the tip of the ostrich feather in her turban tickling his nose.

"What ails you little man? Are you lost?"

John was, very, but dare not admit it for fear of a return to Forester Lodge and thence for the next ship to sail from the docks. He controlled his sobs to a snuffle.

"N...no if you please ma'am. My Mama waits for me in the hat shop and I stopped to play with the animals and she will be cross." Sadly mama had outlived her use.

"But child, I have just spent some time at the milliner's..." she indicated a liveried man standing at a respectful distance behind her, impassive of face, arms laden with hat boxes and parcels. "No other lady was present."

Desperation seized John. "I must seek her. My respects ma'am." Ducking under her arms he ran off.

Mrs Blunt gazed after him, puzzled. "How strange," she commented to the bored coachman. Such a handsome child despite his tears. The childless Mrs Blunt would have loved to take him home, pet him, though realising Arthur might well have had words to say. She too was late, Arthur would have finished his business with a client in the coffee shop and be impatiently waiting.

"We will return to the carriage, Peters"

High time, thought Peters. "Very good, ma'am."

His pleasure in the arcade gone John wandered out into another street. To his dismay daylight was fading and a thin icy drizzle stung his face. He must find shelter, a place to sleep for he was very weary. Some illumination was provided by oil lamps outside large houses, showing their grandeur. No shelter there. He turned into a side street, then another, less respectable, lit only by candlelight within houses. More turnings, the streets progressively meaner, culminating in one where the leprous houses on either side of the narrow road seemed to lean towards each other for comfort. In the middle of the road a wide kennel along which a sluggishly moving stream of sewage emptied into a drain. Though sickened with disgust John could no longer overcome his urgent need, adding his contribution. He hurried to get away from the stench, the desperate nightmare poverty. In one doorway lay a huddled figure. Curious, John cautiously approached it. A man sat up, long filthy hair and beard almost covering his skull-like face from which bloodshot eyes glared hatred. With an animal like snarl he lashed out at the boy. Uttering a shrill cry of terror John fled, followed by unintelligible oaths.

More streets, less and less depraved until one with respectable houses led to another broad illuminated road with shops and stalls, the owners preparing to take them away for the night. Unwittingly John had walked in a semi-circle to arrive further along the King's Road. He bought a beaker of milk and piece of cheese from a buxom farmer's wife. She charged one penny. He drank the not very fresh milk and returned the beaker, unaware of how many had used it, unwashed. No questions as to why he was alone. As well, no mama in a milliner's shop would have been accepted here. No milliners.

On he trudged, on the verge of exhaustion, as if in a dream. Then the first glimmer of hope. An inn, its entrance lamps welcoming customers. John knew little about inns except men drank ale there and could hire rooms for the night. Papa had told of his experience with inns frequented during his journeys, some a disgrace to a civilised country. Flea infested beds, cockroaches and other vermin. John did not consider asking for a room, knowing the astonishment, laughter, questions. But somewhere there might be a nook where he could shelter? At the side of the inn he saw a large yard. A familiar smell came to him. Horses! A stable! He loved horses, from his infancy he had known them, had been taken by Papa to the stables to be made much of by the grooms, lifted up so that he could stroke the horses' soft noses, nuzzled by them, taken for rides by Papa or a groom.

Making himself even smaller he crouched in the shadows of the yard, watching the ostler tending horses of overnight visitors. He had a plan but must wait until the ostler had finished. Soon he returned to the inn with a final click of his tongue. John scurried across to one stall. He had noticed a gap at the bottom of the door, big enough for a small body to squeeze through. Pushing his satchel before him he did so, greeted by a startled whinny. Enough light from the inn to see a fine chestnut stallion with a white blaze on his forehead and white socks.

"All right my dear," John whispered as he had heard Jenkins, the head groom, calm a restless horse. "I only want a corner of your stall if I may."

The horse bent his head to examine his small companion, John stroked him with little murmurs, the horse responded with a gentle snort.

John crept to a corner of the stall, making a bed of fresh sweet smelling straw, his satchel a pillow.

"Good night horse," he whispered. He closed his eyes, started to say his prayers, falling asleep while asking the Lord to forgive his trespasses. Running away from Mrs Caroline? The naughty falsehood of Mama in the hat shop?

John was awakened by the horse nudging him. He opened his eyes, wondering where he was. As realisation came he hastily stood up, imagining the horse had warned him he must hurry, soon the ostler would come to tend the horses. He shook dust and straw from his coat, a warm woollen one with a little cape, selected by Mrs Caroline. Tears stung his eyes but there was no time for that. He added his contribution to the horse's droppings, doubting it would be noticed when the stall was cleaned.

He wanted a wash, would there be time to use the yard pump? If he was very, very quick. Squeezing under the door he ran softly to the pump, pulling off his shirt and under-vest, splashing water over his head and trunk, rubbing his feet, squealing softly at the near freezing water. Then back to the stall, drying himself on a rough cloth hanging on a hook. Should he change his linen? No, it would do another day. It might be some time before he found Papa and he must be very clean then. Papa was always clean. His stockings were filthy, his shoes no more than light pumps not meant for outdoor wear and now almost worn through. He would need stouter shoes, could they be purchased. He pulled on new stockings, wiping his shoes clean with the cloth. About to slip into them he froze with fear. The back door of the inn opened and slammed shut. Two voices, the ostler and a groom come to tend the horses. Where could he hide? Then he relaxed, they were working in the end stall. Hastily he took up his satchel, bidding farewell to the horse who bent his head. John flung his arms round his neck, kissing him.

"I wish I was big enough to ride you," he whispered. "We would gallop through London to find my Papa and I would feed you with the best oats and carrots and apples." The horse grunted approval, John again squeezed under the door. Not quickly enough. As he straightened up the groom emerged from the end stall, shouting:

"Hey there, what goes on?"

Without waiting to reply John fled. The man started after him but he had already disappeared round a corner, no longer visible in the morning mist.

"Why the row?" asked the ostler. "Have a mind for the horses." Also the inn's sleepers though they were of less importance.

The groom shook his head. "Damned if I makes sense of it. Little manakin did appear from under the stall, vanished like a will-o'-the-wisp afore I could catch hold of him."

The ostler snorted derision. "Tosh! Tis the blue ruin vexing you Jack." As Jack strenuously denied touching a drop the ostler opened the stall door. The horse regarded them with calm innocent enquiry. No oats?

"Nought amiss," said the ostler. "Nary a hobgoblin nor elf...."

"Lookee here," triumphantly replied the groom, holding up a greasy packet. He opened it. "Squashed mutton pie and a bun." John had been too weary to eat them the previous evening and had no time that morning.

The ostler held up two small grimy torn stockings. "What make you of that, Jack?"

Jack shrugged. "I be hanged if I knows."

The horse did know but kept his counsel.

John did not stop running until again in a busy street. London was awakening to the misty dawn. He mingled with those going to their work and those finishing their night labour. Linkmen and boys had done with lighting the way with burning torches for night revellers and sober citizens making their way home in the early hours. A cart and stench rattled by, generously bedewing road surfaces with overspill contents - the night soil man off to an outlying farm. Women shuffled wearily back to drear overcrowded lodgings, having secured their rent and daily bread by their trade, some so ill-favoured, their faces blotched by disease that only black night found them clients and only those as desperate as themselves. Innocently unaware John's inbred courtesy prohibited no more than fleetingly covert glances at their ravaged features.

Stallholders were arranging their wares, much shouting, exchanging insults, oaths, laughter. No women shoppers, too early. Respectably dressed men, clerks and other lowly grades, strode to their places of business, their haste suggesting not a moment to lose. Not from eagerness to start their daily toil, they must be in their places before their employers arrived by horse-drawn transport. They jostled aside ambling men, poorly dressed, with no occupation to fill the long day other than watching for unguarded pockets to snatch handkerchiefs, purses, with such skill their victims were unaware of loss. Coffee shops were opening, their customers men reading newspapers and discussing recent events with friends, others concluded business deals in low voices implying possible shadiness, skulduggery.

Discovering the loss of his mutton pie and bun John, now an experienced customer, bought a beaker of milk, bread and cheese. Not experienced enough, the stallholder took a shilling for twopence halfpenny of food from the money John trustingly held out. Drinking the milk he returned the beaker, then sat on the ledge of a large building, a bank, safely out of the way of the increasingly jostling pedestrians. He ate his bread and cheese, watching with wide-eyed wonder the street's activities.

Though the wintry sun feebly shone, the previous day's rain left the litter-strewn road and pavement muddy, with filthy puddles sprayed over walkers by passing wagons and carriages. Sweepers tried to earn a half penny by clearing paths for pedestrians risking their lives crossing the road, but almost immediately the litter returned. Stallholders dumped their waste, those with vegetables peeled off outer leaves, tossing aside rotting fruit. Horses left their droppings.

Carriages, coaches, carts and horsemen crowded past the stalls, sometimes near enough to send wares tumbling, to the obscenities of their owners. Sedan chairs were carried along the pavement, another new experience for John. If the occupant was too corpulent the carriers' meagre frames bent almost double in their efforts to keep the chair clear of the pavement. A man walked past with a wizened monkey on his shoulder, soon to attract audiences with its antics. John had never seen a monkey, wondering if it were a deformed infant. Bending over him a man plucked a penny from his ear, walking away laughing at John's open-mouth astonishment. A fiddler played a merry tune at odds with his woebegone features. How sad most people look, thought John.

He had little cause for tranquillity, now realising the hopelessness of his quest. London was a vast noisy crowded place, how could he find Papa, or Papa find him? As he moved away from his perch, for a heart-stopping moment he believed his question answered. A horseman approached, a soldier in the uniform of a Light Dragoon. Another glance told him it was not Papa. The soldier brought his horse to a sudden halt, almost bringing it back on its haunches. A cart had overturned in front of him, sending the contents across the road. As with oaths the carrier righted the cart and reloaded his wares John ran over to the Dragoon, recognising the horse as his stable companion. Acknowledging a friend the horse lowered his head and whinnied a greeting. John fondled his muzzle, gazing up at the surprised soldier.

"If you please sir, do you know my papa? Captain Edward of the Light Dragoons?"

"Edward who?" asked the Dragoon as had the previous soldier John had confronted.

John felt hope dwindling. "I do not know sir. He is tall and dark such as yourself and has been in India fighting for Mr

Wesley." John could not pronounce Wellesley but chanced on the general's previous name.

The Dragoon obviously had little respect for the general. "Arthur Wellesley, the arrogant bastard, so have I had that misfortune."

John's eyes brightened with hope. "Then you surely know my papa sir."

The soldier laughed. "There were a great many of us. I am of the Twelfth Light Dragoons. And your papa?"

Again John's hopes faded. "Oh I did not know there are so many."

As the carter finished his work the Dragoon prepared to ride off.

"I am bound for Knightsbridge barracks to visit a Foot soldier friend. I will make enquiries there as to a Captain Edward." And much good that would do.

John now all eagerness. "Oh sir I am most vastly obliged. If you see him pray say John is at this place? Oh, where am I?"

"Not far from Battersea Bridge. Run home child, he will more easily find you there. Good day John." He galloped off, John forlornly staring after him. If only he had taken him to the barracks, he could have stayed there, helped the soldiers until Papa found him. What were barracks?

Not knowing what to do John wandered on. He halted at a shop outside which hung a sign depicting a boot. Above the shop he spelt out the words Anthony Barnes, Boot and Shoemaker. He hesitated, looking down at his worn pumps. They could not last another mile. Summoning up courage to face the usual questions he entered the shop. No mama in the hat shop this time, none nearby. A man working at a bench shaping leather with a sharp knife rose to greet him. A tall stooped man, to the five year old very aged, with a kindly face and twinkling friendly eyes.

"Good day sir. How may I be of service to you?"

John bowed as he had been taught to do before his elders.

"Good day Mr Barnes sir. I wish to purchase new shoes to fit my feet." He raised one foot. With an effort Mr Barnes repressed a smile.

"But sir, I do not sell ready-made shoes. I make to order, first measuring the feet and then making them to my customers' requirements. That may take several days and I have much work in hand. My apprentice is ill with the influenza." Now the question. "Surely your mother must know that, so why has she sent you out alone? This city is no place for, if I may say, a very small gentleman."

John had concocted his story. "Oh sir, my Papa sent me to enquire. He is nearby in a coffee shop talking about...things with a friend."

Strange but possible, knowing Londoners as Anthony Barnes did after forty years working in that benighted city. What sort of father allowed his small child to walk unaccompanied even a few yards? He had never done so, children were precious. And in such appalling footwear!

"Pray go to papa," he gently advised. "Ask him to come with you and I will gladly measure your feet, hasten the making of the shoes..." As with murmured thanks the child moved dejectedly away his kindly heart took pity. "Wait a moment. I may be able to help you."

Hope renewed, the boy returned to the shop counter. Going into an inner room Barnes took from a shelf a pair of child's leather walking shoes lovingly crafted for his only grandson. The first surviving boy after four beautiful granddaughters, snatched away by a sudden violent bowel disorder that killed him after three agonised days. A common occurrence in the foul miasma of London. He hesitated, biting his lip. Why keep them when every glance brought renewed grief? The boy so like Peterkin, the same blue eyed trusting innocence. Let him go back to that uncaring father well-shod. The father? Making up his mind he returned to the shop.

"Here young sir. These may fit." He lifted John on to the counter top and took off the pumps. "You do indeed need new shoes. What possessed your father..." He broke off, slipping the left shoe on to John's foot. "Not at all bad, a trifle large but all to the good. At your age feet have a habit of growing. I could slip a little piece of rubber in the heel to prevent it rubbing. There, that is better. Now the right shoe. Good, now ...May I ask your name?"

"John if you please sir."

"It much pleases me. My good father's name. Now John, may I ask you to walk a few paces to try how you like them?" He lifted John from the counter.

John walked around the shop, revelling in the warmth of the fine leather lined with kid, admiring their elegance, the metal buckles that shone like gold.

"They are most beautiful Mr Barnes sir." Anxiety clouded his face. "But I fear I have not enough money to pay for them." He took out his paper bag and reaching up spread coins over the counter top. "This is all I have."

No doubts now in Mr Barnes' mind. No papa in a coffee shop. Such an inexperienced little romancer! He spoke with gentle severity.

"There will be no cost if you say the truth. There is no papa waiting in the coffee shop. You have run away from home?"

John lowered his head as he had when Papa scolded him for some infant mischief.

"Indeed I lied sir. It was very wicked but I dared not say the truth."

Tears trickled down his cheeks. Barnes put an arm round his shoulders, leading him to the bench.

"Sit here John. What dare you not tell? It surely can be no great evil at your age."

John looked up at the kindly face, then his overburdened heart found release in a torrent of words, telling of all that had befallen him since taken from his real home, forced up a chimney and had fallen. His rescue by a family that came to resent his presence when his papa did not come, his only friend Mrs Caroline whom he loved as much as his own mama, his torment at the hands and tongues of George and Rebecca, a torment that led to his flight.

"Do you see sir, if I had stayed I would have been put on a boat today and sent to sea to clean cannons that would fire me out if I got stuck, to climb ropes in a storm and...and the men would do...would do things I dare not tell of so horrid they are."

Anthony Barnes had no doubt the boy told the truth. A child of that age was not capable of such invention. This a gently reared child, no street-hardened urchin.

"John, believe me. You were tricked by wicked George. You are far too young to be a sailor." Trying to hide amusement Barnes lifted up John's hands. "Of what use would these be? Too small to grasp thick ropes and cables. Clean guns? They have special rods. Climb rigging? The first gust of wind would have you sailing through the air like one of Monsieur Blanchard's balloons. Even if you were intended for the sea service that would not be for at least eight years when you would receive training. Sometimes lads of eleven but I believe that is no longer the case. Think, John. Of what use would you be on a ship. Why look, you cannot even button your coat correctly." He adjusted the coat. "Such an infant!"

John was able to smile at his own foolishness, at his new friend's gentle raillery. Then the puzzled look returned.

"But why did George say horrid things that were not true?"

"Because he is an ill-conditioned young wretch, most probably a spoilt pet of his mama and jealous of his father's and Mrs Caroline's preference for you. He deserves a sound thrashing. Now John, I have some advice, take it as from a friend deeply concerned for your welfare. With every respect for your courage you are too small to be on your own, alone, unprotected, unable to recognise danger. Somehow you have survived so far..." Barnes could not attribute this to God's mercy, remembering little Peterkin's agonised cries, the doctors' inability to relieve his suffering. "but the longer you are on the streets the greater the danger. Go back to the house of your Mrs Caroline. Think John of the grief she must feel. You cannot find your father by wandering through unknown streets. The nights are long, dark and cold, where will you sleep? The most dangerous time, night prowlers have no mercy. Mrs Caroline has assured you she will again advertise your presence in her house. You must be there for your father to find. Do you not agree John?"

John's face had taken on the semblance of a tragic mask.

"Oh sir I am truly wicked. I forgot Mrs Caroline would grieve. Yes you are right, I must return." John sighed. Go back to George's torment and Rebecca's spite, Lady Georgina's coldness. But also his beloved Mrs Caroline!

"Good," said Barnes. "The shoes are my gift to you, put away your money – do you know how much you have?"

"No sir, I have never had money. But I can count very well, my tutor is much pleased with my sums."

Barnes smiled at such infant pride. "Now make good your boast. How much had you at the start?"

"A guinea that Sir Edwin gave me for making the robbers run away."

"Such a hero? Now take heed." Again lifting John onto the counter he picked up copper coins. "The little one a half penny, that will buy a beaker of milk, the larger a penny, should buy a small loaf. You have no farthings here, those are the smallest, four to one penny."

John held up a shilling. "What is this please sir? The stall man took one for my bread, cheese and milk."

"That is a shilling, worth twelve pennies or twenty four half pennies. The man robbed you and others will do the same if you are not wary. This small silver coin is six pennies. And this large fellow a crown piece, five shillings. Now Mr Clever John, we will count together to find what you have left from your guinea which is twenty-one shillings. Then you count again to make sure of your lesson while I look for a purse."

Grey and fair heads bent over the coins, Barnes piling them into small heaps as he told the value, then he left John to count as he sought and found a draw-string pouch. Murmurs from John as he made his own calculations. A triumphant squeal.

"Sir! I have a total of seventeen shillings and three pennies"

"Splendid! Now how much have you spent of your guinea?"

John groaned, closing his eyes in anguished thought. Again he smiled.

"I think...yes, I believe three shillings and nine pennies."

Barnes clapped his hands. "A genius! But so prodigal, your money will not last long at such expenditure in so short a time. I cannot fault your amazing ability at counting. I shall keep you as my apprentice, my idle fellow three times your age can hardly add together four and five." Barnes had been apprenticed to his father at the advanced age of sixteen, John Barnes insisting on him being well schooled. He wanted no dunderhead in his shop conversing with highly bred customers. Courtesy without deference, read the daily newspapers to be conversant with current affairs. Even a knowledge of French, useful when aristocratic émigrés flocked to London to escape the guillotine.

As John's face was again puzzled he said: "No, I jest. You are such a gullible little fellow it is a delight to tease you. I foresee a great future for you, but do not lose your integrity. Now put away your money in this purse, a suitable one for a wealthy young man about town. You may proudly display it when you purchase a gift for Mrs Caroline. What is the address of the house?"

Again the dejected look. "Sir, I do not know. It is a large corner house in a Chelsea square and there is a stable on the other side. There is a river near where George told me I would be sent to the docks."

"Well, the name of your rescuers?"

Again John's face creased with agonised thought. "Foster? I am not very good at names though I remember Sir Edwin and Mrs Caroline. The name of her mama is... something like Georgina and...oh yes! Sir Edwin is a very important judge though he does not wear a gown and long wig."

Arthur Barnes shook his head. "Edwin Foster? Not a name I recall. But no matter. A City Police Office is nearby, they will surely know. As I expect no customers yet I shall go directly to enquire. This afternoon I have several due customers, you will stay with me and share my meal which is brought to me from the inn, then this evening we will go to Mrs Caroline's house. Pray mind the shop while I am gone, inform any caller I shall be about ten minutes only. Entertain them with witty epigrams ... er... sayings."

Putting on a coat he hurried from the shop, in too much haste to notice that dread had returned to John's face.

The police! A vivid memory returned of the robbery at his own home. A wretched youth, no more than fifteen, bungling, inept, easily overcome by the servants and taken away chained to a burly night watchman who pronounced: "Lad from the village always up to larks. Gallows meat for sure."

The boy snivelling his fear as he was led away.

That occurred in the days Mama was still with him, and his dear nursemaid Bessie, before Uncle Robert and Aunt Sophie came. He asked Bessie: "They will not hang him Bessie? I should be very unhappy to think so."

Bessie hugged him. "Why bless your tender heart! No, I reckon he will be transposed."

"Transpose? What is that please?"

"Sent to some country overseas, Australia most like. Tis a wild rough country that our rulers want to collimate."

More words to puzzle a small head. "What is that if you please Bessie?"

Bessie's knowledge of Australia almost non-existent, her imagination vivid.

"Well, there are a lot of black heathens there who eat people and our rulers want them convened to worship the Lord Jesus." Bessie crossed herself.

John thought this very strange. "But if they only... er...transpose bad men they will not ...convene the black people who may not wish to be convened and will eat them."

"Oh, not only rogues and vagabonds go there but also saintly mission folk to pray for them if they like it or not, and there are also men who want to work there and wives and children. Also little orphans and foundlings."

"Found things? What are they please Bessie?" Then the part John now recalled with fear.

"Why, little children without papas and mamas who nobody wants. Also transposed are naughty boys who run away from apprenticeships or from their homes. They will be caught by constables and sent in chains to Australia to work picking cotton and such. Tis vastly hot there."

"But if they are small they will be eaten by the heathens!"

"Some I dare say." Bessie's imagination had dried up. "Now stop asking questions Jackie, it does not concern you. We must get ready to walk with your mama, not too quickly mind as her health is in a delicate state."

He had only been four then but remembered it as his last truly happy day, before Uncle Robert and Aunt Sophie came, before Mama and his brother went to heaven, before dear Bessie was sent away. Now he recalled it with dread. If the police could not find the address, if they could not find Papa they would think he was an orphan or found thing, and he had been wicked, left his prentship and run away from Mrs Caroline's home. The police men would take him away in chains and send him to Australia to be eaten by heathens! Papa would never find him as he would be dead.

What must he do? Yes, go to the place where soldiers lived, for that must be what the Dragoon meant. He would go even if he walked all the way, find out from people. Or go in a chaise? Or one of those chairs? He still had a lot of money.

But Mr Barnes was so kind and had given him splendid shoes. How much he would like to stay, to see Mr Barnes make shoes, share his meal, talk and talk for he was very wise. He had never known a grandpa but would have liked one such as Mr Barnes. He must be thanked. Finding a blank sheet of paper and a quill pen on Mr Barnes' desk he hurriedly wrote his second letter.

MOST KIND SIR DO NOT THINK ME UNGRATEFUL BUT IF THE POLIS MEN THINK I AM AN ORFAN OR A RUN AWAY THEY WILL SEND ME TO OSTRALA WARE BESSIE SAYS HEAVENS COOK AND EAT PEEPEL. I HAVE TOO FIND PAPA SO I AM NOT AN ORFAN. THANK YOU FOR THE SHOES I LEVE A CROWN. PAPA WILL PAY THE REST WHEN I FIND HIM. PRAY DO NOT BE ANGRY I WISH YOU WAS MY GRANPA. I AM SIR YOR LOVING FREND JOHN

Leaving a crown piece on the table he quickly put on his satchel and crept from the shop, making sure Mr Barnes was nowhere in sight. Again he mingled with the crowds, this time escaping the black cannibals of Bessie's imagined Australia.

TEN

M uch ado at Forester Lodge when John's absence was discovered. Lady Georgina loudly denouncing his ingratitude. Proof of his lowly birth, he had probably rejoined his associates; had the silver been checked?

Anger replaced Caroline's desolate grief, she could not bridle her tongue.

"That is so ridiculous! Pardon me Mother, I must protest at such outrageous injustice. A small child making off with a heavy pack of silver plate? He took only his clothes, those I provided and of no use to anyone here. You have seen the letter he wrote, the reason for his leaving, his terror..."

Lady Georgina had gasped her indignation at this outburst from her normally complaisant daughter. Such disrespect!

"You...you speak too forward madam," she spluttered. "A little harmless teasing would not have made him leave an excellent home...ah, Sir Edwin," as her husband entered the room. "Why is Rebecca here? It is not the hour for her visit."

"She must be questioned," replied the judge. "Her brother is in hiding, he knows what to expect when he shows himself." He turned to Rebecca. "Now Miss, what torment have you and

George inflicted on John? No falsehoods, the maidservant Mary has on several occasions heard your voices in the nursery, where you should not have been, and saw you in John's room this morning shortly before he left here."

Rebecca stood before them, innocently demure, hands folded in front of a modest long white gown, corn coloured thick hair framing her face, halo-like, angelic. She had already planned her defence, to throw all the blame on George. For Rebecca nothing so foolish as sibling loyalty.

"Yes Papa, it is true that I did accompany George to the nursery..." No sense denying this, there was a witness. Mary would suffer for her betrayal. "...but he insisted I did so, saying he would punish me if I did not. He is such a bully. He told John he was base-born..." Her eyes widened, voice no more than a whisper "and many other names I dare not utter, so foul they are, and he struck and pinched John." With her sleeve she wiped away imaginary tears. "I begged him to stop, John is so small. George told him over and again he would be sent as a sailor to be ill-treated by the seamen. Then this morning he told John that Mama had ordered that now we are near the river tomorrow he would be placed on a craft to the docks to become a sailor..."

"I said no such thing!" Lady Georgina was in high dudgeon. "A five-year-old sailor? Poppycock! The boy must have known George jested."

"John is too young to know it to be poppycock," interrupted Caroline. "So innocent, so trusting." She wanted to weep but not here to invoke her mother's scorn, her father's concern and Rebecca's sniggers. She recalled the last walk with John, his wonder at the delights of Chelsea turning to fear when she spoke of a pleasure craft visit to the docks. Those fiendish brats, for she believed Rebecca no less guilty than George, so tormented her beloved John he had run from their threats. What would become of him, so small, unable to fend for himself, an innocent alone in London! The crowded streets, the predators. Where would he find shelter from winter weather? She had known nothing of his fears, why had he not confided in her? She turned angrily on Rebecca, still demure though now with an unpleasant little smirk of self-satisfaction. Not for much longer, my lady.

"Did you threaten him to silence? Was he in too much fear to tell of your spite, your torment?"

Rebecca was all indignation. "I tell you I took no part in George's teasing." Desire to further implicate George led to self-betrayal. "He told John that if he peached... er told on us...er... George we...no he would set fire to his bed while he slept."

Sir Edwin had heard enough. Experience recognised Rebecca as a liar, a sly little minx. He pronounced sentence.

"Go to your room and stay there Miss, I shall speak to your governess on a suitable punishment. As for your brother George, he will get the thrashing I should have dealt him years ago. I am deeply ashamed to be your parent."

With loud wails Rebecca ran from the room. Caroline sighed despairingly. What use punishing them now? They had driven John away, she might never see him again.

Another thought. That morning she had posted to The Times her fresh appeal. What if a relative now came to claim him? Heard how their child had been driven from safety by cruel lies and torment?

Edward Maltravers' tempestuous homecoming swept away his brother Robert's hopes of inheriting. During his furious ride back from the man and pug lawyers he considered ways of contesting the will but could think of none. Leave it to Sophie's more resourceful brain. It was not on ways to overturn a will her wits were to be exercised.

Returning home after her visits she expected to change for dinner, not to be confronted by a brother-in-law she fondly imagined at the bottom of some ocean. By then Edward had grief and bitter anger under control. After the first violent outburst during which, with a superhuman effort, he had refrained from throttling Robert on hearing his shifty-eyed denial of any part in John's abduction, he had stormed into the house to be brought back to a semblance of sanity by the phlegmatic Sergeant Tom Hart.

"Steady down Captain. No getting to the bottom of these shenanigans by going at it like an enraged bull. Agreed you have cause, no denying a very bad business and my heart shares your grief. But back to your calm reasoning self, treat these ...best not say the word...like they was on court martial."

By the time he confronted Robert and Sophie he had disciplined himself, outwardly indeed his calm reasoning self. He had changed from uniform into a plain coat and trousers of fine grey woollen cloth, linen shirt uncluttered by cravat or neck cloth. He stood before them as Robert and Sophie sat either side of the library log fire, more fearful of his grim calmness than his rage. Still in uniform Tom Hart sat in a corner, the jury. Edward had learned the appalling facts from his household staff, now he awaited the fictional version from his relatives.

"I trusted you with my wife and child, I return to news of...of Harriet's ...demise and Jackie's disappearance..."

Sophie interrupted, inwardly fearing discovery, outwardly pained indignation.

"We cannot be held responsible for either mishap. Poor Harriet died in childbirth, a frail little creature, and John abducted while we visited my brother. We had entrusted him to the care of his nurse and the servants"

Mishaps! inwardly raged Edward. Tragedies, the loss of those dearest to me. What sort of heartless insensitive creature is this... this woman?

"You ensured Harriet received the finest treatment? Doctor Durham attended her with his wife as I requested?" Edward knew otherwise but wanted to hear it from them.

Sophie hesitated, wishing to confirm this though realising it could easily be refuted. Before she could reply Robert blundered in.

"Unfortunately the doctor occupied with a difficult confinement in...um... hang it where... Ah yes, Hampton. We had to summon Doctor Corder who came with a woman from the village as midwife." He quailed before Edward's renewed fury.

"Corder! The man is a quack, a mountebank! He bungled a previous confinement, the child miscarried. I instructed he should never again set foot in this house."

"He was the only available doctor," retorted Sophie, her anger rising against Robert. Corder's fee had been much lower than that of Durham, in keeping with his doctoring. Robert had submitted the account to the steward, altering it to show a higher fee, pocketing the difference. A few guineas lost in one night at the gaming hell. Would Edward discover why Durham had not been summoned, the altered account?

Suspecting deceit Edward had already decided to scrutinise the steward's accounts, to question Dr Durham. Now for other accusations, further lies.

"I shall look further into that. You were away when John was taken. How can you justify that? You were his guardians."

"A household of servants," said Sophie, still defiant but increasingly desperate. "His nurse was in charge, she allowed him to slip away."

Edward had details of Nurse Hunt from the maid Tildy.

"Without my permission you dismissed a faithful loving nurse, employing a creature frequently the worse for drink." His voice had risen, now he almost whispered: "You left my small defenceless child in the charge of a drunkard though you must have been aware of her habit." Another accusation, this time from the testimony of stable lad Will. "Furthermore, you instructed the servants to have no contact with him..."

"Servants should be kept in their place!" Sophie yet more

desperate. "They were allowed far too much familiarity with John."

Edward abruptly waved her to silence. "They were his friends, they loved and would have guarded him. I should have entrusted him to them, not you. Why did you isolate him? What devilry have you been guilty of?" Before they could utter denials: "And the letter to Harriet reporting my supposed death. Why did you pretend to receive it only on your return from South Lambeth when Phillips distinctly recalls passing it to you several days before your departure?"

"He is mistaken," shouted Robert. "Do you take his word before ours? Outrageous! What reason could we have for such a pretence?"

Edward's voice now calm, though with an undertone of menace. "That is what I intend to find out though I suspect vile treachery. There are far too many questions to which I cannot expect honest answers from you. I am grievously at fault for allowing you in this house. Tomorrow I want you out of it. If I find you were responsible for...God knows I cannot believe such evil from anyone, let alone a brother. Now get out of my sight or I shall be tempted to do violence."

With no further attempt at defence and fearful that Edward might act on his threat Robert and Sophie hurried from the room.

"Guilty," was the verdict of juryman Tom. "Guilty as hell to which they should be sentenced to burn in eternal fire. Hanging, drawing and quartering too merciful."

To Edward the air breathed cleaner after the departure of Robert and Sophie back to their Kensington lodgings to face the wrath of their landlord and dunning tradesmen. Having dissipated his father's substantial legacy Robert was dependent on the annuity Edward still allowed him – for how much longer? and on the thousand pounds a year Sophie had from her father. A fraught homecoming, each blaming the other for the failure of their plans. Most of all they blamed Edward for not drowning.

At Maltravers Hall Tom was installed in quarters luxurious for one who had rarely slept in a comfortable bed. He was soon on the friendliest terms with the household staff, especially the comely females. Edward resigned his commission. Tom also gave up soldiering, though still referring to Edward as 'Captain' despite protests.

"I am no longer a captain, call me Edward as I call you Tom."

"I could never do that sir, you will be Captain to me till the end of my days."

Edward's enquiries started with lodge keeper Ned, hearing of the beggar-like woman claiming Captain Maltravers awaited him at the Bell Inn.

"She must have used the same tale to lure away Jackie." Edward surmised to Tom. "How the devil did she know of me? The household deny all knowledge of her and my relatives were away. Even had they been here, what truck would they have with such a woman? I cannot imagine Sophie inviting her to take tea and gossip."

Tom shook his head. "Damned if I know, Captain. Beggars belief." No smile from the Captain, not truly a jesting matter. "What say we make enquiries at the inn? Seemingly the woman claimed to work there."

A decision already reached by Edward. More dashed hopes as the host denied all knowledge of the woman, he would never hire such a creature. As they were about to remount their horses a small pot boy ran up to them.

"Beg pardon Mr Maltravers, but I think I do see the woman you was asking after."

Edward recognised one of the pupils at the school he founded.

"Who is she Clem, do you know?"

"Not to say know sir. But I did see her some time since in the sweeper's cart alongside the climbing boys while the sweeper did go into the inn to ask after messages left by folk needing their chimbleys swept. And then they went off."

Edward frowned his perplexity. "A chimney sweeper's cart? Strange. Have you seen her any other time, Clem?"

"No sir, I only see her that time as I was cleaning tankards at the pump."

"Do you recall how long ago that happened?"

Clem screwed his snub nose in thought. "Must have been harvest time sir as I did help my Pa with the gleaning on my free days from here."

Edward patted the boy's shoulder. "That is very helpful Clem, here is a crown piece. Should you see the woman again, send immediate news to Maltravers' Hall."

Clem gazed in wonder at the crown, the most money he had ever seen. How proud Pa would be, perhaps a sixpence for himself. With a great beam he thanked Mr Edward most kindly and would do as he asked. At that moment his devotion for Mr Edward was such he would have jumped off the inn's roof if asked.

Edward returned to the inn for information on the sweeper. Yes, he was told, Sam Billings used to call every six weeks or so but had since given up the trade and his whereabouts unknown. Then a memory returned to the inn-keeper.

"Come to think on it Mr Edward, he did call at Maltravers Hall say in October of last year and Mrs Robert Maltravers called to enquire about him not so long since but I told her he no longer called here and we knew not where he could be contacted. She seemed fair put out."

Thanking him, Edward rejoined Tom for the ride back to the Hall.

"What mischief is this Tom?" he asked. "Can there be a

connection between the woman and my relatives? And what of the sweeper?"

Again wondering at the unworldly innocence of the Captain, Tom bluntly aired his suspicions. "Mischief it is Captain, or downright evil. Little Jackie was surely abducted for the sweeper's use, his woman used as bait."

Edward stared at him, appalled. "Come now Tom. That is impossible! What use could a chimney sweeper have for a child of barely five? An infant?"

Tom could envisage such a use but would not further distress the Captain, already his face was the colour of parchment.

"We should question the servants, discover what they know of the sweeper's visit."

No comfort for Edward when they did so. Butler Phillips and Mrs Grant well recalled the visit, Mrs Grant little suspecting the effect her revelation would have.

"He was here in late October, Mr Edward. Mrs Robert was right upset by the noise when the little climbing boy fell from the chimney. She summoned the sweeper to reprimand him and Mr Phillips heard Billings say the lad was too big for the chimney which is a narrow one requiring a smaller child....Mr Edward, are you ill?"

Eyes closed, face drained of colour Edward had groaned: "Dear God no!"

Tom was there. "Steady sir, probably not what you fear." But he knew, had heard of similar instances. Small boys some as young as four sold by parents to, or abducted from their homes by, chimney sweepers, despite laws forbidding their use.

Phillips' face had also paled. He took Tom aside and whispered.

"That was the same day I passed the letter to Mr Robert which two weeks later he claimed just to have received, the letter falsely telling of the Captain's death."

The men looked at each other, both with the same appalling suspicion.

Edward's hearing was acute, he overheard. Slumping into a chair he stared unseeingly. Through his tortured brain ran lines of a poem by Mr William Blake, a man of strange visions and fantasies.

"When my mother died I was very young,

And my father sold me while yet my tongue

Could scarcely cry 'weep! 'weep! 'weep! 'weep!

So your chimneys I sweep, and in soot I sleep."

"No!" he cried out in unbearable anguish. "It cannot be! Not even Robert would..." He pushed back the chair with such violence it toppled over. "I shall go to Kensington, wrench the truth from him, with violence if necessary."

Tom Hart tried to calm him but his agony had found an outlet in anger. Though not knowing the child Tom shared his Captain's grief, recalling his own cruelly used childhood. To prevent possible murder and the Captain's arrest he accompanied Edward as, pausing only to don a riding coat and boots, he strode out to the stables where his horse Major was already saddled, word reaching the grooms of his intention. Tom selected a fine stallion, a fast mover essential if he were to keep up with the Captain in his present state.

Edward urged Major to a furious gallop, the horse responding with alacrity, seldom having the opportunity to exercise his full power. Tom struggled to keep at the most two lengths behind. Not until after they rode through Chiswick had Edward's rage abated enough to steady Major into a canter.

The Robert Maltravers lived in the poorer part of Kensington, a street of uncared for houses mostly let out as apartments. Dismounting, Edward left Tom to stand by the horses as he hammered at the door of Robert's residence. A lengthy pause during which Edward again vigorously plied the knocker. The door opened to reveal a woman of indeterminate years, drab long snuff-coloured gown partly covered by an off-white apron, wisps of dark greasy hair escaping from her cap. Her face narrow, lined. A sharply pointed nose and mouth drawn in over toothless gums, her eyes small, dark, suspicious.

"Why the row?" she snapped.

"I wish to see Robert Maltravers," Edward's voice equally abrupt. That of a man used to giving orders, having them obeyed. The woman's eyes flashed anger.

"Aye, so would I, so would the landlord. He took off during the night with his haughty trollop. The landlord was sending in the bailiff's men today, twelve guineas in rent owing. Not a penny paid for months."

"Where did he go?" asked Edward, already knowing the answer.

"To the devil for all I care. I shall be in deep trouble with the landlord when he learns of his escape."

"You did not hear him leave? There must have been much commotion."

"I sleep in the back room of the basement, heard not a thing..." Well lubricated, thought Tom, now with Edward and scrutinising the red veins among the greyness of the housekeeper's skin. She continued: "A tenant on the first floor did hear bumpings and bangings on the stairs. He looked out of the window and saw trunks and bags loaded into a wagon driven away by a man he could not make out in the darkness but surely your friend."

Friend! With barely restrained fury Edward took out his purse and counted twelve guineas into the woman's outstretched hands.

"Here! Give that to your rogue of a landlord. I shall see that his extortionate rents are looked into. Good day madam."

He strode off, the woman gaping after him. How many of those guineas will find their way into the landlord's pocket? wondered Tom. Lord but the Captain was a gullible innocent. Half that money would have been accepted without argument.

They had a more restrained return journey. Edward's anger

turned to deep dejection. Robert gone who knew where, the erst-while chimney sweeper's whereabouts equally unknown. And his Jackie?

That night he could not sleep, whenever he closed his eyes he saw the image of his small son thrust into a chimney, choked by soot, terrified, falling... He was convinced he had heard Jackie's cry for Papa that day at the Cape. Oh God, not his death cry! Torturing himself he paced his room, desperately thinking of ways to trace his child. Advertise? After some three months since the abduction? But he must try; put advertisements in all the newspapers. Trace his detested brother? Robert would have to contact him with his annuity soon being due.

During the day he tried to occupy himself with estate duties. Tom Hart was deeply concerned at his haggard appearance, fearing for his sanity but he had no comfort to offer, convinced Jackie was another of the country's many lost children.

Two equally tortured days, then renewed hope for Edward. His lawyers Harlow and Stanford called on him with documents requiring his signature. Stanford sniffed around for Jeffory, Harriet's cat named after a poem by Christopher Smart that had taken her fancy. Also a favourite with Jackie from his earliest prattling which Jeffory heard with closed eyes and omniscient smile. After Harriet's death another of Sophie's victims, she disliked the cat almost as much as he disliked her. She disposed of him claiming he endangered John's health, cats' fleas spread plague. That the fleas of black rats were the true culprits she neither knew nor cared. Abandoning the search Stanford settled at his partner's feet snuffling sagaciously.

Their business completed, Mr Harlow congratulated Edward on his escape from a watery grave and expressing genuine sympathy for John's abduction. Though not caring for children he approved of John, he did not tease Stanford, treating him with due respect. More importantly Stanford approved of John.

"A sad business," commented Harlow. "I think our only

option is to advertise. Strange, about the time John disappeared there appeared an announcement in The Times newspaper concerning a child rescued from a chimney sweeper. I contacted your brother who assured me he had written to the advertiser via the newspaper only to learn the child had been claimed..."

Edward broke in, face alight with hope. "You did not yourself enquire of the newspaper?"

Mr Harlow's bushy eyebrows expressed surprise. "Why no, I accepted your brother's assurance, why should I not?"

Rage again engulfed Edward. He violently slammed a fist on the table, bringing a started yelp from Stanford and open mouthed surprise from his partner.

"Why should you not?" stormed Edward. "Because my thrice accursed brother is a liar and... and the devil knows what else! I shall go to the Times office now...today..." He trailed off, repentant as he saw Harlow's stupefaction. "I beg your pardon sir, you could not have suspected my brother, I myself can hardly believe..."

Mr Harlow recalled Robert's visit. "I do admit we were not overly impressed when he called on us, but Mr Maltravers, surely he would not be guilty of so heinous an act? Of plotting John's abduction?"

"I may be doing him a grave wrong," admitted Edward to whom family honour was paramount. But the dark suspicion lurked there. If Robert was truly guilty of somehow contriving Jackie's abduction he would equally take steps to ensure he could not be traced.

Outwardly calm he told Harlow he would make enquiries at The Times to confirm the rescued child was not John. With an effort he controlled the urge to set off immediately, inviting Harlow and Stanford to take refreshment before their return to Richmond. Madeira and cake for Mr Harlow, a bowl of water for Stanford with whatever cake his partner chose to share with him. Sensing Edward's inner turmoil Harlow refused for them both explaining: such a short journey to Richmond and they had partook of a light meal midday, work to be done in the afternoon. As they prepared to depart Harlow made the unprecedented gesture of placing a hand on Edward's shoulder.

"I hope with all my heart you discover the child is John. Every good wish my dear fellow." He felt entitled to this familiarity, having known Edward since his childhood.

After the lawyers departed in their gig Edward immediately sought out Tom Hart, in a torrent of words pouring out Harlow's revelations.

"I shall ride Major, you take the chaise. If as I hope the advertisement was to do with Jackie and for some hellish reason Robert prevented anyone here claiming him and the newspaper gives me details of the advertiser we can immediately call on them, bring Jackie back..." He gasped impatiently as with an upraised hand Tom tried to stem the flow of words. "I am determined to go even if I do so alone."

In contrast to Edwards impulsive speech, Tom Hart's was the voice of calm reason. "You know me better than that Captain. Tis only I hate to see you build up your hopes so. It is several months since the advertisement appeared, will the newspaper still have the details? And it is just possible your brother spoke the truth."

Edward shrugged, accepting Tom's caution. "If I court disappointment so be it but I must follow every lead. Please go to the stables and make arrangements while I inform Mrs Grant."

Suitably clad for the cold journey to London Edward rejoined Tom in the stable yard. The lad Will was with him.

"A teaser sir." said Tom with scarce disguised amusement. "Young Will begs to accompany us."

"Please, Mr Edward," earnestly implored Will. "I did promise Master Jackie I would do anything for him. He spoke of me as his brother, begging your pardon sir, I intend no disrespect, and I were not there to protect him. I can be of use sir, see to the horses and such. And I have driven the chaise."

"Have you indeed you young rogue," said Edward drily.

"Sir, I were not taking no liberties, Mrs Robert, she did order me to take her to shop for grand clothes when Mr Robert had took the carriage."

"Doubtless also to buy grand clothes. Very well, but you must inform Mr Jenkins you are taking time off to view the sights of London. I should be interested to know how he takes that." Jenkins, the head groom, fought a losing battle to keep his high-spirited young assistants in order.

Will flashed an abashed yet mischievous grin. "Dare not tell him that sir. Most like get a smacked head. With your leave I shall say you requested my presence." Without waiting for Edward's leave he ran off.

Tom gave a snort of laughter. "Impudent brat! But a game 'un."

Aye, thought Edward. The game's afoot.

Eleven

The journey was accomplished without incident, Edward restraining Major's pace to that of the chaise horses. Few travellers were on the roads on such a bleak winter's day, the trio thankful the snow that threatened to hamper them did not fall though biding its time. Born Londoner Tom knew the district, the brewery where he had been apprenticed near the Times offices. Taking Major and the chaise into the yard of the printing house Edward left Will to tend the horses while he and Tom entered the office, greeted by an elderly bespectacled clerk. They spoke above the clamour of printing presses, the air redolent with the smell of printing ink. Edward enquired about the advertisement, probably early November, concerning a child rescued from a chimney sweeper.

"I do recall it sir. An unusual request. Normally we have appeals from families requesting news of lost children." The clerk shook his head. "A sorry state of affairs."

"Indeed," said Edward, restraining impatience. "Did you receive replies?"

"None, sir." A simple answer; for Edward a wealth of meaning.

Edward exchanged glances with Tom. Scarcely believable though it was, Robert's claim that he had enquired and informed the child had been united with his family was false, vile treachery. Showing nothing of his anger Edward calmly asked: "Would you kindly furnish us with the advertiser's name and address?"

The clerk shook his head. "It is our policy not to divulge the identity of advertisers, we forward replies to the advertiser so that they may - or if they wish may not - contact the enquirer..." As Edward started to protest "but as it is some time since, we probably no longer have the details." He lifted a bundle of papers from a shelf and riffled through them. "No, I regret nothing here...what is it Hammond, can you not see I attend these gentlemen?" A spotty shock-haired inky youth had erupted into the office.

"Sorry Mr Johnson, another batch of personal advertisements." He dumped them on the clerk's desk and went out, whistling to show how much he cared for fussy old Johnson's reprimands. Apologising to Edward for the interruption and his inability to assist, Johnson turned his attention to the advertisements. As with murmured thanks Edward and Tom made their way to the door, Edward sick at heart, they were halted by a sharp exclamation from Johnson.

"Why bless my soul, Mr Maltravers. This is most extraordinary. The very first letter contains another appeal for the family of the child rescued from the sweeper."

With an abrupt turn of the heel Edward returned to the clerk's desk, controlling the urge to snatch the sheet of paper from his hand. He could not restrain the eagerness in his voice. "Pray sir, what does it say?"

Johnson read it out. "Consequent to our previous appeal we repeat the information. A five year old child was rescued by this family from a chimney sweeper who it is suspected abducted him. He is evidently of a good family, fair-haired, blue eyed and refined of speech. He knows himself only as John and claims his father is abroad, a Captain Edward of the Light

Dragoons. Will anyone having information about the child please contact CC at the Times, Printing House Square, London."

Johnson looked up. "Is that the child you seek, sir?"

Tom Hart had clutched Edward's arm to prevent him interrupting. Now he responded with a vehemence that startled Johnson.

"Yes! Yes! that is my son. Here," with trembling hands he reached inside his greatcoat, taking from a fob pocket his watch. Opening the back he showed the clerk a miniature portrait of a solemn fair haired blue eyed child, a likeness taken shortly after John's fourth birthday. He turned to Tom. "This gentleman will vouch for my identity, I am recently returned from India where I served as captain with the Fifteenth Light Dragoons."

Tom nodded, taking from a pocket his discharge papers. "I had the honour of serving under the Captain, he returned to this country to learn of his wife's death and the abduction..."

"I implore you," urgently interrupted Edward, "tell me the name of the family so that I may call on them, claim John. I see you have a covering letter with the details."

"The confidential nature of our advertisers is sacrosanct, Mr Maltravers." Johnson hesitated, finding himself unable to withstand the anguish in the desperate father's eyes, twenty years previously he had lost his only son to smallpox, the memory still with him.

"Very well, in the circumstances I doubt the advertiser would object. A lady, Mrs Claremont. Forester Lodge, James's Square, Chelsea. She writes that the family has removed from Blackheath, from where the child's rescue was first advertised." As Edward, desperate to leave, fervently thanked him he added: "Pray say nothing of this, I am flouting rules but feel justified." Then as Edward moved away: "Please return after you have spoken to the lady, if the boy is not your son we must immediately insert the advertisement."

Edward had not waited to hear, already hastening to the stable yard leaving Tom Hart to make assurances and renewed thanks.

Though Edward fervently desired to set off at a furious gallop for Chelsea he restrained himself to keep pace with the chaise, relying on Tom to ask directions. Not a long journey, they reached Forester Lodge mid-afternoon. Leaving Will with the chaise and horses, accompanied by Tom Hart Edward presented his card to the footman, requesting to see Mrs Claremont on urgent business. His impassive face showing no surprise at Edward's agitation the footman took his card to the upper parlour, after a delay that had Edward fuming with impatience returning to say that Sir Edwin, Lady Forester and their daughter Mrs Claremont agreed to see Mr Maltravers and his companion. He ushered them up the stairs to the parlour, announcing:

"Mr Edward Maltravers and Mr Thomas Hart, Sir Edwin," with a slight bow leaving the room.

Lord help us, thought Tom. What a to-do. Nothing of his amusement showed as he and the Captain made their bows to the family. Like being on court martial save that two inquisitors were female, one more grim-faced than any male.

Sir Edwin rose to greet them, a middle-aged man, grave of face, his finely-boned features hinting at sensitivity. Formal of dress, dark frogged jacket, knee breeches and hose, bewigged. Not knowing this attire was for a special occasion, insisted on by his lady, Edward was reminded of solicitor Mr Harlow. He recognised the name, a judge, he believed. A belief that did not make him feel at ease. Far more formidable was the lady of mature years and severe countenance, her haughty stare one that might have been bestowed on intrusive tradesmen. The younger woman maybe in her early twenties, her pleasant features of the same sensitivity he detected in her father. Her dress the unbecoming black of a widow.

Sir Edwin's appraisal was approving. Maltravers had a soldierly bearing, refined features... surely familiar? Thomas Hart, a stolid fellow with open honest countenance. The mutual appraisal complete Sir Edwin announced: "Good afternoon to you gentlemen. Sir Edwin Forester, my wife Lady Georgina and my daughter Mrs Caroline Claremont. I understand you have business with her...Oh, I beg your pardon, pray be seated." As they did so he said to his daughter: "My dear, I think it as well if your mother and I were present at this meeting."

Fiend take him! thought Tom. Does he suspect we will ravish her? He eyed Caroline, hmm, tempting, a comely lady for all those dismal weeds. He misjudged the judge, Sir Edwin's shrewd mind already anticipated with dread Maltravers' business. The likeness unmistakeable, and the name Edward – Captain Edward? Convention demanded that Caroline be chaperoned.

Caroline inclined her head in assent, no sign of her quickened heartbeat as she too saw the resemblance. John's Captain Edward. How would he take their appalling news? That expression of hope so soon to be extinguished...

"Now sir." Lady Georgina had snatched the reins from her husband, uncaring that this was Caroline's visitor, that her daughter was a woman of twenty-three, not an inexperienced sixteen. "Perhaps you will kindly state your business. Prior notice would have been a courtesy."

Restraining impatience Edward replied calmly: "No discourtesy intended, Madam. I believe that your family may have rescued my small son John after his abduction in early November from our home at Maltravers Hall near Richmond." He again took out his watch, displaying the portrait. "This is my son, is he the child?"

Swiftly Caroline rose, taking the watch from Edward. With a small sob she said:

"Yes sir, that is John." Her John, the child she had come to love.

Drawn features transformed by delight Edward exclaimed: "Wonderful...I...I cannot express ... Where is he? Please. I must see him." As they remained silent all animation left his face. "My God, what is it?"

Tom Hart was beside him, hand on his arm, "steady sir." To Sir Edwin. "Where is the boy sir? Your silence grievously distresses Mr Maltravers."

A stranger to any emotion save displeasure, Lady Georgina again took charge.

"He is no longer here. Despite all our kindness he absconded from this house yesterday. And you sir have taken vastly long enough to come searching for him, ignoring our previous appeal of some months past for information."

As Edward numbly absorbed this latest blow Tom spoke for him. He had no fear of this harridan who regarded him with the hauteur of the Madras fine ladies.

"Captain Edward Maltravers returned to this country from India not a week ago, unaware of his son's abduction. Your advertisement was deliberately ignored by..."

"No more Tom!" snapped Edward. He faced Lady Georgina, head high, eyes ablaze with anger. "My son could never be ungrateful for kindness. What drove a defenceless five year old child from this house?"

Lady Georgina was no novice in anger. "Sir! You dare speak to me in that disrespectful fashion..."

Leaning forward in his chair Edward interrupted, fists clenched in an attempt to restrain anger. "Respect must be earned. I ask again. What unkindness drove my small child out into this inhospitable city and in such weather? A loving obedient child..."

Lady Georgina's wrath equalled his. "An ingrate sir! We took him into our family, showed him every kindness..."

Kindness? Her mother? Never! Her pent up anger finding an outlet Caroline joined the fray.

"You call it kindness madam? Banished to the nursery, isolated as though he were a leper, left to the torment of my brother and sister who drove him ..."

Furious at her normally meek daughter's daring to defy her Lady Georgina commanded: "Be silent Caroline! A little childish teasing..."

Caroline too indignant to curb her tongue. "Teasing! Torment is the truer word. We have heard from Rebecca what form that teasing took. Foul names, blows, threats, terrifying him with lies on what we intended..."

Sir Edwin had tried to intercept the angry exchange. Now he succeeded.

"This wrangling is unseemly and unhelpful." To Edward: "My apologies for adding to your distress sir. I admit we were grievously at fault in not bringing John more into our family life..." Here Sir Edwin gallantly took on himself blame for his wife's neglect, he was seldom at home, "...with the exception of my daughter who indeed treated him with every kindness. A true friend."

Edward's grim expression, his tension, relaxed as he turned to Caroline.

"My most sincere thanks, madam."

Caroline's voice was no more than a whisper, as though talking to herself.

"I loved him as I would my own child had he lived."

Lady Georgina was deeply affronted by such an improper display of emotion. Sir Edwin coughed to cover his own.

"Yes, quite. Mr Maltravers, we will do all we can to trace John, I have already alerted the City Police. In some small way to make amends may I suggest that to aid your search you and Mr Hart stay here as our guests..."

Already outraged by Caroline's accusations Lady Georgina made no attempt to disguise further displeasure.

"Sir Edwin! Perhaps you would have the kindness to consult

me before inviting guests. We know nothing of Mr Maltravers or his companion."

"Indeed we do madam." Sir Edwin turned to Edward. "Your father was John Maltravers of Gray's Inn? A highly respected King's Counsel?"

Edward now spoke more calmly. "Yes sir. He died four years ago. I inherited the Maltravers estate on the death of my older brother Benjamin in a hunting accident. I was then serving with the Light Dragoons but have now resigned my commission to attend to estate duties." He indicated Tom. "Mr Hart is my trusted friend and companion, a gallant gentleman who saved my life at the risk of his own in the Assaye battle." To Lady Georgina: "Does that meet with your ladyship's approval?"

His bitterly sardonic tone robbed his words of any respect. Tightening her mouth Lady Georgina made no response. What could she say? His lineage finer than her own, the youngest daughter of a country squire relieved to have married off his self-willed daughter to a promising young lawyer, eldest son of a wealthy family. She was then handsome with an assumed charm soon abandoned after marriage. But, she consoled herself, Maltravers had no title. Nor had she before Sir Edwin's knighthood.

"Well sir," continued Sir Edwin. "Will you and Mr Hart do us the honour to make this house a base for your search?"

Edward looked to Tom for guidance. Sleepless nights and despair had taken their toll, he could no longer think clearly.

"It would surely be of great assistance Captain...er... Mr Edward. But there is also young Will – our stable lad sir," he explained to Sir Edwin. "Outside with the chaise and horses." The chaise intended to carry John in triumph to his home.

"That will cause no problem," replied Sir Edwin. "There is room enough in the stable block on the other side of the square."

"But we have not come prepared for a stay," objected Edward.

"Easily solved," said Tom. "Will and I shall return to the Hall, make the arrangements and ask Mrs Grant and the maids to pack for us. There sir, how does that suit you?"

Edward agreed it suited him well, thanking Sir Edwin for his hospitality. Lady Georgina could not resist a further jibe. "Surely you have a valet? Or do you require us to provide one?"

Edward smiled bleakly. "I am a grown man madam. I do not need assistance in attending to my personal needs." He glanced at her exquisitely tortured hair, wondering how long it had taken her maid. To work for such a mistress must be purgatory. Then he thought desperately. But my small son cannot fend for himself. He spent last night in freezing temperatures – where? Oh God, protect him until I am able to do so. He would never know how his previous appeal had been answered - the deliverance of a small climbing boy from an apprenticeship that would have surely killed him within weeks, if not days.

Anthony Barnes had been slightly delayed at the City Police office. He did not expect to encounter the Marshal who made only sporadic appearances. Far too important, a portly pompous ass who did little to warrant his equally fat remuneration. Duties were left to two young constables in their smart blue military style uniforms. When Barnes arrived they were attempting to placate an irate householder whose windows had been smashed by young ruffians. Yes, the constables assured him, they were known and would be apprehended, given a good flogging, that would make them mend their ways. Unlikely, thought Barnes. They would move on to more heinous crimes, the gallows. What else was there for them? Semi-starved, untutored, undisciplined since infancy.

"Their flogging will not pay for my windows," grumbled the householder as he fumed out of the office.

The constables showed little concern for his financial outlay.

"I wager the lads' fathers are glaziers," said one.

"You lose," responded his colleague. "They are outcasts,

turned out to live as best or worst they can. If the gentleman does not have his windows promptly repaired he may wake tomorrow to find much property missing."

"Not if we alert the night watchman." The constable turned to Barnes. "You also have problems with the rogues, Mr Barnes?"

"Ah no, I have little they would want to steal. My problem is I hope more readily solved. Do you know of a family by the name of...it may be Foster, Sir Edwin, living in a large house in a Chelsea square with stables?"

The constable shook his head. "An unfamiliar name but I am newly come to the area. Do you know Jerry?"

To Barnes' relief Jerry did know. "Sounds like Sir Edwin Forester's place in James's Square. They have their grand house in Blackheath but spend some months here. An exceeding important gentleman, is Sir Edwin. High placed judge and they do say a fair man." He took up a sheet of paper. "Ah yes, Constable Blake reports a servant calling from there about a missing boy."

Barnes joyfully clapped his hands. "My problem solved! I have the lad and shall return him there this afternoon. I am most grateful for your help."

Returning to the shop his relief turned to dismay, John had gone. He read the note, mystified. What nonsense had the child now got unto his head? Oh the little idiot! Why had he not waited, spoken to him of his fears? How strange that John thought of him as a grandfather when he had been so reminded of his grandson. He ran through the street, questioning passers-by, stallholders. None had seen John, a busy time of day. He hurried back to the police, they promised to alert their mounted men. Deeply distressed, Barnes returned to his shop where customers impatiently awaited him. Not until five o'clock was he free to collect his horse from the hostelry and make the short journey to Forester Lodge. There he asked to see Mrs Caroline.

"Mrs Claremont," haughtily amended the footman. "Kindly

wait while I ascertain if the lady is at home." Knowing full well she is, jackanapes, thought Barnes.

The family was preparing for dinner but after a delay caused by Caroline persuading her mother that she should see Mr Barnes, he might have news of John, he was ushered to the parlour. From John's description he recognised Lady Georgina, looking as if she had a very sour prune in her mouth. No mistaking the grave faced gentleman, Sir Edwin. And the sorrowful young woman in black, John's beloved Mrs Caroline.

Lady Georgina summed up Anthony Barnes as a tradesman. Respectable, but still a tradesman. The sour prune drew her mouth in still further.

"Your business sir? Important I trust, to call at such an inconvenient hour?"

Anthony Barnes stated his business, bringing a small cry of distress from Caroline. No distress from Lady Georgina. Wrath only.

"That wretched child has caused yet more trouble..." An indignant gasp as the quiet measured voice of Sir Edwin interrupted her.

"If you please madam." To Anthony Barnes "May I ask your patience sir. There is another gentleman whose presence is vital." He rang a bell, answered by the jackanapes.

"Please ask Mr Edward Maltravers to join us. Inform him there is a gentleman here he must meet." To Anthony Barnes. "Mr Edward Maltravers, lately Captain in the Fifteenth Light Dragoons, returned from India. John's father."

TWELVE

Allocated a first floor apartment at Forester Lodge Edward Maltravers courteously but firmly requested the house-keeper to prepare similar accommodation for Mr Hart, a friend, not a servant. Stable lad Will was happily accommodated in the stable block.

Edward hoped their stay would be brief, not only was he desperately anxious to find Jackie, he wished the shortest possible acquaintance with his hostess, her hauteur more unbearable than that of the East India Company wives with their absurdly superior airs. He had reluctantly accepted that he should dine with the family and their guests, as a frugal eater having no appetite for a lengthy meal and idle chatter. As Tom and Will were not yet returned he had no evening wear and after a day of travelling felt far from fresh. He was making an effort to remedy this by taking off his shirt and washing as best he could from the supplied ewer of water and basin when the summons came via the footman.

"Sir Edwin desires your presence in the parlour sir," he said averting his eyes from Edward's naked upper torso. As well a maid had not been sent. "He wishes you to meet a...person there." The footman baulked at calling a tradesman 'a gentleman'.

"Do you know the purpose?" asked Edward, drying himself on a towel. Army life was no respecter of false modesty.

The footman was affronted. "I am not acquainted with Sir Edwin's affairs sir."

Are you not! Edward thought with grim humour of his own staff who did not hesitate to acquaint themselves with his affairs. Hastily donning his shirt and jacket he followed the self-important footman, his own thought similar to that of Anthony Barnes, popinjay!

He was duly announced to the company in the parlour, Sir Edwin rising to introduce Anthony Barnes. Lady Georgina also rose.

"We shall leave the... gentlemen to their discussion, Sir Edwin. Our guests are arriving. Come, Caroline."

"I wish to stay, Mama," replied Caroline with unwonted firmness. "Mr Barnes is my caller."

Not desirous of anther family dispute in the presence of strangers Lady Georgina had to be content with a look of extreme displeasure and a curt "as you please" before leading Sir Edwin from the room, with the briefest of nods acknowledging the bows of Maltravers and Barnes.

Anthony Barnes had needed no introduction to John's father. There stood John as he would be in twenty or so years, blue eyes wary rather than trusting, mouth hardened by experience and suffering, the firm chin. The two men stood in awkward silence, each waiting for the other to speak. Caroline came to their rescue.

"I am so sorry you were not asked to be seated, gentlemen. Pray do so." As they obeyed: "Mr Maltravers, Mr Barnes has had the great kindness to call with news of your son John."

Edward impetuously sprang to his feet. "Your news sir?"

"I fear it is not all you may hope for sir." As Barnes described his encounter with John, Edward returned to his seat, gazing at him with sombre eyes.

Caroline said gently: "Mr Maltravers, it is not such bad news.

John is well, he has money, has made purchases, and thanks to Mr Barnes' generosity well shod. The police are alerted, they have his description. Be assured he will soon be found."

An anguished response "But he is so small! Among the crowds in London all occupied with their own affairs who will notice such a scrap of humanity? See how dark it is, where will he find safe shelter?"

Anthony Barnes smiled faintly. "Last night he slept comfortably in a horse's stall. The horse his friend he assured me."

From Edward an equally brief smile, more a grimace. "He has a great love of horses from infancy."

Caroline said eagerly: "Does it not give you hope, Mr Maltravers? Such independence already! He confidently makes purchases..."

"With the tales of mamas in milliners and papas in coffee shops," added Barnes. He took John's note from his coat pocket. "He left me this with a crown to pay for the shoes though I assured him they were my gift. But the note sir? What can he mean? Sent to Australia to be eaten by heavens? Who is Bessie?"

Edward took the note, gazing with an absurd smile of pride at his son's prowess in writing. The last letter he had from Harriet ended with the shakily formed "Love to Papa from Jackie", no doubt his hand guided by Harriet. Now a few months later this letter, misspelt though it was! On her mother's strict instructions Caroline had not shown her own note naming George as John's tormentor, responsible for his flight. That would come when she became better acquainted with his father.

"Bessie was Jackie's nursemaid," Edward answered Barnes. "Dismissed without my knowledge or consent. An ignorant girl but devoted to Jackie. He no longer needed a nursemaid, I had intended finding her another place in my household. She would not have allowed my child to wander on his own as did that drunken nurse...hired by my brother and his wife." Both Barnes and Caroline noted the sudden tightening of his mouth, the flash of anger in his eyes, heard his whispered: "Surely not even Robert would..." Then more calmly: "Not realising the consequences – how could she? – Bessie obviously filled his head with some ridiculous tale of orphans sent to Australia where they might be eaten by heathens, in truth a harmless peaceful people. The true fate of orphan children sent to Australia and other colonies is more likely to be exploitation by white so-called Christian settlers. That is a matter I shall raise..." He broke off before indignation replaced calm reason. "Tomorrow I shall go again to the police, search with my comrade Tom Hart in your area, Mr Barnes. He cannot have travelled far on those small legs." He closed his eyes as if to shut out the vision of a weary little pilgrim, his Holy Grail a beloved Papa. Edward longed to leave the house immediately to search for Jackie, share with him the perils of the night.

Madness! He knew nothing of the area, would soon be as lost as Jackie. If only Barnes had come earlier...no, that was unjust. Barnes had done all he could and by the time of his own arrival in Chelsea Jackie had been gone several hours. As Tom would advise, be his normal reasoning self, wait for daylight. Meantime take advantage of the hospitality offered by Sir Edwin, act the part of appreciative guest.

Calm restored he said to Anthony Barnes: "Sir, I have not sufficient words to express my gratitude for your goodness. Indeed you acted as a fond grandfather would." To Caroline, "dare I ask that Mr Barnes be invited to join the company at dinner as my guest?"

Sparing Caroline the embarrassment of explaining that Mr Barnes' presence at dear Mama's table would be most unwelcome – for she suspected Edward Maltravers establishment would tolerate no such arrant snobbery – Barnes rose from his chair.

"Thank you, but I must decline. Since my wife's death three years ago I have lived with my daughter and her family in Vauxhall, she will be expecting me."

Edward took his outstretched hand in both his. "Again my

thanks. If I may I will call on you tomorrow, I long to hear more of Jackie...and," glancing down at his boots, "These have seen better days, I would be grateful for a fitting. Trading in such an affluent area I dare say you provide the so-called gentry?"

"Indeed sir," replied Barnes with some complacency. "I have royal dukes among my customers. They are a mixed honour, for they're also among my worst debtors. I shall be far more honoured to have the custom of the Maltravers' family. Until tomorrow." He bowed to Caroline. "Good evening, ma'am, I hope to be of service to you."

She held out her hand, a civility that would have given Mama the vapours. Shaking the hand of a tradesman! "You already have sir. Good evening and my grateful thanks."

In his apartment Edward found Tom Hart had returned and unpacking his portmanteau. No gratitude, only exasperation from Edward.

"Tom this will not do! I have already told you I do not require a valet."

"Nor am I but nor do I wish you to disgrace me before the gentry. You are the most careless of dressers, you may go about in open shirt and labourers' breeches at the Hall but not here, Captain. You must try to act the gentleman."

Edward attempted a military reprimand, though anticipating defeat. "That hints at insubordination; Sergeant."

"As you are forever reminding me, we are no longer in the army, Mr Edward. Hurry now, the guests are assembling. On my way here I encountered Sir Edwin who courteously invited me to join them but the look on his lady's face was enough to curdle milk so I declined, I prefer to eat my meat with the servants."

"Insufferable woman! Then so shall I," angrily retorted Edward.

"Indeed you will not, the servants would be scandalised. As stiff-necked a crew as their employers."

Impatiently Edward changed into more formal dress, thankfully kicking off his boots and donning clean stockings and smart though comfortable buckled shoes.

"There, will that do? Or shall I rouge and patch my face, prink and smirk?"

A grimace. "I should deny your acquaintance. A comb through those tangled locks will suffice...good, a gentleman to do credit to any table."

"I have no appetite for food or idle chatter. All my thoughts are with Jackie." Recalling Tom was unaware of Anthony Barnes' visit, Edward told him of Jackie's latest escapade.

"Tomorrow we call on the police, I will have bills posted asking for information, with a reward for his safe return, place another advertisement in The Times. Jackie must still be in this area, from what Mr Barnes tells me he seems to have walked in circles, completely lost. How could he know directions? He has never before been abroad unaccompanied, knowing only our gardens and park, the village. But we will find him." Aye, gloomily thought Tom, and in what state? He knew better than Edward the fate of little strays in London. "... And I shall visit Mr Barnes, I need new boots." He glanced at Tom's. "You also."

Tom placed one hand on his hip, smirking as he twirled the other hand, taking a few mincing steps. "La-la Captain, are we not become dandies! Quizzing glasses and swagger canes? Ah, the bell summons you. Enjoy your meal among the highfalutin, try not to be too much in your cups."

"Have you ever known me to be so Tom?"

"No, there's the pity. It might loosen that damned rigidity of yours."

"And less indulgence on your part might curb that insolent tongue."

Tom saluted. "Touché, Captain."

. . .

The company gathered for dinner was more numerous than Edward Maltravers anticipated, the Foresters were renewing their London acquaintance. He was conscious that what he and Tom considered suitable evening wear was greatly outshone by the male guests, many in frilled shirts, embroidered waistcoats, knee breeches and hose. The ladies in a variety of silks and muslins with a generous display of necks and shoulders, bejewelled, any defect of their features disguised by powder, rouge and patches, their hair styles out-vying each other in bizarreness. Edward did attract attention, not for his lack of fashion, rather his tall erect soldierly bearing, his features, though too lean to be handsome were, some ladies whispered behind their fans, vastly interesting.

Unaware of admiration Edward looked around in the hope of discovering an acquaintance, wishing Tom were there muttering insolent comments on the more outré guests. To his surprise he saw James Black, his table companion on the Pelican. He noted with amusement that though Black had expressed his low opinion of society women this did not prevent his ogling of the prettiest. He too was dressed less formally but as a large well-built man of bold determined features he too attracted admiring eyes, not only from the women.

Edward took Black's mind off the study of white flesh by greeting him.

"James Black! I thought you had gone to Winchester to take up your old practice?"

Black grimaced, waving away the supposition. "Too many doctors vying for patients and my old practice taken over by a quack. There is an opening at St Thomas's Hospital for a surgeon, no remuneration but the opportunity to build up a reputation and a lucrative London practice. It is an affluent area and bloated life-styles have need of medical men."

"Also malnourishment but the sufferers cannot afford

doctors' fees." Realising this might imply criticism of Black, Edward hastily added: "St Thomas's a fine hospital. You are evidently acquainted with the Foresters."

"Yes, Sir Edwin is a friend of my uncle Henry, they are both members of the Royal Society. Sir Edwin is a patron of St Thomas's and offers to recommend me. I am at present acting locum for their family doctor while he is away, I may join him as partner until I have my own practice."

A fast worker, thought Edward, barely a week off the Pelican!

"A fortunate acquaintance. Ah, our summons to the festive board."

Edward noted that Black had expressed no curiosity as to his presence in the company but knew his self-absorption left no room for others, save to criticise. They were neighbours at the table, Edward as a last minute male upsetting the seating order. On his left he was relieved to see Caroline Claremont, her quiet voice balm amid the starling-like chatter. This was not the right time to quiz her on Jackie, he longed to hear of their walks, to know his son through her.

His attention was soon sought by other ladies intrigued by his quiet manner.

"You are in London to enjoy plays, visit Vauxhall and Ranelagh Gardens, or to attend balls?" enquired one eighteen year old chit with bright gold ringlets and sprigged muslin gown, one of James Black's ogles. A few places along the table her Mama cast an approving eye on Edward. An acquaintance to be cultivated?

Not much promise in Edward's dismissive reply. "No madam, I am in London on business. Pardon me for saying this is not the ideal season for parading so called pleasure gardens in icy drizzle, nor to hear indifferent singing, ill-played music."

The chit giggled. "Oh but there are vastly entertaining plays, oratorios and splendid balls,.. .you must find time to dance! The Duke of Westminster is giving a grand ball this very Friday, it will be vastly attended by all the ton."

James Black interrupted. "I attended such balls in Madras and Penang. Intolerable! British folk in that humidity dressed as for a winter ball in England, streaming sweat. A most malodorous affair." Black had a voice to suit his personality, loud. An uneasy silence, not the most appropriate subject for a genteel dinner table. To ease the tension a military looking man asked:

"You stayed long in Penang sir?"

Black was completely unacquainted with tact. "Too long. For senior employees the Company has a sanatorium on the hill, where it is cooler. I had charge of two invalids, both victims of over eating, drinking and ...other excesses. Diseased livers and the rest. One died, buried within hours. In that climate decomposition soon sets in."

More silence. The military man gallantly persevered. "You were acquainted with the Governor, Sir George Leith?"

Take care, thought Edward. The gentleman appears to be an acquaintance. His tongue well lubricated, Black blundered on.

"Indeed I was. Damned dull fellow, pleasant one moment, surly the next. As ineffectual as are most Company people. Almost as stupid as Lord Clive in Madras."

"Clive!" shrilled the chit. "But he is a great hero! I have heard that he captured single-handed, with only a sword, over forty black soldiers and locked them in a hut. Indeed I have seen the painting."

"An unlikely feat," answered Black. "No, this is his son Edward, a complete buffoon..."

Edward muttered a warning that only Black could hear.

"Take care for your recommendation, the gentleman is obviously of the Company and Sir Edwin is not vastly pleased with you, nor is his greatly affronted lady."

"Damn it! Yes." Immediately sobered Black turned to Sir Edwin with a repentant smile, holding up his goblet. "I beg pardon sir, I am not used to such splendid wine and it has greatly loosened my stupid tongue." To Lady Georgina: "I grovel at your feet, my lady." He bowed his head to the military man. "A thousand pardons sir, I spoke out of turn. There are many good reports of both gentlemen." A diplomatic untruth.

Sir Edwin nodded, somewhat mollified by the compliment to his wine. Lady Georgina' s grimness relaxed, Black could be a disarming fellow when necessary.

The Company officer grunted an acknowledgement, then asking Edward: "I understand you are lately returned from India sir. What is your opinion?"

Much as Black's, but Edward decided on diplomacy. He relied on Sir Edwin's support in tracing Jackie. Thus expedience makes liars of us all, he mentally misquoted.

"I was in India too short a time to form an opinion sir, apart from gaining the impression we are building an empire there by the actions of the East India Company..." Plundering crew! "I was wounded at Assaye and had to return to this country."

A murmur round the table. A wounded hero! Black's indiscretions were forgotten as Edward was questioned on his adventures. Then as with all such gatherings their attention drifted away, leaving Edward free to converse with Caroline.

"Forgive me if I also speak out of turn ma'am, I sense you are not comfortable in this company?"

She answered in an equally low tone. "You are very perceptive sir. Fortunately my father is no great lover of these occasions so they are rare."

"Yet your mother seems greatly in her element."

A rueful smile. "Indeed. As you have noticed a very forceful lady." Believing she read compassion in his eyes she hesitated, then confided: "On my marriage two years ago to a naval captain I escaped to our own establishment. After Charles' death at sea and the loss of my child I became so frail in health and spirits I allowed myself to be persuaded by my mother to return here." Flushing deeply Caroline was appalled at the impropriety of confiding personal matters on so brief an acquaintance, and to a man. She had prided herself on reticence, why so off her guard? Perhaps because he gazed at her with the same solemnity as dear John. Such fine eyes, windows of the soul it was said. If so… she looked away, confused, self-reproachful.

Edward lightly touched her hand, too brief to be misinterpreted as an impropriety.

"I have distressed you, clumsy oaf that I am. You are now fully recovered?"

Having her emotions under control she smiled at him. "Thank you, yes. My all too short an acquaintance with your delightful John greatly assisted the healing process. As if with my own child."

"And you a mother to him, I can never thank you enough."

Caroline made a small gesture of repudiation. "No thanks are necessary, a lovable child. But with recovery comes the longing for a more useful life."

"May I ask how do you occupy your days?"

A soft, unamused laugh. "As other women of my class. Calls on ladies I care nothing for, an idle exchange of gossip, the latest novel, piano playing, some embroidery, attending exhibitions, plays…"

With a teasing smile Edward responded: "So much excitement! Can you not go back to your own home?"

Caroline sighed ruefully. "No longer my home, my father-in-law's property, now a daughter and her new husband are settled there."

Edward hesitated before responding, fearing his words might be taken as impertinent. "Do you engage in charitable works? There must be great need in London."

Caroline sorrowfully shook her head. "Mama would be scandalised! Associating with the lower orders? Bringing back who knows what vile disease? Shame on you sir!"

Mentally Edward reproached himself. To ask such personal questions of a woman on so brief an acquaintance. "Please forgive my forward speech, soldiering blunts gentility. You impress me as a lady of character, not one meekly to suffer tyranny. There are two ways of dealing with it, bow your head in submission or confront the tyrant. You are more than a match for Mama, see how your father in his quiet firm way manages her, you are truly his daughter. If you wish to lead a useful life I think you could well enlist his support."

Caroline's laugh now truly amused. "Such a stern taskmaster! I see where John gets his grave air...No, sir," as Edward made as if to apologise for his temerity. "You only say what I have told myself these past months. You evidently abhor idleness, I am sure you greatly busy yourself about your estate, or will do so when you return with Jackie."

His eyes glowing with fervour Edward told her of his plans. Good housing for all his tenants, assistance for needy families, support during the winter months.

"There is a school for the children, evening classes for those who work. Local people are willing to give their time to teach there. Have you thought of teaching? You surely have a way with children."

He was interrupted by a servant taking away his almost untouched plate of roast fowl, in his absorption forgetting to eat. Caroline tutted her concern.

"I see why you are so spare of build Mr Maltravers. Shall I ask the man to bring back your plate?"

"No, I thank you. I have dined well enough. What were those desiccated little creatures accompanying the fowl?"

"Skylarks sir, do you not like them? I certainly do not but Mama considers them de rigueur.

"I like them extremely when they soar free in the air with their joyful song. But on a dinner plate! An abomination!" A dish of cream syllabub was placed before him. "Ah, how Jackie would love this! The very treat for a five year old."

Caroline tapped his wrist with a spoon, hoping other guests -

and Mama - were too occupied in gossip and guzzling to notice. "You are the most impolite of guests! May I say that you are mistaken. This dish would be far too rich for a young child." As Edward showed no sign of repentance: "A hardened rogue I fear. To return to our learned discussion. I have thought of how I would like to teach small children though I'm not qualified."

"To teach them their letters and numbers? Even I could do so. Is there not a ragged school near here? I heard something of the sort."

"Yes, near London Bridge. Founded by Mr Thomas Cranfield. A tailor I believe."

Edward regarded her with mock gravity. "Ah, a tradesman! Mama would most certainly not approve of that!"

"As I suspected you are truly wicked sir! But you have inspired me. I shall…"

Their conversation halted by Lady Georgina rising from her chair, a signal for guests to stand.

"We ladies will now leave the gentlemen to their discussions…" Or to their intoxication, interpreted Edward. "They will join us later for coffee and cards. Come, ladies." She shepherded her meek flock from the dining room. Having no wish to remain drinking with the men or join the ladies' twittering, Edward escaped to his apartment pleading weariness after an eventful day.

He was indeed weary, of over-loud voices, an overlong meal, the overheated room with its cloying odour of perfumes and pomades…and worse. Truly an ungrateful guest! Returning to his room he slumped into a chair, his mind reviewing the day's events, then dwelling on his conversation with Mrs Claremont. Telling her of the improvements he wished to make to the estate brought agonised memories of Harriet, her gentle unquestioning approval of his plans though offering no suggestions. Guilt that his concern for Jackie had lessened the impact on his grief for her loss. Now anguish came, recalling their all too brief and much interrupted seven years together. Their first meeting when she and her parents visited his father. He was on leave, at twenty-four a lieutenant, she two years younger. The attraction mutual, he adoring her ethereal beauty, her porcelain-like delicacy, she seeing in the quiet gravity a strength of character lacking in her. A protector to be trusted. Had he betrayed that trust?

At that time there was no prospect of his inheriting the estate, his elder brother the heir, but with sufficient wealth and status on both sides, the families welcomed the match. His father's sudden death from apoplexy, Benjamin, still a bachelor with a roving eye, in no hurry to settle and produce an heir, breaking his neck in a hunting accident. Edward inherited. Benjamin had sadly neglected the estate. Such plans Edward had, Harriet in smiling fond agreement. Those happy days with her. He had not wanted to put her through the perils of childbirth but she longed for children. Two miscarriages, then the glorious birth of a healthy boy with none of his mother's delicacy. No more, he had decreed. But Harriet insisted, a companion for Jackie. Despite her fragility she had a stubbornness to which he yielded. All seemed to bode well, her letters happy and full of hope. Then silence as he travelled, nothing to prepare him for the appalling news imparted by his household on his return. Now every effort must be made to find their child, her gift to him. Failure equalled betrayal.

THIRTEEN

Edward Maltravers need not have worried where his son would sleep that night. Fate in a quirky mood provided John with a lodging. After leaving Mr Barnes' shop he had determined to find his way to Knightsbridge Barracks. Soldiers lived there, he was a soldier's son so they would look after him until Papa came. The simple logic of a child with no realisation that in a country at war army authorities had more urgent concerns than tracing a Captain Edward no surname serving in far off India. The presence of a parent-less young child in a busy barracks would be less than welcome.

He bought a mutton pie from one stall and milk from another, carefully counting out the correct money. He must spend wisely, not be prodigal. Why, he wondered, had the prodigal son's father given him a fatted calf and the good son nothing? He had asked Bessie, she said that perhaps the good son did not like fat meat, nor did she.

He received no information from stallholders on the location of the barracks, merely arms waved vaguely in a southerly direction. Wandering on he reached the river and Battersea Bridge, staring in open-mouthed wonder at the span, the craft, the docks.

Was this where George falsely told him he would be sent? He had envisaged tall full-sail ships but these were quite small, then he reasoned a big ship would not go under the bridge. The other side of the river was lost in mist but he could discern a windmill. He had seen one in a picture book but surprised to see one in a town. Was Knightsbridge Barracks over there? He asked a man also watching the craft.

"No child, you would be lost in streets of manufactories and vile stinks. Why do you wish for the barracks. To enlist? Too small even as a drummer boy or fife player."

What was enlist, a fife? Guessing the man jested John shook his head.

"If you please sir I go there to find my papa."

The man looked down at him. Polite, well-bred, no street child. But alone at his small age? "A fine long walk you have. You should not attempt it on your own." Then with relief: "Look, there is a constable, he will assist you."

A constable! As the man gaped in bewilderment John fled, in his panic running across the road, dodging between carriages and bringing oaths from horsemen. Safely on the other side he ran along a side road, glancing back to see if he were pursued. No sign of the constable or a hue and cry. Passers-by ignored him, a small boy running no unusual sight, a child's normal mode of progress. His heartbeat returning to normal he walked along the seemingly endless road, legs shaking with weariness, then another traffic busy street. Unable to walk further he sat on a low wall outside a large house. What to do now? Daylight fast fading, Mr Barnes had warned him of London's night time perils. He must find shelter. Another inn?

Abruptly the traffic came to a standstill, the road ahead blocked by an altercation between carriage drivers on the right of way. A chaise with two white horses drew up on the road nearest him, the morose driver mouthing silent curses. Its occupant was the strangest woman of John's limited experience. Her long cloak did not completely cover her scraggy neck. Her face long and narrow, thickly plastered with rouge, black patches around her wide thin mouth. Dyed red hair piled high, topped by a small lace cap. Black eyes glittering she returned John's gaze. Her voice high, almost a screech.

"Why are you alone dear child? Are you lost? Such a sweet cherub!"

The name Mama called him. Encouraged, he approached the side of the chaise.

"I am going to the barracks, ma'am. I seek my papa. Captain Edward of the Light Dragoons."

"Captain Edwards!" shrilled the woman. "Why, he dines with me this very evening!"

So overcome by joy John had to support himself against the chaise step.

"Papa dines with you? Oh ma'am pray take me to him!"

"Willingly dearest child." As John excitedly tried to clamber into the chaise she said sharply to the coachman: "Lift the boy in, can you not see he is too small to mount?"

"See yerself," retorted the man. "Yer cannot take a child off the street..."

"But please," cried John. "I must go to my papa."

"Robin, do as you are bid," snapped the woman. "Or you lose your place."

Muttering, the man jumped down from his seat. He shook his head at John, whispering: "Run fer it, she knows not what she does."

John hesitated, heart sinking as doubt assailed him. The woman ordered:

"Hurry! The traffic is moving. Pull out the spare seat for the child...Now!"

Groaning the driver lifted John onto the seat facing the woman and resuming his seat drove off. John's enquiring gaze met the woman's intense stare.

"My Papa truly dines with you tonight ma'am?"

"Have I not already said so? And many other gentlemen of high rank. The King is sadly indisposed but the dear Prince of Wales..."

"He comes all the way from Wales ma'am? Is that not another country?"

An impatient gesture of her skeletal hands. "Ignorant child! He lives in London and will be our next king."

"Of Wales ma'am?"

"And of England and Scotland also...oh yes and Ireland which is now part of our kingdom. There will also be Prince Frederick, the Dukes of Westminster and Devonshire, Lord North, Mr Pitt and Sir Joshua Reynolds is to take my likeness: and Mr Handel has composed a heavenly anthem which choristers from Westminster Abbey will sing as we dine."

John was not acquainted with any of the names so unable to query them. An anthem by long deceased Handel heavenly indeed. To him princes, dukes and lords sounded vastly important. And Papa among them!

A thought struck him. "Are there no ladies?"

A grimace further distorted her unlovely face. "No, they are such a fidget. I shall be the only lady."

Surely a very high-up lady. "May I know your name if you please ma'am?"

She drew herself erect, holding up her head to the danger of the cap perched precariously on top of her tortured hair. She grabbed it while pronouncing in shrill ringing tones "I am the Duchess of... of..."

"Of fiddlesticks," muttered the coachman. He had listened in grim faced silence to the farrago. She had found an audience who actually believed her fantasies.

"Silence! Of Laputa. You may call me Your Grace." Her much beringed claw-like hands indicated parcels on the seat. "As you see I have made my purchases for the banquet."

John thought there were very few parcels for a banquet and most seemed to contain pastries and sweetmeats at which he had gazed longingly in shop windows but determined not to be prodigal. Perhaps all the food was already purchased, when Uncle Robert and Aunt Sophie had a dinner party the kitchen staff prepared for it all day. Papa did not eat so heartily, oh soon he would see him again... But his first heart-leaping elation now tinged with doubt. Such a strange lady.

The chaise rattled through a maze of streets, some with cottages, tenements, others with grander houses.

He asked timidly: "Where is this please ma'am...er... Your Grace?"

"We are in Westminster, dear child."

"Bedlam more like," muttered the driver, spitting into the road.

"You are uncouth Robin," reproved the duchess. "Mind your manners before my honoured guest."

Robin said nothing, his face its usual grimness.

"Westminster sounds very grand," ventured John.

The duchess nodded her top-heavy head, again rescuing the cap. "Indeed, the seat of our government."

John looked around for benches but could see none in the gloomy mist of late afternoon. What he could see of the buildings they now passed disappointed him, they were not very grand.

The chaise entered a narrow street with tall houses, at one time imposing but now like the duchess in a sad state of disrepair. The chaise stopped at the end house.

"Robin" shrilled the duchess, "assist me and the child to dismount, take the parcels into the kitchen then take the chaise to the stable yard, see the horses are well fed."

The coachman scowled. "Yer knows full well the chaise is 'ired, I shall return it by and by. 'ow many 'ands does yer thinks I 'ave."

A sharp rap on his head from the duchess's fan. "You are

impudent! Take care you do not end in the workhouse. And bow when you address me."

"The devil I will," grunted Robin. He lifted John down then assisted the duchess. Gathering the parcels he went to the front door, having no hands free giving it a hefty kicking. A woman appeared, tall, with severe features, dressed in a long black gown, hair tucked under a white cap.

"She should not have gone out," she snapped at Robin.

Robin replied sullenly: "You was on yer errands, she ordered me ter 'ire the chaise, threatened me with the workus, threw one of 'er screaming fits."

A look of contempt. "You are so weak! You know full well she has no power to dismiss us."

Without answering Robin pushed past her, jerking his head towards John.

"See there, Nell, what she made me pick up?"

"Insolence." snapped the duchess, now in the hall. "Tomorrow I shall ask my man of business to find more amenable servitors."

"Man of business!" retorted Nell. "Whoever he is will not easily find anyone to tolerate your whims and fancies."

Tossing her head the duchess placed her hands on John's shoulders, propelling him into a large room lit by candles in a broken chandelier and in clay holders placed on the small centre table and mantel shelf. They shed a gloomy light on the scant furniture, damp walls, worn carpet and draperies. A log fire did little to combat the air of must and decay.

"There my little one," she said proudly. "Is this not a magnificent venue for a distinguished personages' banquet?"

Having questioned her husband, the housekeeper hurried into the room.

"What is all this nonsense Miss Emmeline, why did you take the child from the street? There will be great trouble for us all when his absence is discovered."

Emmeline tilted up John's chin. "Is he not the most beautiful child? He shall be my page, I will dress him in a little embroidered robe, on his head a turban with a ruby in the centre. He shall carry a cushion on which rests my tiara and will precede me into the banquet, announcing to the gentlemen The Duchess of Laputa."

"Duchess? Fiddlesticks!" snapped Nell. "What banquet? You will be dining here on your mutton alone while Robin and I eat in the kitchen, your grace declining the company of such low wretches as we are."

John listened in growing dismay. "But....but the Duchess is dining with many great gentlemen and my Papa will also be there." He turned agonised eyes on Miss Emmeline. "Is that not so ma'am...Your Grace?"

The housekeeper answered. "She is as much a duchess as I am. There is no banquet, nor has been for many a long year. Nor any guests other than yourself."

Grief and bitter disappointment overburdened John's heart. Covering his face with his arms he burst into an agony of weeping.

"Now see what you have done," berated the housekeeper.

Miss Emmeline put her hands to her ears. "My poor head!" From a small dish she took a sugar bonbon and thrust it at John. "Here child, do stop that hideous wailing."

John turned away from her, tears the only way he had of expressing his deep sorrow, anguish, bereft of hope, of trust.

"Nell, take it away!" screamed Miss Emmeline. "Throw it outside!"

"I shall do no such wicked thing!" angrily retorted Nell. "It is pitch black out there. You brought him here with false promises, you must see he has a safe refuge tonight."

Emmeline waved hysterical arms. "Shut him into one of the bedrooms, anywhere, loathsome little pest. Then bring me a tisane, my head aches exceedingly."

"The bedrooms have been locked for years. I shall see to him.

And as for your tisane you will have tea when I have seen to your foundling. A page indeed!"

Holding John's hand Nell took him into the kitchen. Comfortless though the grasp was, the human contact lessened the intensity of his grief, his sobs quietened to a few hiccups, then despairing silence.

Divesting him of his coat, muffler and cap the housekeeper lifted him into a chair near the fire. For a few minutes he sat with lowered head while she conversed in low tones with Robin, returned from driving the hired chaise to a nearby hostelry. Young though he was John had endured suffering that would have taxed one many times his age, now resilience asserted itself, his father's firmness of purpose present in infant form. With a deep sigh of resignation he raised his head, looking around the kitchen. Large, far less desolate than the room. A dresser displayed enough china for the mythical banquet. A cleanly scrubbed table, tiled floor covered with rush mats, padded chairs. Emmeline's guardians had made a comfortable refuge for themselves. The fire well stacked with logs warmed the kitchen. At one time large joints of meat would have roasted there, now only a small piece of mutton; on the hob a pan of potatoes and turnips. The smell made John realise how hungry he was. Would he be given a meal? Should he pay?

In a corner of the kitchen he saw a basket in which a cat nursed squealing kittens. With a little cry of pleasure he slipped from the chair and ran to her, kneeling to fondle her head. With soft crooning he took up the kittens, holding them against his face. The adults silently watched. Let him take comfort while he may, the cat too, for tomorrow her litter would be bundled into a bag and drowned. A fine mouser but of loose morals, three times a year the cat lost her litters but never learned the error of her ways.

Reluctantly John left the cat to confront the adults. "Please ma'am, sir, what is to become of me?"

"You are to sleep here tonight," Nell indicated a pallet in an inglenook, "It was used by the kitchen boy but he is long gone. I shall find a coverlet, you will be warm enough there. First you will share our meal."

Never having been faced with this situation John was unsure how he was supposed to react. "May I pay for it ma'am?"

Nell laughed, a brief humourless laugh. "Quite the lordling! No child, it will make up for your lost banquet."

John gazed at her with large imploring eyes in which tears still glistened. "Oh please ma'am why did ...the lady tell me such stuff?"

"Because she is demented, she knows not what she does."

Demented? He recalled hearing the servants tell of a village girl who had run screaming through the street before drowning herself in the pond. Why? He'd asked Bessie.

"The poor lass was demented, an affair of the heart."

John believed this to be an illness of the heart. Not made pregnant and abandoned by her lover. He solemnly asked the housekeeper: "It was caused by an affair of the heart ma'am?"

Another brief laugh. "What know you of affairs of the heart? No, she had no lovers. Her head is afflicted, not her heart."

She could not tell this child Emmeline's history. The only unmarried daughter of a wealthy distiller, ill-favoured and from her youth showing signs of nervous affliction, sudden fits, outbursts of wild hysteria. More than fifty years ago her father set up a trust, purchased the house between Charing Cross and Westminster, installing guardians to care for her, servants, a coach. Everything for a comfortable life. But she was not expected to live into her late seventies, few people of her affliction lived beyond their forties - hardly surprising as most were consigned to lunatic asylums. The Trust money now almost spent despite the sale of furniture and furnishings, the chaise, the dismissal of servants save for guardians. There were only three habitable rooms. Enough remained for a very few years of frugal living, nothing for repairs.

Yet if she escaped Nell's surveillance Emmeline spent wildly on frivolities. The Trustees eagerly awaited her death, the demolition of the house and others in the street, mostly uninhabited, to make way for a new development. For her guardians, the workhouse? The child must say nothing of his abduction, were it known Emmeline would be sent to Bethlem, Bedlam folks called it. And the guardians' fate?

Robin took hold of John's shoulders, his voice low and intense.

"See 'ere, young'un, yer not ter tell no one what passed 'ere terday. If yer does the poor lidy will be put in the mad 'ouse ter be mocked by visitors and mebbe killed there by raving lunatics. Give us yer solemn promise."

John would have liked to tell Papa of his adventures but he did not want the poor demented lady to be killed by mad people. He put a hand on his heart. "I promise by the Lord Jesus."

"That will 'ave ter do I suppose." Robin released his grip. "The mutton is cooked Nell, time fer our supper."

Very little was said during the meal, John perched on several cushions so that he could reach the table. When asked where he intended to go in his search for his father he told them of his wish to find Knightsbridge Barracks. Was it far?

"Too far fer your small legs," replied Robin. He marvelled at the incredible innocence of the child. What sort of reception did he expect? The country at war, soldiers constantly on the move, no motherly women to tuck him in bed. True some of the rougher element might find a use for him. But his presence in a busy barracks an accursed nuisance, soon handed over to the police. Best solution, he could not wander alone much longer. Of this Robin said nothing, for all his surly weakness he was not an unkindly man. Talk it over with Nell.

The meal over John faced his usual embarrassment. He whispered to Robin who led him to the back door. Unlatching it he indicated a ramshackle wooden lean-to.

"Privy." He thrust a candle into John's hand. "Do not fall darn the 'ole."

On his return John felt his whole being reeked of the privy's stench. So distressing he found the courage to ask the stern lady: "If you please ma'am, may I clean myself?"

Nell curtsied. "As your lordship pleases." She placed washtub on the floor, poured in hot water from the kettles on the hobs, then cold water from a pail. Robin could collect more from the pump, he was of little use other than the heavy work.

Another curtsy "There, sire, your bath. Be thankful it is not a cold one."

Obeying a shrill summons from Emmeline she left him as he fumbled to undress, making a reasonable task of washing with the gritty yellow soap that rasped his skin. Returning, Nell handed him a towel in which to wrap himself while she examined his clothes. Of excellent quality, warm vest, a fine lawn shirt, snug jacket and nankeen ankle length trousers. Clothes lovingly selected but the child's mother was dead, so who?

She tutted. "Careless child, you have spilt gravy on both shirt and jacket."

He dare not say that though perched on cushions he had found difficulty reaching the table to eat.

"It was very excellent gravy ma'am," he said placatingly.

Nell laughed, her first genuine laugh for many a weary day.

"Quite the charmer! I shall wash your clothes, they will dry by the fire. What have you in your bag?" She examined the contents, again tutting. "No master packer young sir. All creased." She neatly folded the clothes, shaking out a shirt. "Wear this tonight." As he obediently slipped it on, "Now to your bed. You must be up early tomorrow before my lady wakes. I shall direct you to the curate's house, he will care for you, try to trace your papa for he has great knowledge of London. A good Christian man." She lifted him onto the pallet. "Sleep now, goodnight."

She moved away before John could ask more questions. What

was a curate, he wondered. A man who cured? Warm in the kitchen boy's bed tiredness overwhelmed him. He drifted into sleep lulled by the quiet voices of Nell and Robin, unaware of Emmeline's shrill summons for them to play cards at which they dare not win.

At seven the next morning Nell shook him awake. Sleepily he stumbled out to the loathed privy, washing hands and face in a bowl of water and dressing in the cleaned clothes. He inexpertly scraped at his hair with a comb Nell gave him, he had not thought to pack one. Meanwhile Nell broke bread into warmed sweetened milk for his breakfast. He tried to eat slowly, loath to leave the warm kitchen to face the ordeals of another day but sensed Nell wanted him gone. He guessed because of the demented lady. Laying down his spoon he said quietly.

"Thank you for all your kindness ma'am. I am ready to go."

With a sense of shame mingled with relief Nell helped him on with his outer garments. She found the purse in his coat pocket.

"Not wise to keep it there." Finding string she tied it in a loop to the purse drawstrings. "Hang it round your neck under your shirt. Good, now we must leave, the lady will soon be calling for me, hysterics if I do not immediately attend her." Holding John's hand she opened the front door and took him to the corner of the street.

"Walk along this next road, soon you will come to the curate's house. Look, it is that red roofed building. I dare not come further with you."

John looked up at her, trying to disguise his trepidation but unable to control a tremor in his voice. "Thank you ma'am, I wish you well." He kissed the hand that held his.

"Go!" said Nell harshly, fighting the urge to hold him closely, carry him back to the kitchen, keep him safe, hidden from Emmeline. Impossible! She gave him a gentle push. "God go with you."

Her own belief in a merciful benevolent deity had died many years ago, let the child keep his a while longer.

She watched the small figure crossing the road towards the curate's house until a loud scream sent her hurrying into the house.

FOURTEEN

Had John reached the curate's house that good man would have offered him sanctuary while making enquiries, soon learning of the search for a lost child of John's description, reuniting him with his father perhaps that same day. But now in a malicious mood, assuming the form of a large undisciplined mongrel dog Fate decreed otherwise.

The dog escaped from the back yard of a house next to the curate's as a servant opened the gate to empty slops into the gutter. Seeing an easy target the dog, large enough to bowl John over, rushed at him barking furiously. Terrified, John fled along the road into a side street, hiding behind a bush trying to stifle terrified sobs. He was sure the dog meant to kill him, having seen a stable yard dog kill a large rat by shaking it to death. Proud of defending its master's property the mongrel lost interest and when its ungrateful owner stuck his night-capped head out of the bedroom window shouting: "Duke! Come here sir!" it lolloped back into its yard.

Unaware of the dog's retreat John dared not go back to the curate's house. He continued along the road, a quiet one more gentrified with few residents yet abroad. A quiet broken by the headlong clatter of hooves. A horse pulling a cart, the driver attempting to control it by yelled oaths. As the horse careered towards him John leapt for a hedge, stumbled and fell. The horse stopped abruptly to sample the grassy verge, nearly throwing the cart's passengers into the road. A hated familiar voice yelled: "Lookee there Pa, Jacko!"

Before John could scramble to his feet and take flight Barney leapt from the cart and grabbed him.

"Chuck 'im in the cart!" hoarsely commanded Sam Billings. "I gotta few scores ter settle with that devil's whelp."

A few scores indeed. Sam Billings held John responsible for all his ill luck since the failed attempt to make him a climbing boy, an attempt that thanks to Georgina Forester's threats finished Billings' chimney sweeping career. He and Barney – Zack dying from blood poisoning after the untreated cut received while breaking into Forester House – had proved very inept thieves, the loss of their horse restricting them to less wealthy areas within walking distance of St Giles. Competition from other residents of that criminal infested rookery resulted in Billings and son breaking into already ransacked houses.

Then what Billings considered a stroke of luck. Visiting a horse dealer to procure the cheapest nag possible he was offered a young healthy horse at the incredibly low price of six guineas, which he haggled to four. Little did he suspect with what relief the dealer saw the unpredictable creature go. A present from another dealer, he soon discovered why. "Not right in the head" he confided to a friend. John might have agreed, having been present at the Maltravers Hall stables when a dealer brought horses for head groom Tobias Jenkins' approval. He immediately refused what seemed a lively young horse, telling John and stable lad Will: "Untrainable, see how he shows the whites of his eyes, tosses his head too much, paws the ground? Never have nothing to do with the like."

No one to advise Sam Billings. As at first the horse seemed tractable enough, the night before he renewed acquaintance with John he used it for burglaries in a Westminster square he knew from chimney sweeping days, where dwelt high government officials. An all-night sitting, owners not at home, their families and servants retired early. Billings concealed the horse and cart in the stable yard of an empty house. Bored, also hungry from Billings' belief in a light diet for all creatures save himself, the horse broke out of the stable and dragged the cart onto the central grassy square, indiscriminately demolishing grass and emerging delicate snowdrops and bulbs. As Sam and Barney crept from their latest crib they saw an indignant night watchman dragging the creature away. After downing the watchman with a vicious blow from a heavy sack, Sam and Barney hastily clambered into the cart, Sam lashing the horse into a headlong gallop. It needed no encouragement, with mad abandon racing through London streets until wearied it stopped in another square, again wrecking carefully planted beds and young bushes, refusing to budge despite Sam's urging. He dare not raise his voice for fear of also rousing the residents who, like Sir Edwin Forester, might be armed. So he and Barney sat and fumed until the horse decided to move. A gentle trot until out of the grand squares, then faced with more open roads again a headlong gallop, ignoring Sam's efforts to steer it homewards. But a consolation prize awaited them at the creature's next refreshment halt. Jacko.

Before John could scream for help Billings grasped his throat, snarling threats. The frustrations of the night, all of which he traced back to this brat, urged him to tighten his grip, to squeeze the last breath from that fragile body. Too quick a death. Jacko must be made to suffer before the final murderous blow, to be then dumped in some malodorous alley.

Outwardly subdued John huddled in a corner of the cart. But this John was a different child to the trusting innocent lured from his home almost three months ago. Three months in which he had known terror as a climbing boy, endured the taunts and blows of George and Rebecca Forester, and kept himself alive since his flight from their torment. His wits had prematurely sharpened, his trust and innocence had been betrayed too often. He instinctively knew Billings would kill him. He must await the chance to escape from the cart while their attention was diverted, Barney not watching his every move. But how?

Taunting Jacko on his coming fate Barney examined his satchel, gleefully telling pa the clothes and bag would fetch a few shillings in the market. He stripped John of his overcoat and muffler.

"No more yer aint needing these, me fine young cockerel."

John said a silent prayer of thanks that Barney had not found his purse. Without money he would surely starve, not knowing how to beg or steal.

The horse was now behaving itself, wearied after a long hyperactive night it trotted meekly towards home and rest. They entered Oxford Street, passing Tyburn. Billings averted his eyes. Felons no longer hanged there but he recalled as a child revelling in the public hangings of prisoners brought in cartloads from Newgate. Now they were spared that journey, the gallows were in Newgate's precincts. Billings knew that if caught hanging would be his fate but the police had as much chance of finding a twelve year old virgin in the rookeries of St Giles as a particular thief or murderer. Few made the effort, Newgate was already overcrowded despite bulk hangings. But Fate in the shape of another animal was still in a malicious mood, this time on John's side.

The horse. Perhaps sensing it might not fare too well for food at Billings' illiberal hand, in Oxford Street it abruptly halted at a vegetable stall to sample the wares. Yells and waved arms from the stallholder, oaths from Billings as he wrenched its head away. The inevitable reaction. With a mad whinny the horse reared, then raced through the busy street, scattering pedestrians, overturning stalls, the cart's passengers struggling to keep seated, not noticing they had lost John. At the horse's first lunge he had taken advantage of the cart's tilting to slide off, grabbing his overcoat but not the scattered clothes, darting into an alley and hiding in a doorway. No pursuit. The Billings were too occupied in staying upright.

The horse could not long keep up its momentum. A dray emerging from a side street caused it to rear, then come to an abrupt halt, covered in sweat, foaming at the mouth, snorting its frustration while its passengers shakily righted themselves. The traffic was in turmoil, much cursing and manoeuvring to right carts, drays and carriages. So engrossed were they in their own adjustments Sam and Barney did not notice the mounted policemen until confronted by them.

"A fine muddle you beauties have caused here," commented one while his companion examined the cart.

"What have you in the sacks, lad?" he asked Barney. Terrified, he kept silent.

"Stuff ter sell in the market," gabbled Sam, looking around for means of escape but seeing none. An inquisitive crowd had gathered round the cart, not a friendly face among them. Dismounting, the police examined the sacks.

"Market you say?" exclaimed one with heavy irony. "The stall selling silver and gold plate perchance? We say stolen from houses in Lupus Square last night."

"Exactly so Dick," said his companion. "During which a night watchman nearly had his skull cracked open. He recognised this fine fellow as the chimney sweeper who traded round there some months ago. One by the name Sam Billings."

"Billings?" queried Dick. "A gentleman at Forester Lodge is

exceeding zealous for words with you, master sweep. I would not care to cross swords with him. Abduction of his young child, no less. What say you Ben? Settle him in Newgate first?"

"Aye, the gentleman can visit him in his cell. There may be enough of him left for the hangman...Oh no none of that," as Billings tried to escape from the cart but prevented by the crowd avid to see an arrest. He was pushed into the cart and manacled, also the loudly wailing Barney, prepared to sacrifice pa to save his own skin. No love or loyalty due to that brute from whom he had never a kindly word, only blows.

"None of it my fault, 'e made me do them things."

"Of course he did," consoled Ben. "Dick, do you take these beauties to Newgate, I shall bring your horse." He turned to the crowd. "Off about your business, nothing more to see here." Hang around Newgate yard for a week or so, he told himself with grim humour. Strange how folk lusted for the sight of a hanging twisting fellow human.

Recognising a masterly hand the horse obediently turned in the direction of the city and Newgate, its passengers fearfully silent. Their only consolation, John was not with them to bear witness. They forgot the heap of small garments, silent witnesses still in the cart.

And John? He had witnessed all from a shop doorway, thankful to be free of one danger, not realising that had he remained in the cart the much feared constables would have restored him to Papa. Fate had other plans for John.

Edward Maltravers rose early, desperate to start enquiries. Tom Hart joined him, gnawing at a hunk of bread and cheese.

"You will miss your grand breakfast," he warned.

"No matter." With a rueful laugh Edward added: "There are coffee shops for papas awaiting small sons." Not that his role would be so passive.

Accompanied by Tom on a chaise horse, Edward rode Major to the City Police Office where he requested permission to post notices with his son's description, offering a reward for his safe return.

"We already have details from Mr Barnes," said the constable. "He tells us your boy was abducted, is that so?"

"It is," said Edward, keeping his voice calm. "Lured from our home by the woman of chimney sweeper Sam Billings for use as..."

"Billings!" An officer in the uniform of the mounted police looked up from a report. "A coincidence here sir." He flourished a sheet of paper. "A report of robberies in Westminster, a night watchman injured but recognising his assailant as a chimney sweeper once trading there, Sam Billings by name."

"Has he been arrested?" excitedly asked Edward. "I must speak with him."

The officer laughed. "You do us too much credit sir. Our officers are on the watch and I join them as soon as I have checked all reports. Where can you be reached if we have news?" Edward gave them the address of Forester Lodge. "Ah, judge Sir Edwin's place. Very appropriate. Never fear sir, your little fellow is being sought and now we seek Billings. I suggest you return to the Lodge and await events."

"And your breakfast," muttered Tom. "We can do no more now Captain. Return later for words with Mr Barnes, too early for him to have started work. And there may be replies to the advertisement you asked me to insert in the Times newspaper."

"I have no stomach for breakfast..." Edward checked himself from uttering the words nor for the dragon lady breathing fire and spitting venom at every incautious comment. The police would relish such an indiscretion. He held out a hand to the chief officer. "Thank you for your help sir. I shall take your advice."

Outside the office he felt more free to speak his mind to Tom Hart.

"How can I stay in that house doing nothing while awaiting possible news? I detest inactivity. My small son wanders the streets of London, tired, cold and hungry while I eat more than I need and listen to idle mindless chatter."

Tom Hart again took up his role as adviser, checking the reckless impulses of the Captain. "How will you help your small son by aimlessly pacing the streets of this vast city Captain? What do you know of London? Contain yourself for this day at least. As for idle chatter I noticed you were not averse to the company of pretty Mrs Caroline, if not for that of her fire and brimstone mama."

"Guard that tongue Sergeant," replied Edward repressively, "I am mourning the loss of my wife. Mrs Claremont is indeed a very agreeable lady and I am grateful for her great kindness to John. There my interest ends."

The gentleman doth protest too much, cynically thought Tom. The Captain often spoke of his wife. Tom had the impression of a delicate porcelain sort of woman, best kept in a display cabinet. Not the wife suited to the energetic Captain, he needed a helpmate in his high notions of improving his estate, one to steer him on the practical side, prevent folk taking advantage of his good compassionate nature. Now Mrs Caroline... Tom made an attempt at a tactful reply.

"Your pardon Captain, I am a clumsy wretch."

Edward clapped a hand on Tom's shoulder. "And I a tetchy one Tom."

The family were about to take breakfast when Edward and Tom returned to the Lodge. After a hasty change out of riding clothes Edward joined them with apologies. Lady Georgina gave a curt nod, still no softening of her sour prune features. Sir Edwin smiled a welcome, Caroline asked eagerly: "Have you any news Mr Maltravers?"

"Surely after we have breakfasted would be more suitable for such conversation?" icily commented Lady Georgina.

"No time like the present," replied Sir Edwin. "Your news, sir?"

Edward told of his visit to the police and the reincarnation of chimney sweeper Sam Billings as a housebreaker.

"Billings!" exclaimed Sir Edwin. "The rogue who attempted to rob our Blackheath house..."

"An attempt foiled by your brave little son," added Caroline.

Edward had not known of the incident. Caroline vividly recounted the momentous event, her mother breaking in to air her grievance.

"The Billings creature, Mr Maltravers, would have escaped unnoticed had he not attempted to again abduct your son. As we feared he would make another attempt we were forced to move here sooner than planned. We were put to great inconvenience."

Did she expect an apology for the inconvenient abduction attempt? Perhaps she wished it had been successful. Choking back irritation Edward asked:

"Why should Billings wish to abduct John? He could be of no further use to him."

The bizarre truth that Billings wanted revenge on a child he believed had brought him ill-luck occurred to no one. Caroline ventured a possible explanation:

"Might he have needed a small boy for his robberies? One was used to break in the scullery window at Blackheath. He cut himself, there were..." Anticipating her mother's disapproval she checked a reference to blood traces.

"Unlikely," said the expert Sir Edwin. "A child as small as John would be of little use. Too great a risk of injury in a fall from the window and he could not unlock or open heavy doors. I caught a glimpse of the housebreaker's boy, about eight years."

"Idle speculation," observed Lady Georgina as she rose from her chair. "I have calls to make before preparations for my West

Hampstead visit." She gave Edward a curt nod. "I wish you joy of your enquires sir." A softening? Certainly not of her voice or countenance. Edward bowed his thanks as the attendant maid opened the door for her ladyship's imperious exit.

Sir Edwin shook Edward's hand. "I too wish you every success Mr Maltravers. I shall be in the library, do not hesitate to join me there, your company would be most welcome." Not an idle civility. Sir Edwin rarely experienced intelligent conversation in his home, it being one reason for frequent absences. He hesitated, glancing at Caroline. "If you wish to explore Chelsea I am sure my daughter would appreciate an escort. Having lost her small companion she has not yet walked here. And such a fine mild day, almost spring like." With a nod he left the room for the sanctuary of the library.

An awkward silence ensued broken hesitantly by Caroline.

"I... should...er... would indeed appreciate a walk... but you may wish to remain here to await news."

Courtesy demanded one reply, the reply Edward wanted to give.

"I will escort you with the greatest pleasure. It is perhaps too early to expect news, Tom Hart would request any messenger to await our return." Recalling their earlier conversation Edward prepared to ignore Tom's knowing smile. Let him smirk, the walk with Mrs Claremont was no more than a courtesy to a member of his host's family. So Edward assured himself.

Caroline also disguised her pleasure, saying calmly: "We shall not go far, Mr Hart could come to inform you if needed. If agreeable to you I suggest a stroll along the river walk towards Battersea." Edward murmured an assent. "Good. Excuse me for less than ten minutes while I change into more suitable attire for walking. I shall meet you in the hall."

In her room she hesitated over what to wear, something she had not done or wanted to do during many months of wearing black. Surely the time had come to gradually move away from weeds? Mama would disapprove, a year's mourning de rigueur even for a marriage of which she had also disapproved. Insufficient wealth and status. Papa's concern had been for her welfare. Charles Claremont a very pleasant fellow, light-hearted, much charm, a great favourite with the ladies to whom he paid more attention than Sir Edwin thought proper for a betrothed man. Had he depth, constancy? On Caroline's assurance of their mutual love he reluctantly gave his consent. For Caroline an escape from the repressive matriarchal household and two years in her own home, Charles' absences compensated by ecstatic reunions. His loving letters, joy on learning she carried their child. Two happy years followed by a lengthy period of mourning. As suggested by Edward Maltravers was it not time to plan a useful life away from the enervating tedium of Mama's regime? The alternative? Dolorous years as her submissive companion with Mama's death leaving her a defeated middle aged woman, an object of pity and scorn. Impossible!

Without summoning her maid she selected a fine woollen dark grey gown with white at the collar and cuffs. Not that it would be seen under her cloak she somewhat guiltily assured herself as she changed indoor shoes for those more suited to London's damp mired streets. A bonnet over the dark naturally curling hair usually concealed under her cap and she was ready. She dismissed as ridiculous her increased heartbeat. Twenty three, acting as sixteen? And after so brief an acquaintance!

Accepting that a woman's ten minutes was longer than a man's, Edward sought out Tom Hart in the kitchen rightly suspecting he would be ingratiating himself with the female staff. At Edward's request he left them amid a flurry of giggles. No outward sign of amusement when Edward told him of his walk.

"I shall be after you like a gun dog should there be news. Until then Will and I can pass the time in the billiard room. I am assured the family seldom use it."

With a laugh Edward clapped Tom on the shoulder before

going to the hall to await Mrs Claremont, a smile lingering as he imagined Lady Forester's reaction should she learn of a stable boy in the house. He hoped her calls were many. She had much to impart to her doubtless intimidated female acquaintance, including the intrusions into her household. A tradesman! And the father of the wretched child who had repaid her kind hospitality by running off. What appalled gasps would there be had she told of the stable boy in the hallowed billiard room, handling the cues meant for the use of gentlemen!

To Edward's surprise Mrs Claremont took no more than the promised ten minutes. He noted with appreciation her slender figure in its well-fitting cloak. She looked younger, a healthy glow lightening her usually wan countenance. Leaving the library to fetch papers from his study Sir Edwin nodded his approbation. The girl needed shaking out of her overlong mourning. Good for Maltravers should he succeed. Now there was a match even Georgina....Reproving himself Sir Edwin concentrated on his own affairs.

Apart from banalities on the mildness of the weather and the hope of an early spring few words passed between Edward and Caroline until they gained the river bank. There Caroline recalled her conversation with John, how they planned to sit on a bench eating Chelsea buns, commenting on the fashionable folk while watching the river craft.

"So the imp ran off without buying you the promised bun," observed Edward with mock solemnity. "Very remiss, if I see a seller I shall honour his promise. We too could sit munching buns, like naughty children poking fun at the ton."

"We ourselves would attract adverse comments," reproved Caroline. "Reports of our antics reaching Mama. John would have kept his promise had events not forced him from us. Such an earnest solemn child but the greatest delight to be with."

"A pleasure to hear you speak so of him," said Edward. "When I last saw him he was just emerging from infancy, prejudiced though I am I found him even then a delight to be with. So full of questions, eager to learn." The animation left his voice and countenance. "My first duty should have been to my wife and child, resigning my commission earlier. Instead my incredible folly in appointing my brother as their guardian! But who could have suspected such perfidy?" Abruptly checking himself he turned to Caroline, his countenance suffused with embarrassment. "Madam! I do apologise. I have no right to inflict my personal problems on you."

Caroline laid a hand on his arm. "No apologies, please! You did what you believed to be right. Oh if only you had heard John's pride when he spoke of you, known the great love he bears you. Now at his small age he wanders London's streets determined to find his papa. How proud I should be if..." Her voice faltered, she turned from Edward to control her emotion. He said gently:

"Please do not distress yourself. Come, that bench is free." Taking her arm he escorted her to the seat, waiting for her to settle before sitting beside her. "No buns but we can vie with each other spotting the most outrageous... ah, see that young buck? About eighteen but swaggering like the most experienced macaroni..." He broke off as with an embarrassed giggle Caroline lowered her head.

"Oh dear! My brother Joseph. Has he seen me?"

"No, he is with several adoring ladies. He has passed without noticing us." Then as Caroline raised her head, face alight with amusement. "Your brother! Many apologies for my comments. More gaffes. We are unfortunate in our relatives. At that age my brother Robert also would figure away, a ridiculous coxcomb. I hoped marriage would subdue him, his wife being a far stronger character, even domineering... There, more indiscretions, I shall pass to more conventional topics." With an inane smirk: "Pray madam, how do you find the salubrious invigorating London air after the foul miasma of Blackheath?"

His ploy had succeeded, Caroline now laughing, at ease. Tom is right, thought Edward. A very attractive lady. Resolutely he dismissed the thought as disloyal to Harriet's memory.

Caroline also had tried to suppress pleasure in Edward's company with thoughts of Charles, but this absurdity overcame sobriety. She sought words to answer in kind.

"Blackheath's foul miasma sir? A calumny. Our Blackheath air is as salubrious as yours at Richmond. The heath, our beautiful park..."

"I beg to disagree. No air could be more fragrant than ours in Surrey. I cordially invite you to sample it as my guest... er...accompanied by your father Sir Edwin of course. I doubt that your mother would approve of my free and easy household, no bowing and scraping, forelock tugging. My dinner guests are good honest unfashionable local folk and friends made on my travels, intelligent as well as entertaining conversation."

Caroline frowned in mock disapproval. "Sir! Do I scent disapproval of the guests assembled at our dinner table?"

He gave a dismissive gesture. "I would not dare. You have already reproved me as an ungrateful guest. I was particularly entertained by my acquaintance James Black, though as other guests and your mother were not impressed perhaps perversity on my part. And our own conversation made up for much inanity. I would also have welcomed hearing more from your father, a truly intelligent man."

Caroline pleased by the compliment to her father, knowing it to be sincere replied. "He dislikes such occasions as much as you and I. He would I know welcome a conversation with you. And when you find John I...we would willingly accept your invitation to sample Richmond's air. Your estate is large?"

"Fairly so. We too have a fine park, much farmland rented out to competent farmers, orchards and plentiful woodland. My forebears amassed great wealth trading in the East, much I fear by exploitation hence my reason for wishing to spend freely improving the lot of my tenants, as I related at tedious length last evening."

"Not in the least tedious. Your plans seem close to the model villages I have read of in other parts of the country."

Edward eagerly interrupted. "Thank you! A wonderful idea. I had considered how best to proceed. There are fallow fields which could be converted to provide an ideal site for such a village. Replace the hovels with good cottages, enlarge the school..."

"A chapel," suggested Caroline. "A teacher's house..."

"And a green place for children to play."

Caroline urgently interrupted. "Look, Mr Hart with a constable. Oh pray they have good news!"

Rising swiftly from the seat Edward hurried to meet them, Caroline following.

"What news," he demanded. "Is Jackie found?"

"Not that," replied Tom. "The sweeper is taken and is now in Newgate."

The officer interrupted with the news Tom meant to break more gently.

"Officer Collins sir. In the sweeper's cart were child's clothes we think may belong to your boy. Billings denies any knowledge of him."

Edward flinched as if from a blow, his face grey with shock.

"Dear God!" he hoarsely whispered. "What has the...the fiend done with him?"

Caroline was at his side, clasping his arm. "Billings used other children. And...yes of course John took clothes when he left, we think bundled in a table cloth."

Though wanting to shout and rage at the officer Edward's sense of justice checked him. This man was not at fault. With a mighty effort he spoke quietly.

"I must see Billings, force the truth from him. I may see him in Newgate?"

Before Officer Collins could reply Caroline said with quiet determination:

"I also, to see the clothes. I purchased them for John so can tell if they are his."

Collins shook his head. "Newgate is no place for a lady such as yourself. The foulest of pestilent air, villainous inmates foul of speech."

Caroline protested: "But I have read that there are apartments where prisoners move freely, even carry on their business."

Collins allowed himself a brief smile. "Only for gentry not guilty of serious crimes, perhaps too loudly criticising the ruling powers and who càn afford special privileges. The low scum are kept in dark verminous cells before stepping out to the gallows yard. Powerful bad odour reaching many yards around the prison."

"Can he not be brought to some examining place?" asked Edward.

Collins pulled a long face. "Against regulations sir."

Tom Hart knew the implication there even if the honourable Captain did not.

Taking him aside Tom murmured: "Give me your purse Captain."

A bewildered: "My purse? Why?"

"Never trouble that overly-strict conscience of yours Captain. Do you have a chat with Mrs Claremont while I have words with the good officer."

Now realising the implication, with an exasperated sigh Edward handed him the purse. As Tom walked a few yards away, a hand on Officer Collins' shoulder,□he returned to the bench with Caroline.

"Bribery! So much for our splendid new police force, Mr

Fielding would be proud of them! But as it is imperative I see Billings I must condone what I detest."

"Let Mr Hart take it on his less spiky conscience, Captain." Caroline put a hand to her mouth. "Oh I beg your pardon. Mister Maltravers is such a tongue teaser it is not surprising that little Jackie could not say his name."

"I am no longer entitled to call myself captain though it is the custom with some ex-officers to retain their rank. But as you wish, I am Edward to my friends."

"Jackie knows you as Captain Edward. And me as Mrs Caroline. Are we adult and daring enough to drop the titles? Mama would be appalled at such impropriety."

Edward clapped his hands. "Splendid! I applaud impropriety. Dare I say that your mama is easily appalled? We are adult enough though maybe not daring enough to lose titles in her hearing. We greatly flout convention to use given names on so short an acquaintance."

"Are you not the man who advised me to defy convention by finding useful employment? And how conventional are you in not keeping the lower orders in their ordained place, crowded in hovels, barely scraping a livelihood?"

Edward raised both hands in surrender. "Mercy Madam Caroline! I see your papa the judge in you. Guilty, ma'am. There, let us call a truce, we have argued enough to rate as friends." He held out a hand. "To friendship,"

"To friendship," agreed Caroline, placing her hand in his. As Edward was about to raise it to his lips, Tom Hart appeared, grinning broadly. Ignoring Edward's ferocious scowl he announced cheerfully: "All settled Captain. Sam Billings will be taken to the City Office, you and the lady can see him there in less than an hour." He handed Edward the purse. "Less heavy now. Officer Collins' conscience was not easily appeased. I suggest we return to the Lodge so that Will can prepare the chaise with one horse for Mrs Claremont, we take the other horses. Agreed, Captain?"

A resigned gesture from Edward. "As you appear to have taken command have I any choice, Sergeant?"

"None, Captain."

Captain Edward Maltravers saluted. "At your command, Sergeant." Then sotto voce: "We shall have words about this later, when the hurly-burley is done."

Tom returned the salute. "By then the battle will be won, Captain."

FIFTEEN

The City Police Office had a large cell designed to hold prisoners awaiting transfer to Newgate. On a bench sat manacled Sam Billings. In his dirty unshaven face Caroline discerned the cringing wretch questioned by her mother after John's fall, and the robber fleeing from Forester House. Billings also recognised her, averting his eyes from her accusing gaze.

"You know the prisoner ma'am?" asked the officiating Sergeant Clarke. Officer Collins sat beside him, a silent observer. Making sure of his share of the bribe, deduced cynical Tom Hart.

"I do," quietly answered Caroline. "He is the chimney sweeper responsible for unlawfully using a very young child as a climbing boy, leaving him to fall...."

"No I never," loudly interrupted Billings. "Me boy Barney done that, I give 'im a thrashing..."

"Quiet," snarled Sergeant Clarke. "The lady has not yet finished." To Caroline: "He admitted abducting the child?" As again Billings tried to interrupt: "Keep your mouth shut until I give you permission to speak. Yes, ma'am?"

"Mr Billings told my mother he bought the child from a beggar woman, denying abduction. Later I saw him again when he was foiled in his attempt to rob our Blackheath house and abduct John Maltravers, then in the care of my family."

Edward Maltravers had remained grimly silent during Caroline's testimony. Now he abruptly rose from his seat, looming darkly over the scrawny misshapen Billings, his voice menacingly low.

"You lured my small son from his home with evil lies that I awaited him at the inn, as you did the lodge keeper. How come you by information about me?"

Billings glanced sideways at Sergeant Clarke, taking his brief nod as permission to answer. His chains clanked as he held out his hands as if in supplication.

"I swear to Gawd I never abducted 'im. Nah, I was pied ter tike 'im."

Maltravers' voice was hoarse with fury. "Paid? By whom? The truth or I swear to save the hangman a task even if I risk my own neck."

"I tells the truth, the gentleman at the 'all an 'is lidy give me twelve guineas ter tike the boy, wanted rid of 'im, said ter mike sure..." Billings cowered back as Edward clenched his hands, face suffused with rage. His anger not directed at Billings, he had suspected Robert of some wrong-doing, but this abominable treachery?

Tom Hart was by his side, murmuring: "Steady does it, Captain. No way to get the truth by terrifying the snivelling wretch to death." To Billings: "You say that Mr Robert Maltravers paid you to lure the child. But they were away, who arranged the abduction?"

His fear somewhat lessened by Tom Hart's calm tone Billings confessed freely, let the blame fall where it should.

"They said as they would go on a visit but was gonna 'ire a servant ter see the plan went smooth, like putting laudanum in the nurse woman's gin so she slept, then spinning the boy some yarn ter get 'im ter the lodge so me woman could tell 'im 'is pa was waiting fer 'im. The truth, I swear."

"The footman Parker." Edward muttered. "He shall pay dearly for this." Outwardly calmer he asked Billings: "Have you had further dealings with my brother?"

"Nah sir, not clapped eyes on 'im since."

"Then why attempt to abduct my son from Forester House?"

Billings could not say he wanted revenge on the accursed brat for bringing him ill-luck. He desperately sought a credible answer but not finding one he tried the incredible.

"Yer see sir, I took money orf yer brother ter mike sure the boy never troubled 'im agin and as a man of me word I was obliged ter try an nab the boy..."

"A man of your word!" exploded Edward. "You wanted him for some foul purpose of your own. And you tried again, did you not? A child's clothing has been found in your cart." He turned to Sergeant Clarke. "Are the clothes here?"

At a nod from the sergeant, Officer Collins took a small bundle from the seat beside him, spreading clothes on the table, also a satchel.

"In the cart with the bag we believe they were carried in."

Caroline quickly moved over to the table, carefully examining the clothes. Edward watched intently, white faced.

She turned to him. "They are the clothes I purchased for John but," she hastily added as Edward groaned despair, "...not those he wore on the day he left us. As I told you he took others with him, it appears he bought the satchel to keep them in." A brief sobbing laugh. "Oh, such resourcefulness in so small a child. But how came they in this man's cart?" Angrily she turned to Billings. "What have you done with John?"

As Billings glowered in sullen silence the sergeant rapped out:

"Answer or you get no mercy from the magistrates." Not that he would, they were not known for showing mercy.

Again the hunt for the least incriminating answer. "Well arter that...damn nag went mad galloping through the city we come across little Jacko weeping in the road cos 'e was lost an we took 'im on board ter mike sure 'e got somewhere sife. Then the nag took orf agin an when we got ter Oxford Street it did a big lunge, muster tipped Jacko art, never saw 'im go." That, at least, true.

Sergeant Clarke partly confirmed Billings' account.

"Witnesses did see the horse galloping madly through Westminster, and true it did go berserk in Oxford Street. A small child could have been tipped out though no sign of one. But it is a very busy street, he could have hidden anywhere without attracting notice."

"John's coat is not here," said Caroline. "That is a very hopeful sign."

Billings interrupted, giving no thought to the purport of his words. "Muster grabbed it back arter Barney took it..." Too late realising he had tightened the noose he fell silent.

"So," said Edward grimly. "You gave my son a ride out of the kindness of your black heart, rummaging through his clothes doubtless hoping to sell them." His pent up fury and anguish exploded into action. Grabbing Billings' shoulders he shook him violently, setting chains rattling. "Where is he? Tell me or..."

Hastily Tom Hart moved to drag him away from Billings. Sergeant Clarke and Officer Collins made no move to protect their prisoner, seemingly indifferent to what violence the furious father inflicted on the man who had so cruelly treated his child. His punishment trivial to what awaited Billings at the even more merciless hands of the law.

Hart muttered: "Calm yourself Captain. You know how you will regret it later."

Edward already regretted it. Attacking a defenceless man whatever his crime. Despicable! Pushing Billings back onto his bench he sat beside Caroline, head lowered. She put her arm through his, murmuring: "You had every provocation but I do believe that whatever Billings intended he was prevented from harming Jackie."

Calmed by her quiet reason Edward relaxed, even managing a wry smile. "Prevented by a horse! But Mrs...Caroline, how much longer can he survive the perils of this accursed town? I am desperate to find him but where, how?"

Tom Hart asked the still fearful Billings: "Where were you when the horse lunged?"

"Told yer," Billings sullenly replied. "Middle er Oxford Street. We was on our way ter St Giles. Along there somewhere."

"St Giles," muttered Tom. "Pray God not among that ..." He bit off the words "cut-throat crew."

"St Giles?" asked Edward. "Where is that?"

Unwilling to further distress the Captain, Tom kept silent. Sergeant Clarke was not so sparing of Edward's sensibilities.

"The worst part of London, saving Spitalfields. Thieves, murderers, footpads, whores. All the lowest scum hide out there, derelict buildings swarming with vermin and even more vicious human. Stinking alleys..." Belatedly noticing Edward's despair he added: "Seems your boy was some way off, our men are searching Oxford Street, plenty of places round there he could find shelter." Not that Oxford Street is all that genteel, he told himself. He privately held out little hope of finding one small boy among the hordes of homeless urchins wandering the streets.

Edward had listened to the sergeant in appalled silence. Now he spoke with impassioned urgency.

"We must search now, before Jackie reaches..."

Again Tom Hart took charge, his steady common sense like an icy douche on Edward's near hysteria.

"What now Captain? Rushing into action like an impetuous green ensign, deserting your usual calm assessment and planning? Not to mention your lack of courtesy to Mrs Claremont. Is she to make her own way to Forester Lodge, lacking an escort?"

Suitably chastened and remorseful Edward stammered:

"Madam...Mrs Caroline, forgive me. Such discourtesy after your kindness."

Caroline longed to hold him, comfort him as she had Jackie. Scandalous! Instead she reassured him: "No apologies Captain. Your concern for John is understandably paramount. But Mr Hart speaks truly. The search needs careful planning - our search, I insist on being one of the party."

Edward violently shook his head. "Mrs Caroline! I greatly honour your courage but cannot allow you to take such a risk."

Caroline laughed. "This from the man who scolded me for not leading a more useful life! Indeed sir I can be of use, enquiring of shopkeepers if they have seen my naughty little son who slipped away while I indulged my vanity in the milliner's trying on ridiculous hats."

Edward had relaxed enough to smile and answer in kind. "And I the neglectful papa in the coffee house allowing my son to wander off while I chatted tosh to friends. Tom, as always you are right. Back to the Lodge and make our plans in a less heated manner." To the sergeant: "My grateful thanks sir. Your help has been invaluable." He looked over to the huddled wretched Sam Billings, asking in a low voice: "What is to be his fate?"

The sergeant replied indifferently: "Men are hanged for much lesser crimes."

Edward grimaced. "Barbaric. Agreed he has done my child great harm, bribed to do so by those supposed to be his betters who have so far escaped the law though doubly treacherous. His death will not be of benefit to my son or myself."

The officers exchanged wondering glances at such leniency.

"Well sir, a plea for clemency might help him at his trial, have him transported with his oafish son. Though why the colonies should be infested with our rogues and trouble makers baffles me."

With that semi-assurance Edward had to be content. A memory returned of Jackie's note to Anthony Barnes expressing his fear of transportation to be eaten by heathens. Another look at Billings' unappetising form told him the former chimney sweep would be safe from the hungriest cannibal. Anthony Barnes! He had promised to visit him that morning. To Caroline and Tom Hart he said: "Before returning to the Lodge may we call on Mr Barnes, his shop is very near. He will be anxious for news of John."

A courtesy call for which Edward would be forever thankful.

While his father planned how best to search for him, including further monetary inducements to the police, John Maltravers was negating those efforts by evading the police, keeping to alleys and side streets. He purchased bread and ham from a cook shop. No stories of mama awaiting him were necessary, the apathetic shop woman served him in silence, giving him the correct change from the proffered sixpence. He ate the food seated on a low wall outside the shop, eyes ever wary for danger like any other street urchin. At a stall he drank milk from a none-too-clean beaker, then tried to decide on his next move. How near was he now to Knightsbridge Barracks? He could not know that had he taken the direction to the park, a long walk for small legs, it would eventually have led him there, but he dared not ask, trusting no one.

Fear again assailed him as he turned into another alley. At the far end a blue uniformed constable was talking to a man carrying a basket of fruit on his head. As John turned to flee he tripped over the feet of an immensely fat woman squatting on the doorstep of a small house wedged between tenement buildings.

"Mind what yer at, clumsy cub," she wheezed. "Running orf from the polis are yer? What yer done?"

Scrambling to his feet John mutely stared at her, astonished at the immensity of her body spreading the width of the doorway. Seeing the constable leave the basket man and start to walk along the alley he again turned to run.

"'ere," croaked the woman. "Git behind me, I got no love fer the bastards neither." She moved a few inches so that he could edge into the house, crouching in a passage made dark by her bulk. A minute or so later he heard the constable's voice.

"Good day Mrs Jemima, behaving yourself I see, no drunken brawls at the inn." As she merely grunted he asked: "Have you seen a little lad, four or five years, fair haired, blue eyes. Not the usual type of street brat?"

"Nah, I seen no such moppet. Plenty of thieving little bastards making a mock of me. What's he done? Stole an apple orf a market stall? Want ter 'ang 'im does yer?"

"No," said the constable, moving away. The flabby immensity of the woman prevented John hearing his next words. "Lost child, his father seeks him. A reward..."

When he was out of sight Mrs Jemima heaved herself to her feet, grunting and wheezing. Entering the house she slammed the door and turned to stare long and hard at John, at the tangled fair hair, frightened blue eyes. So, the lost boy's pa was giving a reward for him. Her sluggish brain activated by lust for money she considered the best way to procure it. What if she went to the office the next morning, said she found the boy wandering the street at dusk, cold and hungry and taken him into her home? They would have to collect him, she could not risk his slipping away if she brought him to the office. She would have to keep the brat locked in until morning....

Made uneasy by the mountainous woman's prolonged stare John interrupted her thoughts. "I am much grateful to you ma'am. If you please I shall be on my way."

The woman shook her head, making her chins wobble. "Yer will not git far, chick. The polis is rounding up stray childer, have a cart waiting in the street ter tike 'em ter the foundling 'ome. Best stay 'ere a while." She smiled at him, not a pleasant sight as she displayed two rotting teeth in an otherwise toothless mouth. "Poor little feller, yer must be weary. Come into the kitchen, share me meal then yer kin be on yer way." To bed after a few drops of laudanum, she mentally added. Keep him quiet while she went to Players Street, collect the takings from the bawdy house she owned, then a few gins at the inn.

Torn between dislike of the horrid woman and fear of the Foundling Home John knew he had no choice, meekly following her into the kitchen.

Very different from the scrubbed neatness and comfort of the afflicted lady's kitchen. Small, dark, malodorous, table littered with unwashed dishes and pans. On the log fire sat a cauldron, on the hob keeping warm a dish containing belly of pork.

"Cook shop roasted it fer me," explained Mrs Jemima, pushing it onto a chipped platter. Taking two chipped plates from the table she rinsed them in a bowl of greasy water, drying them on her apron. "Gotta lass what cleans fer me but ailing." An eleven year old from the tenement paid a shilling a week, a small contribution towards the keep of her parents' numerous offspring. "Most like on 'er way art, real poorly. 'er sister Mercy is coming tomorrer." Two older sisters satisfied clients in the bawdy house. Jemima had hopes for twelve year old Mercy but still too scrawny to tempt customers.

She sliced the fatty meat, three portions for herself, one for John. Out of the cauldron she ladled potatoes boiled in their skins, too much fuss to wash or peel them, also carrots. She piled her plate, a potato and two carrots for John.

"Some wine ter wash it darn," she said, rinsing two tankards. "Plenty of water in yours chick, or yer might fall orf yer chair." A few drops of laudanum added to the water would make sure he slept sound.

Like the good son in Bessie's version of the prodigal son parable John did not like fat meat but heroically consumed his portion and the earthy tasting potato and carrots. Mrs Jemima wolfed her large helping, occasionally pausing to belch, something John had been taught was very ill-mannered. She drank copiously of the wine, urging John to do the same. He drank a little, spluttering over the sour taste to the mirth of his hostess.

"Never git ter be a man at that rate! Give it a good swaller."

Feigning obedience he raised the tankard, pretending to drink, then as she went over to the cauldron for more potatoes and carrots he hastily tipped the contents into the bowl of water, again raising the tankard as she returned to slice more pork. She nodded approvingly as he replaced the empty tankard on the table.

"What a good chick. Soon as I finishes me dinner I will put yer ter bed. Reckon yer tired arter all yer wandering."

Indeed John was weary. He had not ingested much of the liberal dose of laudanum, lethally liberal for his small frame, but that minute amount, with his eventful day, made him long for sleep, he cared not where. Mrs Jemima lingered long over her meal, finishing with sweetmeats from a box, none finding their way to John. His tiredness grew, eyes and head heavy with fatigue. He could fight it no more, slumping over the table in profound sleep.

Nodding her satisfaction Mrs Jemima wiped her mouth on her apron, gave a belch and fart as she rose heavily from the table. Without effort she carried him upstairs to her bedroom, dumping him on the unmade feather bed and drawing a counterpane over him.

"There manakin, sleep well until tomorrer when I gits me 'ands on pa's reward."

Jemima could not foresee that the chick's actions would ensure her own chickens would never come home to roost.

SIXTEEN

Returning to Forester Lodge after his distressing meeting with Sam Billings, Edward Maltravers regained his captain's efficiency, dividing his search party. He and Caroline Claremont to take one end of Oxford Street, Tom Hart and stable lad Will Cooper the other, including every side road, alley and passage. A mammoth task, gloomily predicted Tom whose knowledge of London far exceeded that of his companions. The flagrant impropriety of Caroline's inclusion in the search party made easier by the absence of her mother, that afternoon departed on a week's visit to a sister in West Hampstead, an annual duty neither enjoyed and made more onerous for the sister by the addition of equally unlovable Rebecca. George had been sent back to his academy in the hope he would receive the discipline lacking at home. Joseph disported himself as he pleased, indifferent to family affairs so there was no one to report Caroline's transgression to Mama. Sir Edwin readily entrusted his favourite child to Maltravers, welcoming the opportunity of leaving the young couple in each other's company. His shrewd brain had quickly assessed and approved of Maltravers' character, a man of honour and integrity he would gladly accept as a son-in-law...after a decent period.

As the assembled search party discussed tactics Edward informed them that with the aid of the police he and Caroline had received several responses to their appeals for information. The day John ran away from Forester Lodge a woman had seen him weeping in a King's Road arcade with a story of mama awaiting him in the milliner's shop, a story she knew to be untrue as she had just left there. A Dragoon officer reported a young child halting him to ask if he knew Captain Edward of that regiment. The officer had informed him he was on his way to Knightsbridge Barracks and would make enquiries. A man claimed a small boy answering John's description had spoken to him on Battersea Bridge, asking the way to Knightsbridge Barracks but had run to the opposite side of the road at the sight of a police constable.

"Why did Jackie believe I might be at the barracks?" wondered Edward. "There are Foot soldiers there, none of my regiment."

Caroline smiled, fondly recollecting John's naivety. "He is too young to realise the vastness of the army, believing that as a soldier's son he would be welcomed, efforts made to trace his papa."

"Little idiot!" scoffed Edward, though with affection. "Imagine the consternation of high ranking officers at having to deal with a small child during intricate planning of troop placements."

"Jackie is no idiot," warmly protested Caroline. "Any other five year old would curl up in a corner weeping for his mama. Your courageous little innocent faces the perils of unknown streets determined to find you."

"Because he is innocent of the perils," said Edward. "You are right, a son to be proud of. What greatly concerns me is his fear of the police, thanks to dear Bessie. They search to restore him to me but he evades them! It is imperative that we seek him ourselves.

He will not run from us or his friend Will. The reason I am arranging for him to accompany Tom who Jackie does not know."

The only reason? Tom asked himself. But good luck with the lady, my captain. She is as eager for you as you are for her but your wretched probity will take some breaking down. Aloud he said. "Before we start our search I shall ride to the barracks to warn them an infant may arrive asking for his papa and advise them where papa is to be found, to send him post haste to Forester Lodge. If he is on the park side of Oxford Street he may have been directed and on his way. As I ride through the park I may encounter him."

"I should be the one to go," protested Edward. "He does not know you."

"No Captain, you stay here for any news the constables may bring. An opportunity to plan your strategy with Mrs Clare-mont..." As Edward glowered at him, knowing full well the import behind Tom's words, he hastily added: "I shall take Will, as you say he and John are good friends. We should not be above an hour, then able to start our Oxford Street search. You will agree, Captain, no point doing so if your boy has found shelter in the barracks."

The Captain did not agree. Irritated at Tom's taking over his leadership Edward repelled the usurper. "We shall not wait for your return, it will be nearly dusk by then." To Caroline: "If you are willing ma'am we will start our enquiries at the St Giles end of Oxford Street, working towards the street centre. Mr Hart and Will from the park end. We must take the chaise with one horse as Mr Hart and Will have the other mounts," Another glare at Tom who gave an unrepentant grin.

"Gladly," demurely replied Caroline. "Though I fear it will take more than an afternoon to complete our task."

"Aye," said Tom. "The Captain has no concept of how many side streets, alleys, nooks and crannies there are in the street." Tom forgot the Captain's ability to bring insubordinates to heel.

"Sergeant, guard your tongue against insolence. I have as much if not more experience in charting unknown territory. The search will be thorough no matter how long it takes."

"Aye Captain," said Tom with a smart salute. However wrong-headed, praise be a Captain back to his normal tetchy self.

Edward Maltravers and Caroline Claremont had dispiritingly little success at the start of their search. They questioned every shopkeeper and stallholder, posing as anxious parents of a naughty child who had slipped away while...mama tried on hats at a milliner's, papa advising on what suited her. Those questioned did not openly express surprise that such a well-dressed couple should shop in an area where the only milliner sold poor quality hats mostly purchased by servant girls. Neither Caroline nor Edward were aware of the incongruity.

Then one small success. Enquiring at a cook shop in a side road the dejected shop woman recalled that about midday a small child answering their description purchased bread and ham, sitting on the wall outside to eat.

"Did you see where he went after eating?" eagerly asked Caroline.

The woman shook her head. "Had customers. Never noticed. Lots of side alleys and such where he could have gone. Regular maze."

"How was he?" asked Edward. "Did he seem well?" A strange question about a child supposedly missing a few hours but the woman too lethargic to wonder.

"Better than most brats round here. Well-spoke and polite. Cleaner too." She brightened somewhat when presented with a half crown for this heartening information. John still had money and in good health!

The shop woman had spoken truly. A maze of small side roads and alleys with a mixture of buildings: cottages and small houses wedged between tenements inhabited by many families. This was the poorer end of the Oxford Street area, eventually merging with the squalor of St Giles. The tenants Edward and Caroline encountered told them that earlier a constable had also questioned them about a lost child but how were they to distinguish one lost brat among the district's many waifs and strays no one usually cared a fig for. Too busy rearing their own brood. Would not the lady and gentleman care to take one if they could not find their child? A few guineas only, for their choice.

Hastily refusing and realising the futility of further questions Edward and Caroline decided to abandon the search until the morrow.

"We should return to the chaise while there is still light enough," said Edward. "These gloomy alleys have no illumination."

Caroline agreed. "I doubt John will have taken shelter in any of these buildings. As the shop woman said he seemed well he must have found a warm bed last night and we know from Mr Barnes he spent the first night in a stable. Presumably not visited by kings or shepherds."

"Perhaps we should question horses," feebly jested Edward. As they passed a small ramshackle house he indicated an immensely fat woman waddling some twenty yards ahead of them, her way lit by a link boy, his torch casting a grotesquely menacing shadow behind her. "She nearly takes up the width of the alley. Is she not the fattest creature you have ever seen?" murmured Edward.

"How gallant!" reproved Caroline. "She is indeed gross but her link boy's torch shows that we are nearing Oxford Street's better lighting." She turned to look at Edward's despondent countenance. "Take heart Captain, I am certain your enterprising little son has found another warm bed."

A warm bed, yes. They had just passed the ramshackle house in which John lay in profound slumber. His hostess the gross creature waddling before them to her night's bawdy house activities.

Their own evening activities were far more decorous. They dined with Sir Edwin who insisted Tom Hart joined them, profusely apologising for his exclusion from the previous evening's party, adding he would have welcomed his own exclusion. No trivial chatter on this occasion, Sir Edwin asking to hear of Edward and Tom's army experiences, agreeing with Edward as to the overweening ambitions of the East India Company. Tom Hart argued for the magnificent empire that would emerge from those ambitions. Caroline grieved for the lost lives of young men of both nations. When would mankind realise the futility of war? Never, replied her father, men delighted in the invention of increasingly sophisticated weapons to slaughter their fellows, the only species in the animal kingdom intent on destroying their own environment. Then lightened the conversation with anecdotes of his own legal experiences.

The one lady was not expected to retire while the men continued their conversation. They retired together to the drawing room for coffee, then, as no one wished for cards Sir Edwin challenged Tom to a game of billiards while Edward and Caroline quietly conversed on their tactics for the next day. Tom Hart had earlier expressed his doubts as to the wisdom of the Captain and Mrs Claremont searching the poorer parts of London dressed like the gentry, they should blend more with their surroundings.

Caroline enthusiastically agreed. She felt as she imagined a prisoner might when released from shackles. An escape, however brief, from a dreary existence. "I shall borrow my maid Betty's walking out gown and shawl. And you, Captain Edward?"

Edward glanced at Tom's stocky figure. "No match there, nor with stripling Will. I have no suitable clothes with me..."

Caroline interrupted: "Betty's beau is Frederick, the under footman, more or less of your build. For a small consideration I am sure Betty could persuade him briefly to part with suitable garments, Betty will be vastly entertained that we shall walk out dressed as servants on their day off. How will that do, Mr Hart?"

"Vastly entertaining, Mrs Claremont, do you not agree Captain?"

With his fellow conspirators of one mind Edward dared not voice objections, relieved that this conversation took place out of Sir Edwin's hearing. His tolerance might be overstretched by the thought of his daughter abroad in mean streets dressed as a servant girl on her day off. His reaction would be tame compared with the hysterical vapours of his lady. As well she was testing her sister's endurance in West Hampstead.

Mrs Jemima was returning home later than she'd intended, two clients at the whore house had perversely demanded her personal service, a demand unknown since her younger days. Nothing loath she obliged...several times, in between bouts drinking with them amid raucous jests and laughter until a night watchman hammered at the door bidding them to restrain their merriment, they disturbed their neighbours' sleep. Having a special reason for not spending the next day in a lock-up Jemima refrained from shrieking foul abuse and emptying the contents of the communal piss pot on him, sweetly apologising for the disturbance and continuing her duties in a more subdued fashion, weaving her ponderous way home by the first misty light of dawn.

Stumbling and wheezing to her bedroom she found the boy lying as she left him, curled in sleep. To make sure she shook him. "Awake are yer?" No answer, merely the light steady breathing of sleep. "No need ter give yer another dose then." After noisily using the chamber pot she threw off her outer garments and slumped onto the outsize bed, fortunately for the boy's safety he lay at the opposite edge. The long unaccustomed exertions of the night and plentiful gin had exhausted her, she needed no laudanum to help her sleep. Soon her snores filled the house with discordant sound.

John was not asleep, waking to Jemima's wheezing unsteady progress along the alley. He sat up, a tiny figure in the immense bed. Where was he? Then the recollection of the fat woman saying she would put him to bed. About to climb out he heard the front door slam and wheezes, groans and curses as the woman slowly heaved her bulk up the stairs. Swiftly he curled up on the bed, feigning sleep. Though his heart pounded he kept his breathing steady as she bent over to shake him. How her breath stank. She believed he slept, muttering about another dose. Of what? The bed shook as she dropped on it groaning and muttering. Soon after came her snores that seemed to rock the bed. When they became regular, accompanied by more grunts and wheezes he cautiously sat up to stare at her. Even more horrid than he recalled, rolls of mottled flesh under her grubby petticoats, greasy hair straggling from her cap, mouth wide open to expose that near toothless mouth, foul smelling breath. John's first sharing a bed with a woman was one he would never forget, for the wrong reason.

Now he dared to leave the bed, urgent necessity forcing him to use the repellent, large, half full chamber pot. His hostess had dumped him on the bed fully clothed save for his shoes which he rescued from where they were thrown. He felt unclean but no sign of a wash bowl. No matter, he had seen a pump in the alley where he could rinse his face and hands – and drink, for his mouth was dry, he believed from the sour tasting wine. He had only to find his coat then escape, so he thought.

He crept down stairs that creaked even under his light weight, but Mrs Jemima's snores echoed through the house, drowning all other sounds. He found his coat in the kitchen, disturbing mice foraging among the used dishes on the table. Hardly daring to breathe he crept to the door, standing on tiptoe to pull down the handle. The door did not move, it was locked. For a few despairing moments he stared at the obstinate wood. The windows? Going into the small front room he tried to open them. Rusted shut. No back door. He hunted for a key, then recalled hearing the woman unlock and lock the door. She must have it with her.

Taking deep breaths to give himself courage he returned to the bedroom. The woman still snored, now lying on her side. Her eyes were half open, glinting. John imagined she was watching, would leap from the bed to crush him under her enormous weight. With trembling hands he searched the tumble of garments on the floor, suppressing a crow of triumph as he found the key in a pocket of her cloak. Also a heavy purse of money he left untouched. Thou shalt not steal, he wondered about the key but he would only borrow it, though without her permission.

He did not intend waking her to obtain assent. A snort and gulp from the woman momentarily froze him, the snoring resumed in a different key as she again shifted position. Abandoning caution John ran from the room down the stairs. Taking a footstool from the front room he stood on it to have better purchase on the key and door handle. More despair when the key would not turn. Wrong way! He tried again, another little crow as he heard the lock click. Using the handle he pushed...no, pull. The door opened, nearly knocking him off his perch. Pushing aside the footstool he stumbled out into the alley. He did not resist the imp of mischief urging him to lock the door from the outside, leaving the key to one side of the doorstep, not easily seen among litter and weeds. He ran along the alley into the road, leaning against a wall to calm his trembling. He had no idea what the woman intended for him, no matter, he was free! Freedom at a cost. From the worst of intentions Mrs Jemima would have informed the police of his presence in her house, then collected the reward when he was reunited with his dear papa. Fate again leading John along her chosen path.

• • •

John could not easily shake off the memory of his nightmare awakening in the bed of the hideous fat woman. She reminded him of the stories Bessie told of ogres whose favourite food was the tender flesh of little children they ensnared. He thought of the meat the woman had eaten so freely, sparing him one fatty slice of what she told him was pork. Had she intended fattening him for her next meal? But she told him the cook shop roasted the meat, they surely would refuse to cook a child.

He was safe from her, when she woke he would be far from the house and she was trapped until someone found the key. The cleaning girl? It would need an army of girls to clean that horrid house.

The word army reminded him of his mission, the barracks. He had no other hope of finding Papa. But John was no longer the trusting innocent lured from his home by false stories. Now he trusted no one, dared ask no one. And he was no longer the neat clean child who had run from Forester Lodge. His coat bore evidence of his night in the stable and the food purchased from stalls. His jacket and trousers crumpled from sleeping in them, his hands and face grubby. An attempt to wash at a pump in a stable yard brought furious yells from the ostler. The water was for drinking, not for washing a filthy diseased street brat. Would the soldiers in the barracks also take him for a filthy diseased street brat and chase him away? If they did he would never find Papa and roam the streets begging like an urchin until he died of hunger.

Dejectedly he wandered on, no knowledge of where he was or where to go. He paused at a booth with a Punch and Judy show. He had never before seen one and for a while forgot his woes staring in fascination at the puppets, seemingly moving and talking as if they were alive. He turned to a boy standing beside him.

"How do they move like that?"

The boy was pleased to air his superior knowledge. "A cove in the booth moves them on sticks, talks in squeaky voices. Why, ant yer never seen one before?"

"No, never." Encouraged by the boy's friendly reply he asked: "I wish to find Knightsbridge Barracks, do you know where it is, if you please?"

The boy, a few years older and taller than John, took him by the shoulders and turned him to face the opposite direction. "Go to the end of the street then through Hyde Park to Knightsbridge. Why, want ter join the army? Best wait a few years, you need more size."

The jest was not ill-natured, the boy amiable, about nine or ten, poorly but cleanly clad. By now John was an expert if not a convincing liar. "My father is there. My mama is ailing and asks me to go to tell him."

"Breeding is she? Mine always is but Pa needs no telling."

John did not understand so replied evasively: "I think she is not but my Papa does need telling. I must be on my way."

"And me to yonder eating shop where I work as kitchen boy." The boy jerked a thumb at a row of shops. "They open shortly. Goodbye... what is yer name?"

"John, and yours?"

"Billy. Knightsbridge is a long walk fer a little 'un like you, John. I wish yer well." He held out a hand.

John clasped it. "And you Billy. God be with you." His first friendly encounter since leaving Mr Barnes brought tears to his eyes, he hurried away before they could fall. Billy set off to his long day's labour which would be interrupted in an unexpected way.

Elation soon replaced dejection as John believed his quest nearly at an end. The length of the walk did not matter, a park would have plenty of places to rest, as there were in his own park. Tears again threatened but he must not be childish. Then more thoughts of his urchin appearance. How could he present himself as a Dragoon captain's son? He must find somewhere to wash. Would there be a pond in the park? There was one in his park on which he sailed boats when someone was with him. Papa had jested: "You may be a gallant naval captain but I love you too much to have you go down with your ship." Again childish tears threatened.

Then salvation. Above the door of one building he spelt out 'Cold and Warm Baths." Dare he? Yes, he must. Taking money from his purse which the fat woman had not discovered under his shirt he approached a man seated by the door. In a shaky voice he ventured: "Please sir I should like a bath."

The man stared at him. Not an impudent brat joshing him, for all his grime a well-spoken polite child. He glanced around for an accompanying adult.

"Indeed you need one. Why alone? Where is your mother?"

The old lie. "If you please sir she is in the hat shop and is very angry with me for getting dirty playing with rough great boys who knocked me into the mud." He held out sixpence. "She has given me this to have a warm bath. How much must I pay?"

The manager found his tale strange but had heard stranger. And the boy had money, a customer was a customer however young.

"Three pence for a cold bath, four pence for warm. Have you a towel and soap?"

"No sir but if you please I wish a warm bath with soap and towel."

That will be six pence in total." Not true, the soap and towel were included in the four pence but the manager rightly suspected the child could not read the scrawled price list on the wall. From a shelf he took a rough towel and a piece of yellow soap. "Through that door, you are the first customer so the water is clean. Take care how you lower yourself into it, use the steps and keep to the shallow side, shout if you are in difficulties." There should have been a bath attendant but the manager considered this an unnecessary expense for the few customers, collecting the payment for a mythical attendant from the owner who had several far more lucrative baths in London, rarely checking the poorly attended one in Oxford Street. He planned to sell it for a large profit to those wishing to develop the site.

John revelled in the reasonably warm water. Sitting on the bottom step he made a creditable task of washing his hair, dipping his head under water to rinse off the soap. His ablutions completed he inexpertly rubbed at the marks on his coat and jacket, grieving the loss of his bundle of clean clothes. How much would it cost to buy some from a market stall? His money fast disappearing but he would not need any at the barracks, soldiers would look after him until Papa came. He cleaned his shoes with the towel, an action not pleasing to the manager who had planned to use it for the next customer, scowling when John returned it and the sliver of soap with an angelic smile and "My most best thanks sir." Leaving the baths he was disorientated, setting off in the wrong direction, towards St Giles. The end of Oxford Street searched the previous afternoon by his father and Mrs Caroline.

Had she encountered them in the street Lady Georgina would not have spared a

disdainful glance at the male and female in their inferior ill-fitting dress. Even a haughty stare would not have recognised the young woman with the cheap over-beribboned travesty of a picture hat, drab gown and tartan shawl as her elder daughter. Nor the young man in the tight-fitting cheap cloth greatcoat and jaunty cap as the father of the wretched child who had so disrupted her well-ordered life.

Not only had Edward and Caroline to adjust to their costume, they also needed to modulate their speech pattern, to roughen their voices. Easier for Edward, used to conversing with soldiers. Caroline found it more difficult to shake off the accents of her select finishing school for young ladies, a school more adapted to training pupils on deportment, dancing, drawing, playing the piano and polite conversation than associating with the lower orders.

Their morning was unproductive until Edward, ever mindful of Caroline's comfort, suggested a halt at an eating-house for refreshment, one in keeping with their apparel. Ordering coffee and cake Edward asked the proprietor if he had seen their small son. Little wretch took off while they was choosing his Ma's hat. Five year old, fair hair blue eyes. Name of John or Jackie.

"Nah, no young'uns like that come in 'ere," the man assured Edward. "I would soon chase them off. Young limbs only up to mischief."

They were served by a young boy in an overlong apron he was in danger of tripping over. Glancing round to make sure the proprietor was in the kitchen he whispered:

"I've seen a boy like what you said mister. Was watching Punch an' Judy earlier, said 'is name was John. But mister, 'e said as 'ow 'is ma was ill an 'e was going to the barracks to tell 'is pa. So not your boy, was 'e."

Controlling elation Edward gently took hold of the boy's arm, saying quietly: "Yes, he is my son, he mistakenly believes I am at the barracks and made up a story that his mother ails. Tell me, is he well? How did he seem?"

The boy looked bewildered. John's ma not ailing, had been trying on hats, his pa not at the barracks but here with ma. He replied hesitantly:

"Yes sir, 'e looked well though untidy an' was very friendly, I told 'im the way to the barracks but..."

Aware of his confusion Caroline said gently: "You are of great help... what is your name my dear?"

"Billy, ma'am. Kitchen boy but the waiter is ailing so I also have to serve.

"Billy," said Edward. "You saw John set off in the direction of the barracks?"

"Yes sir, but sir I did see 'im stop at the bath place an a bit later 'e passed this shop going in the wrong direction. Must of turned the wrong way leaving the baths. I wanted to run an tell 'im but Mister Martin yelled at me to serve."

"Bath!" exclaimed Edward. "Did he say anything to you about baths?"

"No sir but 'e looked a bit unwashed, wanted ter look 'is best for pa ...you..."

"Billy, get on with your work," shouted the proprietor.

Before he hurried away Edward pressed a half guinea into his hand, many weeks wages for a kitchen boy. "Bless you Billy, you have given us fresh hope."

"Thank you kindly sir." Not daring to look at the coin in Mr Martin's presence, hitching up his apron Billy scampered to the kitchen.

"He can be no more than ten years," whispered Caroline, sorrowfully gazing after the boy. "Such work for a child!"

"I agree, but he is better off than many working children. Warm and fed, unlike those crawling through coal mine tunnels dragging heavy trucks, never seeing daylight or among dangerous machines in manufactories. Remember Jackie intended as a climbing boy at the age of five, I have heard tell of boys even younger, surviving but a short time. Monstrous!" Edward's voice had risen in anger, causing other customers to stare at him. He spoke more calmly. "When he is safely home I shall campaign against the employment of young children."

"There are already such campaigners," Caroline gently reminded him. "But cheap labour seems a cornerstone of our new industrial age, they are voices in the wilderness."

"The more voices the greater the volume." Edward shook his head self-reproachfully. "I know Tom would say I talk through my hat. But now we know that a short time ago Jackie was well and still determined to find me at the barracks. Shall you rest here while I enquire at the bath house?"

Caroline resolutely shook her head. "No indeed, I am intrigued to see such a place."

Leaving coins to pay for their refreshments Edward replied: "So shall I, our enterprising boy has the advantage over us."

Caroline's heart quickened. Yes, our boy! They exchanged glances, then quickly away. Edward muttered awkwardly: "You are such a support, Mrs...er... Caroline. I do not know how..." He faltered into silence, his code of moral conduct unaffected by his changed appearance.

The baths manager well remembered the child with his story of a cross mama in a hat shop. He glanced at Caroline's hat, unsurprising the brat had run from such a monstrosity. Yes, he had taken a warm bath, ruining a towel the manager knew not how. No, he had not noticed what direction the boy took after leaving the house. Would the lady and gentleman care for a warm bath? No one there so their privacy guaranteed. Hastily refusing and leaving a shilling for the purportedly ruined towel, money that would find its way into the manager's pocket, Edward and Caroline hurried from the baths stifling laughter and both with pleasurably guilty thoughts.

"No luck there," said Edward when gravity restored. "Apart from the knowledge Jackie managed to bathe without drowning. I should have berated the man for allowing so small a child to bathe unattended. Such self-sufficiency, soon he will have no need of a papa, I would not be surprised to learn he has set up his own establishment." He added more soberly: "In the meantime I fear we must retrace our steps, renew the enquiries we made yesterday."

Caroline said quietly: "And pray he has not wandered into St Giles."

Seventeen

John had not achieved his own establishment, that would have been difficult with his few remaining shillings, nor had he yet wandered into St Giles. After walking some distance with no sign of a park he asked a man selling baked potatoes from a shovel over a brazier.

"Tis the other direction, young master," the man replied as he put two potatoes in a bag. "One penny your grace. Take care not to eat them until they have cooled a little. Buy some cheese to have with them. Food fit for the gods."

Thanking him John sat on a nearby bench to eat the potatoes, no cheese, he must not be prodigal with his remaining money, already today he had spent seven pence. As he ate he pondered over potatoes as food for the gods. He knew of only one and had not thought he needed food. Did angels bring it to him as he sat on his throne? Potatoes and cheese on golden dishes, other angels singing and playing on harps. Mama's friend Mrs Redmond played the harp and sang so shrill his ears hurt, but perhaps God liked such music. Mama's singing had been low and gentle, was that why God had taken her into heaven? Did he like hearing her sing lullabies to his baby brother?

His Revelation-like thoughts were replaced by the realisation he had walked a long way in the wrong direction and was weary. A short rest before starting off again. Curling up on the hard bench he snuggled under his coat and soon slept.

Half an hour later his father and Caroline passed the bench without a second glance at what seemed to be a small pile of clothing. They approached the potato seller, asking the usual question.

The man nodded assent. "Oh aye master, quite recent, he bought potatoes and asked the way to the park. I told him he walked in the wrong direction and he set off on the right way. I was busy with customers so lost sight of him."

Tipping him a shilling Edward and Caroline turned in the park direction. Again concerned for Caroline's welfare Edward asked:" You must be weary, please rest awhile on that bench."

Though indeed weary Caroline thought the bench uninviting, liberally bedaubed with bird lime that would soil Betty's shawl and gown.

"Thank you but we should continue. As Jackie was here so recently we may overtake him. Those little legs will not have carried him far."

"True, Tom and Will are near the park end, he could be caught between us."

They walked on, leaving behind the despised bench on which their boy slept in blissful oblivion.

John woke with a start as two large persons thumped down on the bench. A farmer and his wife, resting after selling their dairy produce, chickens and suckling pigs at the market, their horse and cart at a hostelry. An amiable couple they regarded with amused surprise the small head popping up from the coat like an infant genie out of a bottle. Startled blue eyes stared at them from under a tangle of fair curls.

"My faith Jenny," said the farmer. "Is this a naughty elf come to spirit away our gold?"

Jenny, her round cheeks as rosy as apples, smiled comfortably at John.

"More like a cherub from a church window. Are you lost, my pretty?"

John's fear subsided. These were good people like those on Papa's farms.

"If you please sir, ma'am I am not an elf or cherub. I have slept too long and...and my Mama..." He paused, realising the hat shop story was no longer credible. "My Mama sent me on an errand and now it is late and she will be cross."

"And so should I, naughty monkey," said Jenny. As John clambered from the bench, hastily donning his coat: "What was your errand?"

John's brain quickly provided another fabrication. "To buy cheese for my Papa's supper to have with his baked potatoes."

Jenny turned to the basket next to her on the bench, covered with a clean check cloth. She took from it a wrapped slab of cheese, breaking off a generous wedge and placing it in a bag. "Here, take this to mama, enough for her too, and you if you are allowed."

Consumed with guilt John stammered: "Oh... indeed you are too kind ma'am. I must pay you." He fumbled under his shirt for the purse.

Jenny waved a plump dismissive hand. "No, no, child. It was left from our sale and will not be fresh enough tomorrow. Now run home before mama comes for you with a switch." She and the farmer laughed as John ran off, homeward they thought.

How John wished he were running home. The light was fading, a chill wind blowing. Would there be snow as in the rhyme Bessie taught him? He must again find shelter, then tomorrow set off to Knightsbridge. He wandered on, now flares were lit at intervals along the street. Shops were closing, stallholders packing their goods. He bought a half penny of bread to eat with his ill-gotten cheese, sitting on the doorstep of a harness shop, inconspicuous in the shadow cast by the large hanging sign of a horse's head.

Now the people of the night were appearing, women stood at street corners screaming abuse at rivals attempting to depose them. Furtive men tailed respectable citizens hurrying home from their employment. The night soil man's cart rattled along the cobbles, his over-full pails swishing trails of sewage. Link boys and men offered pedestrians some protection from dangerous obstacles on the narrow pathways, huddled sleepers and vomiting drunkards.

John watched fearfully. The flares threw giant shadows, his over-active imagination conjuring up the demons and apparitions of Bessie's stories, she was an addict of Gothic tales. His new-found self-sufficiency deserted him, he was again a very young defenceless child longing for Papa's strong protective arms. Here again was hell, his punishment for running away from his loved Mrs Caroline, from kind Mr Barnes, for all the lies he had told, for not saying his prayers. He shut his eyes and clasped his hands but the words would not come. He could only murmur: "Dear Jesus please help me."

He shivered as the wind penetrated his coat, he must find shelter. He walked warily along the street seeking a warm place to hide away from the terrifying night. In another doorway he saw three huddled children a few years older than himself. About to approach them he halted, daunted by the hostility in their starveling faces. One small ragged girl swore and spat at him. He was clean and warmly clad, a hated alien. Rejected by his own kind he walked away, quietly sobbing.

A passing drunkard lunged at him, grabbing his arm. Uttering a shrill piercing scream, with sturdy shoes John kicked at his attackers' legs. The man yelped and released him. John ran until he stumbled to a halt. He glanced fearfully behind him. No pursuer, the drunkard too befuddled to give chase. In a quiet side road John crouched beneath the covered entrance of a low build-

ing. When fear of pursuit subsided he examined his refuge, illuminated by oil lamps hanging at either side of a brass studded
panelled door. On one panel a large notice warned.

BE SURE YOUR SINS WILL FIND YOU OUT.

John stared. Was it meant for him? He had indeed sinned
while out. On another panel he spelt out the invitation:

KNOCK AND IT SHALL BE OPENED UNTO YOU

He knocked, like many before him receiving no answer, no
opening. Tentatively he twisted the iron ring handle and pushed
hard at the heavy door, peering in. A small chapel similar to the
one at his home, was illuminated by candles. No one there. He
entered, quietly closing the door and bobbing his head towards
the altar cross as he had been taught. He drew a deep breath,
expelling it in a sigh of relief. Silence, no sound of the noisy street
life, the strengthening wind. Peace and safety. Dare he stay? Dare
he not? Here was shelter, not warm or comfortable, the pews too
hard. But if placed together the cushions for kneeling on would
serve as a bed for his small stature. With a guilty glance at the altar
and whispered "Forgive me Lord", in the darkest corner of the
chapel he arranged into a bed the hassocks embroidered by the
good ladies of the parish. Still hard but less so than the pews.
Requesting the Lord his soul to keep he again snuggled under his
coat and slept, safe from the terrors of the night.

His awakening was not so terror free. A nudge from a foot again
caused his genie-like appearance from under his coat, gazing up in
fear at the tall thin black clad figure frowning down at him. A
dark angel come to carry him to hell? No, not an angel, a man
dressed like the chaplain at home. Mr Jordan, a kindly man who
had christened John and always spoke gently when he was taken
into the chapel to share the end of the service, too young to
endure the rites and long sermons which Papa said in his naughty
way would have had him snoring but for the hard discomfort of

the pews. No kindly concern from this man of God, no questioning as to why so young a child was on his own, forced to seek sanctuary from bitter weather. Suffer children to come anywhere other than his neat well-ordered chapel. John saw no emotion other than anger in the long stern face, dark fanatical eyes. The thin indrawn lips reminded him of Nurse Hunt when he displeased her, which was often. And Lady Georgina's face when she looked at him.

"Good morning sir," he piped, innocently beguiling. No beguiling this man.

"Wretched child, how dare you desecrate the Lord's house," his voice loud, harsh, echoing around the chapel.

What was desiccate? Something very bad? "I beg pardon sir, I did not mean to... that word."

"Silence!" thundered the chaplain. As he had asked a question John thought that unjust. But he obeyed, bewildered gaze imploringly meeting the chaplain's darkly intolerant glare.

"Raise yourself," commanded the chaplain. "Come to the altar and confess your wrongdoing to the Almighty, implore his forgiveness."

Bending low to grasp the small offender's shoulders he marched him to the altar.

"Kneel! Clasp your hands, close your eyes and repeat after me."

As John obeyed, the chaplain – 'Ranting Rowley' to his cowed flock – loudly declaimed the confession. In his child's piping voice John deplored his grievous sins and wickedness, justly provoking the Lord's anger and indignation, pleading for mercy and forgiveness. He understood very little, stumbling over unfamiliar words. Seemingly unaware of the child's bewildered incomprehension Ranting Rowley absolved John, adjuring him to sin no more, satisfied he had plucked another brand from the burning.

"Now replace the hassocks and leave the chapel," he

commanded. No interest in the child's bodily welfare, no offer of pastoral care from this unloving shepherd.

Mutely John obeyed, retrieving his coat and escaping through the door held open by the chaplain, vowing never again to enter a church.

But the chapel had served him well. The piercing wind of the night had subsided, a thin layer of snow covered the ground, slowly thawing under the weak morning sun. He thought of the children in the shop doorway, how had they fared in their thin rags? His early maturing conscience troubled him. His own awakening after a night's tranquil sleep had been frightening but unlike them he was rested and in health, also forgiven his sins and wickedness. What new sins would he have to commit today to survive? One sin he had been spared, the urgent desire to relieve himself during his confession. As he now did so in a secluded passageway drain he permitted himself a sinful giggle at the thought of the loud man's horror had he given in to that need while confessing.

John's panicky dash from the drunken man, finding refuge in the side street, had again disoriented him. The streets he now traversed had strange names, Harley Street, Wimpole Street. Thoroughfares of grand houses where passers-by regarded his now dishevelled state with suspicion. No shops or stalls, nowhere to appease his hunger and thirst. Then a good Samaritan among the passers-by. As John stood weary and forlorn a man carrying a basket of bread halted, gazing down with kindly concern.

"Lost your way, young feller?"

John instinctively knew this was a good man, one to be trusted. "Indeed I have sir. I wish to find the park to Knightsbridge."

The man laughed, though not unkindly. "Oho! You are vastly off the track. Tell you what I can do, come along while I deliver these last loaves and cakes, then I shall take you to my shop in Oxford Street, set you in the right direction. All correct with you...what is your name?"

A beatific smile lightened John's woebegone face. "John sir. Indeed I should be very much grateful."

This was no ordinary street child. Taking his hand as they walked the baker asked:

"How comes it such a little feller is on his own and planning to walk so far?"

John had sworn to sin no more. So no mama in a hat shop or ailing.

"My Mama is in heaven and I seek my Papa at the barracks. The soldiers will care for me until they find him." The simple truth as he knew it.

The baker thought this an odd story, but in that time of wars there were many orphans wandering the streets though none as well-spoken and polite as this one.

"Too far for your little legs. There is a shop near mine that delivers dairy food and such to the barracks, has loaves from me. The delivery wagon goes daily. Do you ask the shopman to allow you a seat with the driver. Have you any money?"

About to say "Some ten shillings" John realised this was a large sum for such a shabby child to have. The true story so involved he gave an abridged version. "Some shillings... er... a kindly gentleman gave me for warning him some bad men were about to rob him."

The baker gazed down at the limpidly innocent small face. An odd story but had the ring of truth. London was full of dips waiting to pick the pockets of gentlemen or snatch purses from ladies. He laughed, patting the boy's head. "Such a hero! And such wealth. Offer a sixpence to the driver, that should do it. I will point out where the shop is. Ah, this is one delivery."

He bounded down basement steps of a large house and

banged at the door, exchanging banter with the kitchen maid who told him not to be saucy.

After two more deliveries in a similar manner the baker led John to his shop where customers waited, enticed by the smell of freshly baked bread. After serving them he presented John with two buns, refusing payment.

"I have two lads about your age, ever hungry." Outside the shop he pointed to a shop some fifty yards away. "There you go, little John. God be with you."

Another radiant smile as John clasped the baker's hand in both his.

"You are a very best man. I shall never forget you."

The baker laughed and ruffled his hair "Nor I you, manakin."

The shop was large, outside were suspended dead hares and game birds. Inside a variety of food including dairy produce, eggs, sides of bacon, venison. Unlike the baker the shopman was not amiable, regarding John with suspicion as he made his request.

"I do not allow passengers on the wagon, especially mischievous imps. Hire a carriage or sedan chair." He guffawed loudly at his own wit.

No smile from John. He knew he was mocked but must make the man listen.

"Sir I should be ever grateful, also my Papa. Look, I have a sixpence to pay." He opened a hand to reveal the silver coin he had previously taken from his purse.

The shopman hesitated, not so much for the sixpence as the mention of papa. He might tip handsomely to have his little darling returned. The imp was well-bred so papa probably wealthy. Avarice won, though his reply was still ungracious.

"Make it a shilling and my deliveryman will take you. He leaves here at midday, if you are not here he will leave without you."

Though elated at the thought of the journey, John faced another problem. "Sir, I have no watch and cannot read the time. How shall I know midday?"

In haste to attend customers the shopman waved vaguely.

"St Giles' church clock tells the hour, listen out for it. Almost ten o'clock now, you have two hours." He walked away to attend his customers.

Two hours! A long time to John. Where was St Giles? He must be close enough to hear the chimes. Memories returned of the chapel clock at home. If the wind was in the right way one heard the chimes clearly, other times they were blown over the hills and far away, Bessie had said. She could not read the time but told him that when the two clock hands were together at the top like praying that meant midday or midnight and there were twelve chimes. He could now count to a hundred so twelve would be easy. If he was near the clock he could see the big hand – why were they called hands, because they pointed to the time? Why not fingers? – getting near the small one so he could run back to the shop to be ready for the wagon...to take him to the soldiers and Papa!

He walked towards St Giles, still further from the area his Papa and friends now searched.

Edward Maltravers' party had combined forces, having evidence that John was at last heading in the right direction for the barracks. Edward, Tom and Will scoured both Hyde Park and Kensington Gardens while Caroline, now in her own clothes as they were at the wealthier end of Oxford Street and Bayswater, sat in a shelter in Kensington Gardens, watching the fashionable folk and recalling how in Blackheath she and John had laughed at the more outré. Oh dear little John, why run away, why did you not trust me with your troubles? But she knew in her heart he would soon be found.

Her regard for his father had strengthened over the past days of close proximity. Guiltily she realised he was replacing Charles in her thoughts. Not just regard, but...she must inwardly confess it...love. A more mature clear eyed love than she had at eighteen for Charles, so vastly more exciting and dashing than other men of her limited acquaintance. She had dismissed as spiteful gossip tales of his flirtatious nature, ignoring her father's warning that he lacked depth or substance. Edward had both... Her reverie was cut short by the approach of Edward and his friends. As they dismounted she asked Edward, though from his dejected countenance knowing the answer: "No news?"

Edward sat beside her. "None, nor at the barracks. Tom suggests you and I return to Oxford Street to take some refreshment while he and Will watch here at the gates. Then we stand guard while they have a meal."

"Aye," said Tom. "Will and I are more than ready for a tankard of porter with bread and ham. You are more likely to find superior eating places in Bond Street where Mrs Claremont may wish to see the grand shops."

Caroline assented. Although the sun shone it gave little warmth, she shivered, chilled despite her warm cloak. Noticing this Edward was remorseful.

"I am so thoughtless, you should have been spared this wearying search."

Caroline replied more sharply than intended. "You speak as though I were a fragile flower. Women may lack men's strength but we have as much if not more stamina. So far you have treated me in the same manner as you do Mr Hart and Will. Pray continue to do so."

Edward said quietly: "My apologies, I intended no disrespect. I have the highest regard for your fortitude, your unflinching support. My wife was a delicate lady, I fear I mistakenly judge others..."

Caroline put her arm through his as they walked towards Bond Street.

"I spoke too hastily, you are only concerned for my welfare."

Edward turned to her with a smile of such affection her heart missed several beats.

"Enough of mutual apologies. Now to choose a pleasant place for refreshments and gossip...Good Lord!" He broke off, staring at a fashionably dressed woman emerging from the side door of a gown shop, about to enter a waiting chaise. "Sophie!"

With a guilty start Sophie turned to face him, her eyes wary.

"Edward! You here? Why...What do you want of me?"

Murmuring to Caroline: "My sister-in-law, please excuse me while I have words," he replied: "Not knowing where you were I have not come here seeking you. I would much prefer to have no dealing with you. Where is Robert?"

Sophie shrugged. "I know not and care less. I left him; he expected me to live in a mean Clerkenwell apartment, he may still be there if he has not endeared himself to some hideous but wealthy old crone. My protector found me an apartment above this shop. He will be here shortly so no more questions, I have told you all I know."

Out of consideration for Caroline, Edward kept his fury at bay. In a low controlled voice he replied: "You know far more, so now do I. Believing me dead you and Robert plotted John's abduction, sure he would die at the sweeper's hands. A small child..."

With a startled gasp Caroline drew back as with snake-like swiftness Sophie thrust her face within inches of Edward's, hissing furiously: "Do not dare lay that at my door. Robert plotted it without my knowledge." Moving away and averting her eyes from his contempt she spoke more calmly. "Sooner than bully me, confront your brother at Lancaster Buildings, Clerkenwell. He may still be there, I have no news from him, nor do I wish any further connection with him."

Still controlling anger Edward replied: "I have spoken with the sweeper and know you are equally if not more guilty; Robert is weak, without the wits to plan such a monstrous act." He broke off as an elderly well-dressed portly man strutted from a nearby tobacco and snuff store.

"My apologies for keeping you waiting my dear." To the liveried coachman. "Westminster, Martin." He glanced incuriously at Edward and Caroline. "My apologies for interrupting your conversation. Good day to you sir, madam."

He assisted Sophie into the chaise where she sat staring ahead, her face set with fury. Clicking his tongue at the two chestnut horses the coachman drove off in the direction of Westminster, Edward glaring in frustration after the chaise.

Caroline was again at his side. "A dreadful woman! I can quite believe her capable of such a vile act. To plan the... the disposal of an innocent child entrusted to her care!"

Edward replied with more of self-reproach than condemnation. "Madness on my part to have left Jackie in her care, but as you imply, how could any woman be suspected of such vileness. But she unwillingly provided one piece of information. When Jackie is safe I now know where to find Robert."

Caroline asked fearfully: "You will not use force against him?"

Edward shook his head. All anger spent, now a weary resignation. "No, he is already brought low enough. God knows, Caroline...er...Mrs Claremont, I could find it in my heart to pity him."

"Caroline if you please, Edward. Did we not agree that we are now well enough acquainted, good companions? Your brother indeed deserves some pity for having such a wife." Smiling at him, she again tucked her arm into his. "Now, where are the refreshments you promised me? Then back to the hunt for our elusive little Jackie."

Eighteen

Their elusive little Jackie had wandered even further from them, now nearing the infamous depravity of St Giles. He could see no church but in the distance heard the sonorous chimes, counting to eleven. With apprehension he noticed the meanness of the area he traversed, dilapidated tenements, passages awash with swage, the thin suspicious faces of poorly clad inhabitants. Grimy children furtively lurked in shadows, poised to sneak behind unwary travellers and pick their pockets or steal from barrows while their companions with taunts and jeers distracted the owners' attention. Intimidated by the scowls he received, for though his clothes were dishevelled and grimy they were of good quality, far from those of the inhabitants in this desolate area. John dared go no further, he must return to the shop, wait for the delivery wagon. As he stood, fatefully irresolute, a weak voice greeted him.

"Jacko? That you?"

Fearfully John looked round. That hated name had only been used by the sweeper Billings and his bully son Barney...and one other. Cautiously he approached the thin ragged boy crouching in a tenement doorway. Nothing to fear from that grimy starveling.

"Tad, I hardly knew you. Why are you in this horrid place?"

A racking cough shook the child. When it subsided he said feebly: "Knew you right enough Jacko. What yer doing 'ere? Fought like yer was nice and cosy wiv them grand folk."

John squatted beside Tad. "I was but ran away and have had many strange adventures. You have left the chimney sweeper?"

Another cough shook Tad's skeletal frame. When it subsided he spoke jerkily, taking occasional painful gasps for air. "Not wiv Billings no more. 'E give up the sweeper tride, took up thieving. Chucked me art, said I weren't no good at it. Got 'is own boy fer shoving through winders an I wasn't strong enough ter carry sacks of stuff. Got nowhere ter go, slept in doorways until the watchman moved me on. Gotta place nah, not much but better than the street. 'Ad a crossing sweep pitch, earned a few pence clearing road of muck fer folk ter cross but a boy give me a clout, nabbed me broom. Do some begging but no one gives me nuffin." Another rasping cough, wiping his mouth with a ragged sleeve Tad stared at John with his sore sunken eyes. "'Ow did yer come 'ere? Not fer the likes of you."

John related all that had happened to him since the fall from the chimney, ending: "The sweeper found me in the street and took me in his cart, I got away, then I saw him and Barney taken by the constables."

"Good, 'ope they both swing." Another fit of coughing, closing his eyes Tad leaned back against the door, his breathing loud, rasping.

At a loss how to act John gazed at passers-by, mutely imploring help. Seeing not a flicker of concern on any of the stony faces he turned his attention back to Tad.

"Oh Tad you are ill. Have you eaten today?"

A weak shake of his head. "Not terday, knocked a bun orf a barrer yesdy."

John stood up. "I will get you food, where are the shops?"

"Ant no shops. A market darn yonder, sells most fings. Yer got money?"

Experience had taught John caution. Nothing to fear from Tad but some passers-by had given them hard looks. He said very quietly: "Enough for food. Stay here while I buy some."

A feeble laugh. "Ant likely ter move far. Why yer doin' this Jacko?" Tad was puzzled, never in his eight years had anyone shown concern for him.

John said simply: "You shared your gingerbread with me and I said we were friends. Friends help each other."

"Never 'ad a friend before. Could do wiv gingerbread or even that manky broth what they give us."

"I will get better than that." Noticing how Tad shivered John took off his coat and wrapped it round him before running to the market. At one stall a woman sold broth from a large pot over a brazier. He asked: "Some broth if you please."

"Got a bowl?" she asked. As he shook his head. "Yer needs one. Get it from the stall yonder." She jerked her head to a large stall on which John saw pots and pans.

The stall also had a great variety of wares. Standing on tiptoe John reached over to pick up a thick china bowl, asking the price.

"Six pence," grunted the stallholder, expecting John to haggle, but he did not know how. Noticing his look of dismay the man took up a chipped bowl from the side of the stall. "Two pence. Want a spoon? There, three pence in all. Suit your lordship?" He had intended throwing out the bowl but this infant pigeon made easy plucking.

Thanking him John handed over three pence. About to return to the broth seller he was diverted by the loud voice of a seller of medicines. He joined the crowd of mostly cynical jeering onlookers as the man held up a bottle of brown liquid.

"Here we have a remedy for all ills. Headache? Toothache? The rheumatics? Coughs and sneezes..." He was interrupted by the loud rasping cough of a man standing close to him. "Ah sir, you are suffering?"

"I am," wheezed the man, with another explosive cough. "Life-long sufferer. No cure from any doctor." Sniggers and nudges from the cynics.

"Have a draught," invited the salesman. The sufferer shuffled forward, snuffling and wheezing. Taking the bottle he drank deeply, spluttered, took a deep breath and straightened to his full height. In a clear strong voice:

"God bless you sir! I am cured!"

Jeers and whistles from the cynics, recognising a toad-eater, the mountebank's accomplice. The more gullible, including John, paid sixpence for the miracle cure. If the empty bottle was returned the buyer would receive two pence – if the mountebank and his toady had not moved to another site, as they surely would.

Convinced he had the cure for Tad's cough John paid another penny for a bowl of broth and returned to Tad. He still had a bun from the two the baker had given him. Breaking it into the broth he helped Tad spoon it into his mouth. As he did so the church clock struck twelve. So intent was he John did not notice until the final chimes. A pang of dismay, too late to reach the shop but he could not leave Tad. Tomorrow, when Tad was cured of his cough, they both could go on the delivery cart, wait for Papa.

Tad managed only half the broth, sinking back exhausted against the door. John finished it, his only food since the baker's bun. He had been too excited at the thought of reaching the barracks to eat. After another fit of coughing, persuaded by John Tad took a drink of the magic potion. At first it seemed to work, the rasping of his breath lessened, then Tad vomited into the gutter, his face damp with sweat.

"I better git back ter me room," he muttered. "Git some kip."

"You live here?" asked John, looking up at the drab tenement.

"Nah. Remember where we was wiv Billings?" Too distant

and unpleasant a memory for John, he shook his head. Tad continued: "Well, not in that room, near it is a cellar, mebbe used fer stores or fuel in time past. No one knows I sleeps there free." The talking had tired him. Again his eyes closed. John shook him.

"Show the way and we will go there, we cannot stay here. See the black sky, it will snow soon." Without his coat he shivered, they must move to shelter.

With his own meagre strength he helped Tad to his feet, supporting the frail boy as he directed him to the direst tenement of St Giles At a corner of the building Tad pointed to a small door, the lock of which Tad had wrenched from its rotten wood frame. Fearfully John opened the door, exposing a small cell like room, dimly lit by one small cracked window, abandoned by the tenement owners as too damp and vermin ridden for storage. This was Tad's home, his bed coarse worn blankets, salvaged from the street rubbish heap. Wearily slumping onto them he pulled what once had done service as a hearthrug over himself.

John felt more helpless than at any time during his wanderings. They would have to shelter from the snow in that horrid room. He could not leave Tad while he was ill, Papa would never leave a wounded comrade, would stay by him until help came. When Tad was better they must both go on the delivery wagon to the barracks to be looked after until Papa came to take them home, Tad would be his brother. But how to make Tad better? Another memory of Bessie, after he was ill with spots she said he should eat much to be strong again. He must buy food, none in the cellar, Tad said he had not eaten anything but a bun yesterday. Hurry before the snow came. Taking his coat from the floor where Tad had dropped it he put it on, he would need it in the now bitterly cold weather, telling Tad he would not be long. Tad murmured indistinctly, half asleep.

Outside a few snowflakes were falling. John ran to the market where stallholders were already packing their wares. Quickly he bought bread, cheese, pies, goose fat to spread on the bread. That

would do until the next day. Their drink must be water from the
pump he had noticed in the yard. What else? Gingerbread! Tad
said he would like some. Charging him only one penny for a large
slice, more than enough for two, the kindly woman stallholder
gave him a bag with string handles in which to carry his packets.

"Shopping for your ma, my pet?"

Forgetting his vow to sin no more, John told her Mama was
ailing, his innocent countenance shining with virtue. Then
recalling the darkness of the room he took further advantage of
her good nature to ask where he might buy lanterns holding
candles such as illuminated her stall.

The woman pointed to a stall on the other side of the street.

"There, my duckling. Take care he does not overcharge you,
pay no more than a shilling with candles. And ask him to light a
candle to go in the lantern, phosphorous matches are too
dangerous for a little fellow." She was puzzled, had his mama no
lights? And to send such a poppet to shop in this weather. Later
she was even more bewildered to see the polite well-spoken little
lad, lantern swinging in one hand, food bag in the other, running
towards the most horrid of the tenements. Then she dismissed
thoughts of him as she hastily completed the packing of her wares
before the snow fell in earnest.

Tad was still asleep when John returned. Realising there were
no coverings for his own bed he decided to wait until all the stallholders had gone, then return to pick over the pile of rejected
wares, not anticipating others might have the same idea. The heir
to the wealthy Maltravers estate had to scrabble among the heap
with other desperate tenement dwellers, elfin among them,
pushed, jostled, sworn at. But his very smallness became an asset,
he could wriggle under searching hands to drag away remnants of
carpet and a length of damp-spoilt curtaining, also a large jug with
a broken handle. Too much for small arms to carry at one go, he
secreted the carpet cuttings under an upturned barrow for collec-
tion after dragging the curtaining through the market mire with

one hand, grasping the jug with the other, safely depositing them in the cellar. Snow swirled in the blustering wind as he completed his second journey with the carpet cuttings.

Though exhausted he still had tasks. The food must be protected from vermin, but how? He looked round the room with the aid of the lantern, for which he had purchased extra candles. There were several hooks out of his reach. Ah, a large nail projected from a panel in the door. On it he hung the bag the kindly woman had given him. Going outside into the yard he first swilled his head and hands with the icy water, then filled the jug. Returning to the room he spread out the carpeting, placing a piece over Tad for extra covering, then having reached the limits of his puny strength he lay down to rest until Tad awoke and they could eat. He too fell asleep, to be wakened after an hour by Tad's coughing. Helping him to sit up against the wall John poured water into the bowl for him to drink. Taking food from the bag he shared a mutton pie, broke bread into small pieces and dipped them in the goose fat. Tad managed to eat, drinking more water, then ate a piece of gingerbread. The first proper food he had taken for days. John thought he looked better, mistaking his feverish flush for returning health. Refusing another dose of the miracle cure Tad told John he was a proper green un to fall for that gammon. The cove was a sham, seen him before with the same cove coughing his guts up. The medicine was water coloured by strong smelling brown stuff. Sixpence wasted. The effort of talking tiring him, he lay back on the blankets. John made his own meal, lit another candle from the first and settled himself for sleep, confident that by the morning Tad would be better. His care was not entirely altruistic, John no infant saint. He must make Tad better so that they could take the journey to the barracks – and to Papa.

. . .

Forced by the snow to abandon their search, Edward Maltravers and his party returned to Forester Lodge, Tom Hart assuring the Captain his boy would have found shelter so a search useless until the weather improved. At the Lodge Tom and Will refused to take genteel tea in the parlour, preferring banter in the kitchen with the female staff. Caroline and Edward were alone, no one to comment on this impropriety, that Caroline should be chaperoned. She took advantage of their privacy only to assuage Edward's fears for his small son's welfare, reminding him of John's self-sufficiency.

"Edward, we know that he has survived three nights in good health. He has been seen by several persons."

"But he is little more than an infant!" protested Edward. "Up to today the weather has not been severe, now a blizzard threatens. How much longer can he survive? His money must be almost spent."

Caroline smiled as she recalled the gravely thoughtful child, mature beyond his years. "He was little more than an infant when you last saw him. I can assure you he is now an intelligent resourceful child. How I wish you could have heard our conversations, at times it was as if I spoke with an adult. You would be so proud of him, as I would if he were..." She broke off in confusion.

Longing to reach over and comfort her Edward spoke gently: "His own mother could not have shown more concern, and your selfless unflinching support during our search... I cannot express..." His turn for confusion, then recovering equanimity: "Caroline, when we find Jackie...excuse me if I presume too far, I hope we shall remain friends...that..." He faltered, not a man to easily express his emotions. "Er...Jackie obviously loves you, he also would not wish you to be lost to him...er... us." As Caroline was silent: "Your pardon, I have been too forward."

Caroline hastily interrupted. "No indeed Edward. I have greatly welcomed your company these past days. When Jackie is found I too would be desolated should our acquaintance be at an end." She broke off, her father had entered the room. As Edward stood to bow a greeting, Sir Edwin saw by the happiness shining in Caroline's eyes that he had interrupted a promising tete a tete. Pity, but it appeared his secret hope would be realised. Maltravers also looked well pleased with himself.

Had Tom Hart been present he would have groaned in frustration. Why must genteel folk make such a to-do, not say outright what they desired? He had already done so with the prettiest of the maids, an obliging lass.

John's sleep of exhaustion made him oblivious to the noises of the night, the furtive scrabbling of vermin, the shriek of wind as it penetrated the cracks in the window, and the whimpers, moans and harsh coughing of Tad as he restlessly twisted on his hard cold bed. Not until the wintry dawn filtered through the dirty window did John open his eyes, adjusting to another strange waking, the very worst. By then Tad had fallen into an uneasy sleep, muttering incoherently, his breathing harsh. Now fully awake John's first thought was for the guttering candles. Swiftly he ran over to the lamp to light another from the dying flame. His next task was to refill the water jug. At the door he halted with a cry of dismay, the food from the bag lay scattered on the filthy floor, ravaged by vermin and covered in insects. The pot containing goose grease had tipped, its contents soaking the bottom of the bag, causing its collapse. The food now uneatable, he must buy more. What hour was it? As he cautiously opened the door, peering out to ensure he would not be observed going to the pump, the church clock obligingly struck eight chimes. Surely food stalls would already be serving customers.

The blizzard had blown itself out leaving a couple of inches of snow. John saw with interest that his shoe prints were the only ones, it seemed no other tenant was interested in water. After relieving himself in the corner of the yard, evidently a popular venue as sewage seeped through the snow, he rinsed hands and face, then filled the jug thankful the pump had not frozen. Returning to the room he bent over Tad to see if he still slept. Even to his inexperienced eyes it was obvious that Tad's condition had not improved. John touched his face. Despite the damp chill of the room he was hot, as John had been with the spots and Bessie said he had a fever. Tad too had a fever, he would not be able to travel that day. The thought of leaving him, to travel alone was speedily dismissed as wicked, a bad sin to desert a friend. Bessie had said how wicked of the disciples to let Jesus be taken by the Roman soldiers and Peter to deny him three times though Bessie said he had chopped off a soldier's ear and Jesus put it back again. Nor did John dare ask help of anyone, they might tell the constables who would send them both to Australia to be eaten or to the found things home where they flogged children. He must make Tad better with proper medicine. Near the market he had seen a shop window with large jars of different coloured liquids and the word Apothecary. That was a sort of doctor, one visited him when he had a cough and had given him some nice tasting medicine that made his throat feel better. He would go there with the bottle the sham doctor had sold him, but first he must go to the market to buy breakfast.

Taking the bowl and jug he went to the broth woman, then to a milk seller to have them filled. Back in the cellar Tad was now awake, fretfully whimpering he was thirsty and thought Jacko had took off. John helped him to sit, spooning warm broth into his mouth as Bessie had done when he was ill. It seemed to revive Tad, he spoke more clearly, asking why Jacko was not having any broth.

"I must go back to the market to buy food," said John. "The mice have eaten what we had."

Tad was wise after the event. "Could of told yer so, I never kept no food 'ere." After drinking the milk he said he had to piss, doing so into the jug which John emptied in the yard, washing it

under the pump. He must find something else for that. On his
return Tad stared fearfully at him.

"Yer not leave me Jacko? Gonna die if yer does." Another fit
of harsh coughing, prolonged and alarming to John. When it
subsided he covered Tad with the carpet and curtaining to calm
his violent shivering.

"I vow not to leave you Tad. I must buy food now but will
soon be back."

Tad relaxed and closed his eyes. John emptied the medicine
bottle in the yard and slipped it into a pocket before returning to
the market. By the entrance he incautiously removed the purse
from around his neck to check how much money remained. Malicious Fate again, now in the form of a hulking youth who
violently struck John to the ground, snatching the purse from his
hand. No one moved to stop the theft, the youth too large,
menacing and it was all too common an occurrence in that criminal infested area.

Dazed, John lay in the snow. A good Samaritan among the
uncaring lifted him to his feet, brushing snow from his coat.

"There now little lad. Run home to your mother, she should
not have sent you out alone in these parts."

John wanted to cry out that his mother was dead and also his
father as he had not come to find him, but the man had hurried
off to his employment. Still dazed, for he had struck his head
when falling, John slowly walked to a low wall bordering the
market and sat, staring unseeingly at the stalls and their customers.
He wanted to weep but no relieving tears came. Desolation and
despair numbed him. After his flight from Forester Lodge he had
overcome every obstacle, spent three nights in reasonable comfort,
on the fourth exhaustion made him oblivious to discomfort. But
survival had been possible by the possession of money, he had not
thought how he would survive without it. That time had come,
no money for food not only for himself but also for ailing Tad. He

could not beg, large boys had their pitches and would chase him off. He was too small to rob stalls or barrows, too fearful to pick pockets or steal purses. Already hunger gnawed, so confident of buying more food he did not share Tad's breakfast. Would they now starve to death? In his childish despair and anguish his thoughts turned to the one he loved and trusted.

"Oh Papa," he whispered. "Help me or I shall surely die." The words he had used when in the chimney of Forester House... before rescued from the sweeper by his beloved Mrs Caroline. His confused brain visualised her and Papa together, smiling at him, telling him to be brave. He imagined Papa's voice: "Very soon, my little Jackie."

The vision consoled him, restored his courage. He must think hard how to get money without begging or stealing. What else was there? A memory flash of passing a booth, seeing a woman handing a bundle of clothing to the owner who gave her money. But he had nothing to sell, too cold to part with his coat and no one would buy such a grubby thing. He stared down at his feet. His shoes! Almost new, good sturdy shoes showing very little wear for all his walking, so light of foot was he. Most street children went barefoot, as did Tad.

Taking off the shoes he rubbed them on his coat until they were clear of mud and snow. The ground was icy cold to his tender feet, his stockings had long worn out. Taking a deep breath to give himself courage he ran to the booth, holding out the shoes to the owner. A gaunt sour faced man, eyes as grey and wintry as the sky.

"Please sir I wish to sell my shoes, how much will you give me?"

The man took the shoes, recognising their excellent crafting. He stared suspiciously at John.

"Where did you steal these?"

John responded with a dignity coming oddly from his child's

piping voice. "Indeed sir I am no thief. They were given to me by my...my grandfather, a most good maker of shoes."

The man was still suspicious. "Why are you selling them?"

The simple truth. "I have need of money sir."

The logical question. "Why not get it from your grandfather?"

"I have lost him sir." How John wished he could find kindly Mr Barnes, he would help him.

The man took his words to mean the grandfather was dead. The story rang true, the boy not the usual street child. Yet another orphan struggling to survive. The shoes indeed well made, quality wear, might fetch a guinea or more, not in this mean area where he purchased goods from penurious inhabitants for the least money, he had a sales pitch among wealthier folk.

"I will give you one shilling," he offered.

John was dismayed. A shilling would not last two days, as well as food he must buy medicine for Tad's cough from the doctor's shop. He recalled leaving Mr Barnes a crown for the shoes. How great a sum that now seemed. Not to be gained from this man but he must try to obtain as much as possible.

"No sir, please. See, they are very well made, they are worth a lot more. My...grandfather made shoes for very important people, some were dukes."

Not such a little innocent, decided the buyer.

"Very well, one shilling and sixpence, I shall not sell for much more, they are worn."

"Two shillings and sixpence if you please sir." Desperation had made John an expert haggler. So was the buyer, but after more offers were refused he settled for two shillings and sixpence, realising he might sell them for ten times that price. Grudgingly, for he disliked being outbid and by a child, he gave John the coins.

Clutching them John ran off. He could not leave Tad too long but must buy medicine and food. First the doctor shop.

He entered the apothecary's where a young man mixed powder in a bowl. Again a look of suspicion at the grubby urchin.

"What do you want? No mischief, mind."

"Please sir, are you the apoth...the doctor?" Even to John he seemed too young.

The youth, in fact sixteen, acne scars adorning a sharp featured countenance, close set evasive eyes indicative of an untrustworthy character. He said loftily: "If you mean the apothecary he is out." Though he did not think the brat wished a visit he gabbled the prescribe information: "If you require a visit his fee is seven shillings and sixpence plus the cost of medication. I am his apprentice."

John knew the word apprentice, he and Tad had been apprentices to the chimney sweep. This young man was training to be a doctor so must be wise. John too young to recognise an untrustworthy character.

"Please, I wish a medicine to cure a cough. How much does it cost?"

The apprentice had no right to sell medication but often did so, pocketing the fee. He was bound to the apothecary for seven years, his father paying two hundred pounds. He received no pay, only his board and what small allowance his tight-fisted father doled out. All other sums he could contrive when the apothecary was on his visits were very welcome, the jars diluted with water, powders with chalk to disguise his thefts.

"I can give you a draught of honey, liquorice and balsam, vastly efficacious, it will cost you one shilling."

One shilling! John's heart sank. That would leave only a shilling and sixpence and he had to keep a shilling for the journey to the barracks. Taking the sham doctor's bottle from his pocket he offered it to the apprentice.

"Sir, that is too high. Here is my own bottle, will that make it lesser?"

The apprentice hesitated, the apothecary might return at any time now and he would be in deep trouble if caught supplying medicine.

"Very well, as a great favour I will supply a draught for eight pence."

"Four pence," said John firmly.

Grabbing the bottle the apprentice filled it three quarters full from a large container. The mixture a rich golden brown, aromatic.

"There, that is all I can give you for four pence. Where is your money? Hurry now." No way to speak to a customer, however small.

Thanking him John gave sixpence, waiting while the apprentice doled out two pennies from his pocket. Strange, thought John, why did he put the sixpence in his pocket and not in the money box on the shelf behind the counter? And why did he put water into the container and shake it? His puzzled stare was answered by a glare from the apprentice.

"Why stare so? Be off with you."

Putting the precious medicine bottle in his coat pocket John hurriedly left the shop, almost colliding with a grey-haired sad looking neatly dressed man about to enter. Murmuring "Your pardon sir" he ran back to the market.

Staring after him the apothecary entered the shop, asking his apprentice: "What did the child want?"

The apprentice's sluggish brain managed to summon up a lie. "Impudent brat asked for a free liquorice stick, I sent him on his way sharpish."

The apothecary eyed the youth with shrewd suspicion. "Make sure you do not oblige anyone with shop items or your father will find you back on his doorstep." The father would not welcome the idle oaf, probably thinking two hundred pounds a small price to pay for getting rid of him. Two hundred? grieved the apothecary. He should have demanded three.

The child...polite, well-spoken. No guttersnipe. A memory

stirred, a notice... The apothecary shrugged. A busy day, more calls to make for this was a sick season. He dismissed thoughts of the child. Soon he was to be reminded of that brief encounter by a doctor acquaintance, and to hear of his apprentice's lethal misdemeanour.

NINETEEN

At the time John Maltravers haggled over the price for his shoes, his father and companions were searching the opposite end of Oxford Street. Earlier, beset by troubled thoughts Edward begrudged the time taken over breakfast, the obligation to converse politely with Sir Edwin made more endurable by his host's genuine concern for John's welfare. Sir Edwin knew better than Edward the hazards facing even the most hardened street child. In his profession he heard of children murdered by their drink-sodden parents or sold for a few shillings to work in mines, perilous manufactories and, like John, to chimney sweeps. Boys as well as girls snatched from the streets for abuse in brothels or shipped abroad. Though keeping his counsel he secretly feared the child would not, could not, survive alone among London's many predators.

When alone with Caroline, Edward confided: "Earlier I sensed Jackie is in trouble, that he called to me for help. I hope it is my own fear giving such gloomy thoughts."

Concealing her own pangs of anxiety Caroline tried to console Edward.

"Your love makes you sensitive to his need. But Edward, that he could reach you means he has survived last night's severe weather. Have you still the impression he is in trouble?"

"Less so." Edward hesitated as though anticipating incredulity. "I... I sent him a thought that he must have courage, we shall soon find him."

Caroline took his hand, holding it to her cheek.

"That would have comforted him."

Edward kissed her hand, longing to embrace her. But the phantoms of his Harriet, her Charles hovered between them. Remorse and guilt engulfed him. Harriet, was he so inconstant? No, he excused himself. Despite many temptations, during their long separations he had remained faithful. True, not only from virtue, a fastidious nature and fear of disease restrained him. A long celibacy he now hoped soon to be over. His acquaintance with Caroline, brief though it was, made him realise his love for Harriet had been as for an exquisite work of art. If Caroline consented to be his wife she would be a staunch companion and friend, sharing his ideals. Harriet forever a treasured memory.

Their preparations made, he joined Tom Hart and Will, in good spirits after their breakfast with the household staff, Tom still refusing the stuffiness of the breakfast room and genteel conversation with Sir Edwin, having to mind his language.

"We must again enquire at the barracks," said Edward. "You and Will, please Tom. Mrs Claremont and I will question Oxford Street shops and stallholders. We will meet about eleven for refreshments at the coffee shop near the Pantheon."

"Aye Captain." Then in an attempt to lighten the Captain's woeful countenance: "Enquire at the Pantheon, Jackie may have found employment there as an elf or sprite in their masquerades."

A wry smile from Edward. "Puck or Ariel?" To himself, or in a tableau depicting the slain children of Macduff? My pretty chick? He shook himself free of morbidity. If indeed he and Jackie were in thought contact, for his son's sake his thoughts must be of optimism and encouragement.

Leaving the chaise in the stable yard of an inn, asking the ostler to care for the horse – Tom had taken Major and Will the second chaise horse – Edward and Caroline enquired of all stall-holders and shopkeepers. No success until they came to the baker's shop, the amiable owner having returned from his delivery round.

"I usually have a lad for deliveries," he explained as he opened the shop. "But he has the influenza, a great deal of it about. How may I be of service to you, madam, sir?"

Edward asked if he had seen a young child – again showing the miniature portrait in his watch. The baker gave a great beam of delight.

"So you are his papa! Indeed sir I have seen the nice little fellow, only yesterday I came across him while making my deliveries. He told me how he sought you. I brought him back here, advised him to enquire at the food shop a few doors hence, they make daily deliveries to the barracks. He could go with the wagon. I intended to ask at the shop how he fared but being on my own was kept busy with customers and baking."

Edward fervently shook his hand. "God bless you sir! He seemed well?"

"Somewhat dusty, lost and forlorn, but he perked up when told of the delivery wagon, and a couple of freshly baked buns... no, no sir," as Edward held out a shilling. "It gave me pleasure, polite little lad as he was. I wish my own were as courteous."

Leaving him with renewed thanks Edward and Caroline called at the grocer shop where they received not so amiable a welcome. The shop owner confirmed that a boy had asked for a ride to the barracks with the delivery wagon.

"I told him to be here at twelve midday but the brat never come. I decided it was some sort of mischief."

"No mischief," said Edward. "For some reason he believes I am at the barracks. I cannot understand why he did not come." He fought back that earlier premonition of Jackie in trouble.

Sensing his fear Caroline hastened to dispel it. "He may have mistaken the hour, at his age one has no idea of time and no means of telling it."

"I told him to listen out for St Giles church clock," said the shop owner, now deciding more civility was advisable to genteel folk. Possible customers?

"St Giles!" exclaimed Edward. "Surely some distance for a child to walk."

The shop man shrugged. "You can hear the chimes clearly enough – hark, there it strikes eleven."

Caroline turned to Edward. "He may come today. After we have taken refreshments with Mr Hart and Will we can return here at noon. If Jackie comes earlier I am sure this gentleman will detain him until we arrive." Her most charming smile had the morose shop man agreeing to do as she requested.

They returned before noon. At twelve the wagon departed, without Jackie.

After leaving the apothecary shop John bought food in the market. Bread, cheese and a pork pie. Later he would return with jug and bowl for milk and broth to break the bread into. He must spend wisely. One shilling to be kept for the delivery wagon, of the remaining one shilling and sixpence he had spent four pence for medicine and three pence for food, after buying broth and milk he would have only nine pence to last perhaps two days. No housewife with a large family could have fretted more than John as to how he would manage if Tad needed more medicine or could not travel by the second day. They would also need more candles. At dusk he must again scrabble in the street rubbish pile for extra bed coverings and something to use as a piss pot as Tad called it.

Returning to the tenement cellar with the food, he found Tad still asleep, a restless whimpering sleep, breathing still harsh. Until he awoke John dare not leave to buy broth and milk for fear of vermin dining on the unattended food. Realising his own hunger he broke off a piece of bread and ate it with cheese, washing it down with water. The pork pie must be kept for their main meal.

As Tad slept on, John wearily sat on the carpeting, leaning against the damp wall. His bruised head ached, his throat was sore. To keep awake he chanted the rhymes Bessie taught him and the poems Mama loved. That made him sad but no tears came. He looked round the dimly-lit squalid smelly cell, recalling his warm nursery at home, even of the room at Forester House where he was tormented by George and Rebecca. Walks with his beloved Mrs Caroline. Now this horrid place. But children like Tad lived in these places all the time, how...?

An explosive outburst of coughing from Tad, so violent it shook his meagre body. As he wiped his mouth on his hand John saw blood there, the coughing must have hurt his throat. He showed Tad the bottle of cough cure.

"I got it from a true doctor's shop," he said. "It has lots of good things, honey, liquorice and...and other things." One of the other things the apprentice forgot to mention was opium. Had the apothecary been present he would not have prescribed without checking the patient's symptoms, nor would he have sold such a potent draught to a small child, to an adult he would given strict instructions on dosage. Not to be given to young children, a small spoonful only at Tad's age. Tad took a gulp.

"Tastes real good," he said feebly.

John was greatly relieved. Soon Tad would be better. How could he know, child that he was, that Tad's ailment, his consumption, had gone beyond recovery, his constitution too enfeebled by years of neglect, abuse, semi-starvation, his lungs damaged by soot clogged chimneys. He lay weakly back on the blankets.

"Please keep awake," begged John. "I have to buy broth and milk for our meal, you must guard our food from the mice."

Tad murmured what John believed an assent. Again he took jug and basin to be filled. More money from his precious hoard, but enough for tomorrow's food, then Tad would be well enough to travel. As both sellers were busy with customers he had to wait to be served. He hurried back, the day was cold with fresh flurries of snow, the broth cooled rapidly. As he opened the cell door he heard a flurry and scamper. Tad was deeply asleep, mice and rats disappeared into holes and crevices, the packages of food John had left on the carpet beside Tad ripped open, scattered, spoiled.

Trying not to weep John shook Tad in an attempt to wake him. He slept on, his breathing deep and laboured. The broth almost cold, John drank it from the bowl, thirstily for his throat was very dry. When Tad woke he would have to buy more, if the woman was still there. If not, they would have bread broken into the milk, nothing more until the morning. They had only money for two days frugal meals. And candles, without them at night the room would be black, and the rats would come....

With a piece of the carpeting he swept all the spoilt food away from their bedding into the furthest corner, where several holes in the walls were visible. He recalled seeing Will filling holes in one of the stable walls with plaster he said would harden.

"Stop them pesky rats getting at the oats," he told Jackie. "Dare not use poison for fear the horse will get at it." Would the doctor shop sell rat poison? But he had not enough money, not even for more four penny cough medicine. He pushed bread hard into the holes. That would stop them until he and Tad could leave.

The vermin greatly enjoyed the unexpected feast rammed into their homes.

Tad slept on. Soon the market would close, no more food until the next day. Running out he bought candles and bread which he buttoned into his coat while rummaging in the rubbish pile. A large pan with no handle would serve as a piss pot. As he was about to pull out another length of stained carpet a tall thin

man with a face as sharp as a ferret cuffed John's head and tore it
from him with oaths still foreign to John but which he recognised
as bad words. The man gave him a violent shove which sent him
sprawling.

"Be off wiv yer, thieving little bastard."

Head ringing from the blow John scrambled to his feet and
scurried away, waiting behind an empty stall until the man
departed with his spoils. He crept back, the ferret man had taken
most of what might be of use. Not everything, John triumphantly
dragged out a small blanket, a child's, worn thin but still protection from the coldness of the cellar's filthy brick floor. Also a stout
cudgel-like piece of wood, with that he could scare off vermin,
human as well as animal. How he would have the strength to
wield the club against an attacker did not occur to him.

The flurries of snow promised another storm. His arms
aching from their load John wearily returned to the tenement in
time to light another candle from the dying flame of the one in
the lantern, rashly lighting another, placing the lantern nearer
their bedding, the cudgel within his reach. Papa said that in the
army he slept with a pistol under his pillow, not cocked or he
might have blown his own head off. Mama had begged him not to
speak of such horrid things but Jackie laughed, for he knew Papa
jested.

Tad stirred from his deep sleep, whimpering. He struggled to
sit up, John used his small strength to help him.

"Thirsty," he murmured. "Real thirsty."

John poured milk into the bowl and held it while Tad drank.
Then another fit of coughing, this time John was alarmed to see
more blood. Emptying the remaining milk into the bowl he ran to
the pump to fill the jug with water, damping an edge of the
blanket to clean Tad's face.

"Oh Tad," he grieved. "I fear you are very ill. I will go now to
the doctor's shop and ask him to come." The fee, he thought.
Seven shillings sixpence with medicine extra. But surely he would

come to see a very ill boy? The apothecary's philanthropy was not destined to be tested, Tad responded with an urgent spurt of energy.

"Nah, no doctor. When one come ter me Ma, Pa said as 'ow 'e killed 'er wiv the medicine. Charged 'im ten shillings, week's wage. They kills yer, does doctors. Give me more cough stuff." He took a large gulp, then exhausted by his vehemence lay back on the blankets. He closed his eyes, then opened them, staring pleadingly at John. He whispered feebly but urgently: "Yer will not leave me Jacko? Not alone? I fear something dreadful." He held out his arms, John hugged him, Tad's first embrace since his mother died.

"I swear not to leave you Tad. But you must eat. Look, I have broken bread into the milk, it is soft so will not hurt your throat."

Tad wearily turned away his head. "Not 'ungry, very tired. Not scared no more...feel kind of...safe." His last words. Again his eyes closed.

John managed a few mouthfuls of the bread and milk, he too felt weary, his head throbbed, his throat hurt. Not daring to leave the remaining food in the room, on shaky legs he walked unsteadily to the door, placing the bowl outside. Returning to his bed he picked up the medicine bottle. A dose might make his throat better. He gulped down a large dose. Yes it was good, soothing. Another dose? No, only enough left for Tad tomorrow. Placing the bottle beside Tad he lay down, pulling his coat over him and snuggling up to Tad for mutual warmth. Murmuring "Please Jesus make Tad better" he drifted into an opium-induced semi-coma, one arm stretched over Tad as if to comfort and protect the dying boy.

The following morning Anthony Barnes left his daughter's Vauxhall home early, embracing her and his clamorous grand-daughters. His son-in-law, a barrister's clerk, had already set off for Gray's Inn to arrive before his ill-tempered employer whose only pleasure was finding fault, justified or not. Anthony Barnes was very happy to be his own man, though finding much to reprove in his ham-fisted apprentice. The addlepate was still absent, poorly with the influenza claimed the small sister who brought the news, rewarded with a halfpenny for toffee. Barnes suspected the youth was kicking his heels with other idle apprentices but did not worry over much, apart from having to open the shop and no one to mind it while he visited clients. He preferred his own company, his own thoughts uninterrupted by the banal chatter of Samson. Samson! No Delilah would wish to trim the greasy locks of that pimple-faced gawk.

As he crossed Battersea Bridge stallholders were setting out their wares. He slowed Pegasus to a walk as he watched, as always astonished at the tawdry items for which folk paid extortionate sums... He pulled Pegasus to such a sudden halt the horse gave a whiny of indignation, snorting his displeasure as Barnes hastily dismounted, dragging him to a stall. The owner had just placed on it a pair of small black leather shoes, buckles glinting in the weak rays of a wintry sun.

"Where did you get those shoes?" demanded Barnes, his voice made abrupt by his alarm, his fear.

The stallholder reacted with unsurprising indignation.

"No need for that tone, they was purchased fair and square."

Barnes modified his tone, he must not antagonise the man. "I beg your pardon, but I recognise the shoes. From whom did you acquire them?"

Slightly mollified the dealer saw no reason to conceal the truth, unlike some other deals he made. "A young child yesterday, said he had need of money."

A young child! Surely John. Barnes asked urgently: "Where was this, I mean the place of purchase?"

Again no reason for concealment. "St Giles market, I purchase goods there twice a week." Then impatiently: "Why these questions? I have work to do, customers waiting."

Barnes held out an imploring hand. "Pray, a moment more. It is of the utmost importance I assure you. The child, describe him please."

The stallholder frowned in concentration. "Aye, unusual customer. Small, four or five, well-spoken..."

"Fair hair, blue eyes?" urgently demanded Barnes. The stall-holder nodded. "Does he live there do you know?"

The man shrugged. "That I cannot tell you. He seemed too well-spoken for the area but must live nearby. Ask other stall-holders there, they may know."

Barnes thanked him. "I shall buy the shoes. What price are you asking?"

"A guinea and a half."

"Certainly not, half that, fifteen shillings."

"Certainly not, I can easily get a guinea for them. See, other customers are taking an interest in them."

In too much haste for further haggling Barnes gave a guinea for his own shoes. Putting them in his pockets he rode pell-mell to Chelsea, living up to his name Pegasus almost flying.

Over breakfast that morning Edward and Caroline despondently discussed how to proceed in the search for Jackie. The previous day they had abandoned their fruitless enquiries when the snow fell. John was not on the delivery wagon, nor had he reached the barracks. They had walked towards St Giles questioning passers-by, residents; no one had seen him. Like Fortunatus in a story Edward had read as a child he seemed to have donned a cap that made him invisible.

Now their spirits were further lowered by a no less gloomy Sir Edwin looking up from a letter to inform them that Lady Georgina and dear Rebecca would return late afternoon with her sister on a reciprocal visit. Heroically resigned he quitted the breakfast room to make arrangements with the housekeeper.

Caroline told Edward that her aunt was only marginally less disagreeable than her mother. She sighed ruefully.

"I pray I shall have the courage to withstand their combined shock and horror when they learn I have taken part in the search for Jackie." She added more defiantly: "Not that they could forcibly restrain me, I am not a child."

Edward was equally down-hearted. "My own fear is that our search will end in failure, no word of Jackie since the storeman saw him two days ago..." He broke off as a maid hurriedly entered the room.

"Ma'am, sir, there is that shoemaker person in the hall asking very particular to see you urgent like."

Exchanging glances of hope renewed, Edward and Caroline hastened to the hall where Anthony Barnes waited in great agitation.

"You have news, Mr Barnes?" Caroline asked eagerly. "Oh, your pardon, please come into the morning room."

In too much haste to impart his news Barnes dispensed with the usual formalities.

"I have news indeed." He took the shoes from his pockets. "Yesterday a child of Jackie's description sold these shoes, the same I gave him, to a buyer in St Giles market who put them for sale on his King's Road stall where by the greatest good fortune I saw them. The man thought the child too polite and well-spoken to live in the area but advised asking stallholders there."

Edward clasped Barnes' hand. "We had almost given up hope. Now again you bring us great news, your name should be Gabriel!" Realising the import of Barnes' words he added: "But St Giles? He intended going to the barracks, how came he to that infamous place?"

Caroline's excitement was unabated. "No matter how." She added impulsively: "We must go there at once, I shall again borrow Betty's gown and shawl, you the footman's..."

"No Caroline," implored Edward. "St Giles is no place for a lady. I shall go with Tom and Will..."

Caroline indignantly interrupted. "Indeed you shall not, Captain Edward! The search for Jackie has been as much mine as yours, do not dare deny me the happiness of being present when he is found."

"Your mama, your aunt.." weakly protested Edward, recognising defeat, welcoming defeat as he wanted Caroline by his side – then and always.

Refraining from retorting "A fig for Mama" Caroline replied: "Mama does not return until late afternoon, by then we shall have found Jackie." With a gasp of self-reproach she turned to Anthony Barnes. "How thoughtless of me. You bring us precious hope and we leave you standing while we argue. May I ask a maid to bring you breakfast? As you hear, Mr Maltravers and I are eager to start our search."

"Thank you," replied Barnes. "I have breakfasted and must open my shop, I expect customers." To Edward, "please take the shoes and inform me when the little fellow is safe. I have every confidence such a gallant lad will have found a way to survive even amid the rookeries of St Giles."

Clad in the under-footman's walking out clothes Edward summoned Tom Hart and Will from the kitchen. Apprised by Betty the servants knew of the fresh search for runaway Jackie, so cruelly tormented by horrid George and Rebecca. Giggles behind hands at Edward's disguise, whispers that he cut a deal more handsome figure than did Frederick, they would happily walk out with him and more than walk.

Tom had instructed Will to prepare the chaise, as they joined Caroline he advised Edward: "Best not stable the chaise in St Giles, the villains there will rapidly descend on the horses and slaughter them for meat on sale in the market, use the chaise for firewood. We should leave it at the hostelry near the Pantheon though..." He looked at Caroline. "'Tis a fair or should I say unfair walk from there to St Giles..."

"I am a grand walker, Mr Tom," Caroline assured him. "These past days should have proved that."

"Aye. But the pathways and roads are muddy and with the thawing snow ankle deep in dirty slush. Your...er...Mistress Betty's gown will be greatly soiled."

"Then I shall hitch up my skirts." Caroline did so, revealing sturdy walking boots and brown stockinged ankles. "I trust the sight of my ankles does not distress you, gentlemen?"

Edward bowed, responding with mock gravity. "Indeed ma'am I assure you my sensibilities are unstirred."

Hello, thought Tom, the nearest I know the Captain come to a naughty remark.

I have hopes for him yet. The lady has succeeded in destarching him.

They set off, Will driving the chaise with Caroline as passenger, Edward on Major, Tom on the second chaise horse. Though the sky no longer threatened snow, as Tom predicted the night's fall had been churned up by traffic into a muddy slush. Leaving chaise and horses at the hostelry they continued on foot towards St Giles, Edward and Caroline, her arm tucked into his, leading the way. Not to arouse curiosity, much as they wished to do so they did not hurry, occasionally pausing to glance at the wares in shops and on stalls. These were fewer as the area became meaner, the inhabitants furtive, menacing. Street urchins lurked in the shadows awaiting the opportunity to rob. Though clad in servants' clothes Edward and Caroline were clean and respectable, normally prime targets, but Edward's lean athletic build, Tom's bulldog sturdiness and even Will's youthful vigour provided Caroline with a formidable bodyguard. As they approached the crumbling leprous tenements of St Giles Edward groaned.

"Surely Jackie cannot be here! How is it possible humans live in such squalor? I have seen better in the poorest parts of India."

"What choice have they?" replied Tom. "Country folk are often not paid in the winter months, they must seek work in the towns. It will get worse as more manufactories are built and more folk flock to London. Have you not seen the cartloads of families coming from the country? They have to live somewhere, they have very little money so are crowded several families to a room by avaricious landlords. They have too many children to feed, turn them out as soon as old enough to work or thieve...gallows meat." He turned to Caroline. "Beg pardon ma'am, I grew up among such folk, know their suffering."

"The wretched place must be demolished," angrily retorted Edward. "Decent housing, the children educated..."

"Aye, it will come sometime," predicted Tom. "The villains will take refuge elsewhere. But not in our lifetime Captain."

"Do not wager on that Tom. And I have a son..." He broke off as the narrow street opened onto a wide area of stalls illuminated by lanterns. "Ah, the market." He quickly decided on a strategy. "You and Will speak to the stallholders at the far end, Tom. Mrs Claremont and I at this side."

Saluting, Tom set off with Will. Edward and Caroline moved among the stallholders nearest the tenements, receiving negative responses. A great many waifs haunted the market, mostly awaiting the opportunity to steal. Then hope. A woman selling broth from a cauldron over a brazier confirmed that a small child had indeed bought broth over the last two days, though she had not seen him that morning.

"Did you see where he took the broth," asked Edward. "Where he lives?"

She shook her head. "I be too busy to watch where customers do go. Cannot be far as the broth would get cold...ah, I do recall the first time he had no bowl and I did tell him to purchase it from the stall yonder." She indicated a stall on the opposite side of the street. Thanking her they crossed to the stall. The owner did remember, such a little feller to be on his own. Also bought a spoon but no, he had not noticed where he went.

"A bowl and spoon!" exclaimed Caroline to Edward. "What an experienced little housekeeper! His several purchases of broth proves he has found shelter."

"In one of those foul buildings," groaned Edward. "But why, when he had arranged a ride on the delivery wagon?"

"We will know when we find him," replied Caroline. "See there, a seller of gingerbread, Jackie may well have been tempted." With Edward she hurried over to the stall. The kindly woman well remembered her small customer.

"Laden with food parcels he was, poor lamb. Shopping for his ailing ma. I gave him a paper bag with strings so the little love could carry them."

"That was kind of you," said Caroline. "Did you see where he went with his parcels?"

The woman was eager to help. "Yes indeed. He asked about the lantern I have here and I directed him to the stall yonder. Then later I was vastly surprised to see him with his lantern and food bag trotting towards the most horrid of those buildings." She pointed towards the tenement, as she said the most horrid. "Such a polite child but perhaps his family has come down in the world."

Edward glanced down at his borrowed clothes. Yes indeed they had. With expressions of sincere gratitude he passed the woman a crown piece.

"Bless you sir, no need for that, but times are hard so I shall not refuse." She slipped it into her apron pocket. "The child is a relative of yours and the lady?"

To prevent an outright lie Caroline merely bent her head as Edward replied: "He is, we have sought him a long time. With your help I pray our search is nearing its end."

"Amen to that," said the woman. She wrapped a slab of

gingerbread and passed it to Edward. "Here sir, take him this with my love and best wishes."

Summoning Tom and Will, Edward arranged a thorough search of the tenement the woman had indicated. Though he would have preferred that Caroline was spared the surely vermin infested fetid squalor of the wretched dwelling he dare not leave her unattended, nor did he believe she would have taken kindly to such unwanted protectiveness. A determination to match his own, he foresaw many a battle of wills should they... So different to the placid acquiescence of Harriet. A twinge of guilt as he recalled the times that had irked him, wretch that he was. But he had never shown her his impatience, truly loving her gentle nature. He resolutely put aside regrets, to concentrate on finding their son.

They mounted the rickety ordure reeking wooden stairs to the top floor, three rooms each with two or more families surrounded by their meagre possessions, some with ragged curtains providing minimal privacy. While Tom and Will made enquiries in one room Edward and Caroline faced the overt hostility of the people huddled together for warmth in another, their questions answered in surly monosyllables. No, not seen no child like what he said. One woman in a ragged gown, a child at her breast, another whimpering at her side, glared hatred at Caroline.

"Git art an leave us be, ant nuffink 'ere fer the likes of you."

With tears in her eyes Caroline begged Edward: "Please, can we do nothing for her...and the others?"

"Not yet," quietly answered Edward. "Only with money, but I swear such poverty will become a public scandal." He dropped silver coins on the child's blanket, she seized one, crowing delight at its brightness. With no sign of pleasure the woman nodded her thanks, transferring the whimpering baby to her other meagre breast in the hope enough milk remained to satisfy its hunger.

They left the room to join Tom and Will on the landing, they were less emotional about the condition of the families, nothing new to Tom. They had no more success on the lower floors, shouted drunken abuse from one pock-marked cripple who raised a crutch at Caroline in an obscene gesture. Tom prevented Edward from an explosive reaction.

"Leave him Captain. The cove is fuddled with the drink."

"Money enough for that!" bitterly commented Edward.

"You know the saying about blue ruin...gin that is ma'am. Drunk for a penny, dead drunk for two. His only escape, has to beg for a living such as it is."

Edward flung down a florin, the man scrambled after it. More gin, more escape.

They descended to the basement. One room only, cleaner than the others used as a communal kitchen. A large fireplace in which a small log fire gave out some heat, worn pans in the hearth. The only means tenants had of heating water, soup or broth, if lucky to fry sausages. Cleanly and neatly dressed the housekeeper sat at a scrubbed table embroidering a handkerchief by the dim light of two candles. Asked if a child answering John's description lived in the tenement she replied no, but she had seen a child she did not recognise at the yard pump quite lately.

"Plenty of brats up to mischief round here, not that there is anything to steal." As Caroline bent to admire her embroidery: "A way to earn my bread, wretch of a husband went off leaving me with three young ones. Girl now kitchen maid at the inn, one lad in the dye manufactory, the other helps or hinders on a market stall. I buy bargain lots of kerchiefs and silk threads from the market, embroider the kerchiefs for sale at four pence each to the gentry in Bond Street."

Edward bought three for Caroline, giving the seamstress a florin.

Sick at heart they left the room. Again failure, Jackie was not in the building.

"We shall have to try the other tenements," said Edward despondently.

Will had prowled round the outside of the building, poking among rubble as though expecting to find some evidence of Master Jackie's presence. He would have ignored the small door, taking it to be a storeroom or fuel cellar. But the bowl outside?

Pushing the door slightly open he peered in. A scrabble as rats and mice disappeared to their holes. The interior barely discernible, but enough to see... Sickened, with a piercingly anguished cry Will stumbled back to the yard. About to cross the road to another tenement Edward halted, assailed by sickening dread as he saw Will's anguished face.

"What is it Will?"

Will ran up the steps. Too shocked to speak he pointed a shaky finger to the cellar door. Leaving Caroline to comfort the now weeping boy Edward and Tom cleared the steps in an instant. Edward threw the door wide open, shedding more light into the cellar. The vermin had been deterred from their prey by the guttering candles, now the last flickers died in the gust of wind through the open door. A choked cry of horror from Edward. Two children lay there, the older boy's eyes open, unseeing, the smaller child huddled against him, seemingly lifeless.

"Oh God," Edward cried out in anguish. "Please, not Jackie!"

Alerted by his cry Caroline now at his side, her arm round him, with heart-broken sobs gazing at the huddled children.

At the sound of Edward's voice a feeble stirring of the bedding. A small tremulous voice piped: "Papa? Oh Papa?"

Edward stood transfixed as the child shakily stood. His heart sank. No, this pitiful grimy scrap could not be Jackie.

As he had when taking his first steps the child tottered on shaky legs to Papa with outstretched arms. Into his opium fogged brain filtered the memory of their favourite game. He feebly piped:

"God for Harry..."

With a great shout of exultation Edward swept his son into his arms, tears of joy unashamedly streaming down his face.

"England and Saint George!"

TWENTY

The boy who for five days precociously survived the perils of London, condemning himself to a filthy disease-ridden slum to tend a sick friend, by an unwitting overdose of opium mercifully easing Tad's inevitable end, now reverted to infancy. He nestled in his father's arms, cooed over by Mrs Caroline. Still befuddled by opium he did not immediately recall Tad. As memory foggily returned he called weakly to where Tad lay.

"Wake up Tad. Papa has come to take us home." No answer. Gazing imploringly at his father he whispered: "Oh Papa Tad is very ill, he must be made more better."

Edward looked over to where Tom Hart knelt by the small wasted body, his impassive face disguising compassion, rage. After gently closing the child's eyes he stood, with a shake of his head signalling to Edward that Tad was dead.

"Tad is no longer ill," Edward murmured to Jackie. "His suffering is over."

John misunderstood, believing Tad had recovered. "It was the cough stuff." His own cough came, harsh, rasping. Wiping his nose on his jacket sleeve he again reverted to infancy, whimpering:

"My throat hurts, I want some of the cough stuff that made Tad better."

Tom Hart took up the bottle and sniffed the contents. "Hell fire! It reeks of opium. The children have drunk nearly a bottle between them, a miracle Jackie survived."

Unaware of Tom's meaning John drowsily croaked: "Bottle not full, the apoth... doctor's prentis gave me only four pence of cough cure." Another harshly racking cough shook him. Gasping for breath, again he whimpered: "Thirsty, want... some... of the... cough stuff."

"He is ill," murmured Caroline, stroking Jackie's flushed face. "We must return at once to the Lodge, send for our doctor."

"I shall fetch the chaise," offered Will. He had joined the general rejoicing, furtively wiping away unmanly tears.

"Thank you Will." Edward turned to Caroline. "Where is your doctor? Will may be able to collect him."

Still caressing John's head Caroline replied: "Mr Hardy but he is visiting relatives. Your acquaintance Mr James Black is covering for him."

"I understood he was to be surgeon at St Thomas' Hospital?" queried Edward.

"That will be next month, but he also joins Mr Hardy's practice in Welbeck Street..." Caroline paused, then with animation: "Oh, that is easily reached from the hostelry."

"You wish me to call on Mr Black, Captain?" asked Will, anticipating Edward's instruction.

Now recovered from emotion Edward was able to give decisive instructions. "Please do so and ask him to come here. If he is out leave a message that he is needed with the utmost urgency at Forester Lodge. Then return here so that we may take Jackie to the Lodge and prepare him for Black's arrival." Edward put a hand on the boy's shoulder: "my deepest gratitude for my son's life. Without you we would never have found him." To himself: Left to die alone amid this filthy squalor, undiscovered for who knows how long, as would the other child had Jackie not been with him, sought by us. Who would have searched for that sadly neglected unloved boy? How many others had perished, unknown, unsought?

Flushing deeply with pleasure at the Captain's praise, with stammered words of thanks Will hurried from the cellar.

Edward again looked over to where Tom stood by Tad's bed. He asked Caroline,

"would you object to holding this grimy smelly brat a brief while? I must speak with Tom."

"Very willingly. No smelly brat, our Jackie restored to us by a miracle." Caroline knew Edward did not wish Jackie to hear what he had to say to Tom. Tenderly she took Jackie from him, the drowsy child nestled against her as if she were his own mother. "I shall be very soon," she whispered.

Joining Tom, Edward stared down at the dead child, unable to speak for the compassion that engulfed him. He had no need for words, Tom knew his Captain.

"You wish me to wrap him in the blanket and take him to the undertakers so that a decent burial can be arranged. He cannot go in the chaise with your boy and Mrs Claremont, I will carry him on the horse, he is no weight, a starveling."

Edward now found words, his hand on Tom's arm. "My excellent friend Tom! Yes, the least we can do for the pitiable child. I shall arrange with the undertaker that he should be bathed, suitably clad, his coffin taken to the Hall for burial in our Chapel grounds so that Jackie may visit him."

Thus in death Tad received more attention than in all the eight years of earthly life.

The chaise arrived without James Black, out on a visit. The servant assured Will she expected him shortly and doubtless he would call at Forester Lodge with all speed. A lucrative call, cynically thought Edward as he and Caroline conveyed Jackie to the chaise for the journey to Forester Lodge. Though not enamoured of Black he believed him to be a good doctor. How he wished for a medical man the like of his Cape friend Mark Halliday who, with his healing herbs, had saved him from an amputated leg, possibly death.

Edward's trust proved justified. Despite his lack of reassuring bedside manner James Black was an excellent doctor. Before his arrival Jackie had been bathed, his hair cropped to rid it of lice. All this he endured with silent lethargy, the events of the past days taking their toll of his small frame. His cough worsened, he was feverish, confused by the effects of opium.

On hearing of the cough cure taken by the children, James Black expressed incredulity. "Obviously it hastened the other child's end, as it would your boy had you not found him in time. I know the apothecary, Mr Daniel Mason. I briefly assisted him after completing my apprenticeship. I will tell Mason in no uncertain terms that his feckless apprentice is responsible for the death of one child and a close call with another. We shall see how long the lad's apprenticeship lasts. No telling how many other lives his thieving has endangered."

"And my boy?" asked Edward, less interested in the apprentice's fate than Jackie's welfare. "Is he badly affected by the opium?"

"Unlike the starveling street brat his constitution is sound. He has a grievous chill and may ramble awhile but I have no doubt as to his complete recovery."

And so it proved. For two days Jackie tossed restlessly in his fever, tended by a nurse recommended by James Black. Edward and Caroline were frequently at his bedside, hearing with incredulity the feverish rambling account of his adventures, his night in the stable, the afflicted lady, his escape from Billings, the very vast fat lady he locked in her own house, the angry church man, Tad, shoes...cough stuff...

James Black frequently called to check on his progress. Though disliking children as much as he disliked most of humankind, thankful his marriage had no issue, he admired the way Jackie endured his suffering uncomplainingly, with none of the usual grizzling and whining he so detested in patients young and old. No gentle compassionate healer, Black's unemotional ministrations proved effective. On the third morning Jackie greeted his father with a feeble but chirpy: "Good morning Papa."

Edward sent a prayer of thanks to a God he had believed indifferent to human misery and suffering. Gently he stroked his son's face.

"Good morning Jackie. I am vastly happy you look so well."

With an effort Jackie sat up in his bed, hands to his cropped hair.

"Do I now look like a boy, Papa?"

Edward stroked the head of his shorn lamb. "You do indeed Jackie. A fine handsome lad."

A solemn dignified response to match his new status. "Then if you please sir I wish to be known as John, Jackie is a baby's name."

Lifting him from the bed Edward hugged his precious, precocious brat.

"From hereafter my son John. Am I still allowed to kiss you?"

John returned the hug, covering his father's face with damp kisses.

"From hereafter and ever and ever, Papa." A serious look. "Or should you wish me to address you as sir?"

Edward laughed. "And bow? Save that for your tutor, son John."

Another two days and John was well enough to return to his own home in Richmond. Much rejoicing for Lady Georgina, appalled on her return to find the wretched child again an unwelcome resident, also his father and companions. And with that tradesman creature Barnes a constant visitor her home no longer her own. Sir Edwin somewhat mollified her with assurances of the respect and admiration of their acquaintance on learning that her family had been responsible for the rescue of the lost Maltravers heir, her home a sanctuary for the ailing child. That she took no part in the rescue, had resented his sojourn in her home, even planned to turn him away, were truths unspoken by Sir Edwin, pulling down a shutter on his shrewd judge's mind. Tact also prevented him suggesting that in due course the wretched child could well be her grandson. He allowed himself a wintry smile at the thought of her reaction.

No rejoicing for Edward and Caroline at the separation. Since John's rescue they had more leisure to further their acquaintance, escaping the trite conversation of Lady Georgina, her sister and other genteel lady visitors by taking walks on the river paths or in the Physic Garden. On the day before his departure they strolled through the Garden, Edward not only discussing his plans for the estate but also his determination to bring pressure on Parliament to ease the suffering of the deprived classes, to enforce laws on child labour, laws flouted by too many employers. How did Caroline think they should proceed, and urgently?

Her heart quickening at the "we", Caroline responded with seeming equanimity:

"Perhaps a letter to the Times citing Tad as an example. Just think, Edward, at six years sold by his father for a few guineas to be illegally apprenticed to that Billings fiend, half-starved, flogged, then callously abandoned to fend for himself. Ailing, he would have died alone and friendless, starving in that loathsome cellar, prey to vermin, his body perhaps never found, unmourned, had it not been for the devoted attention of a young child easing his last hours."

"Surely an account to move the stoniest heart," agreed Edward. "We will write it today!" Despondency replaced enthusiasm. "They may not print it, there are so many similar instances. But we shall continue our campaign..." He broke off. Tomorrow he would leave the Lodge...and Caroline. True, she had agreed to their future relationship...when the requisite time had elapsed. To hell with convention! He could not wait months, he needed Caroline by his side – now and always. He must speak boldly or risk losing her for ever. Intolerable prospect!

"Caroline," he said abruptly, holding her shoulders so that they faced each other. "I wish we should marry, will you have me? Forgive my lack of flowery words, I am a rough soldier but speak from the heart."

No affectation of maidenly coyness. Caroline responded with heart-felt simplicity.

"I wish it as much as you. But Edward we cannot yet think of marriage. Your loss, mine..."

"I want you with me," protested Edward. "Not just on occasional visits. My dearest Caroline, what are we to do?"

They were silent, resuming their walk round the almost deserted Garden. Two children ran past, with their swinging bags of school books, hurrying to their classes. Naughty boys, thought Caroline, Late for their lessons, I hope not the strap from their teacher... Teacher! Her turn to halt as wonderful hope filled her heart. Dare they? Dare they not!

"Edward, you spoke of a house for the teacher of your estate's school. Is it ready and have you appointed a head teacher?"

The import of her words pierced Edward's gloom. "My steward writes that the house is ready, all it requires is the head teacher, we have educated people willing to give some time to teach on subjects they are competent in, but need someone to supervise, to plan.... But Caroline, such flouting of propriety! Your parents...your precious mama!"

With a wave of her hand Caroline dismissed propriety, dear Mama. "I have previously announced my wish for a more useful life, to teach. My thoughts were then of the ragged school. Such vapours from Mama at that, she had determined my fate as her meekly acquiescent companion. I expect no opposition from Papa. Have you not seen how he takes every opportunity to leave us alone? He has you marked as a son, and Papa in his quiet manner usually has his own way."

"And you are his true daughter!" Edward made a gallant sweeping bow. "Ma'am may I offer you the post as head teacher at Maltravers school? The annual remuneration one hundred pounds with excellent free accommodation. The house is at a respectable distance from the Hall. You will be well chaperoned by your personal maid and housekeeper. That will prevent any scandalised gossip."

Caroline's eyes widened in mock disbelief. "Scandalised gossip sir? Fie! Are you not respected as an honourable gentleman?"

"I am indeed ma'am," replied Edward with a virtuous smirk.

That settled, now more mundane matters. Caroline asked, "am I to take my meals with the family?"

"That is a requirement. At present the family comprises myself, Tom Hart and a few guests, one of the most honoured will be Anthony Barnes whom Jackie...er... John has adopted as grandfather. We are so deeply in his debt. John will join us for dessert."

Mock outrage. "Fie sir! How is John to learn the manners of a gentleman if he is excluded from your table except to partake of a little fruit and bonbons?"

"Ma'am," feebly protested Edward, scenting defeat. "He is too young. We often have matters of importance to discuss, tiresome and fidgety for a child."

"I predict that child will listen in silence, absorbing everything, regarding us with solemn eyes, speaking only when spoken to which I shall do often." Caroline emulated her mother's imperious tilt of the chin. "If he does not dine with us nor do I. My affection for John equals that which I have for you."

Edward also with a show of dignity, "Ma'am, am I not to be master in my own house?"

Caroline bobbed a curtsey. "Indeed you are sir. An enlightened master not enslaved by convention. A kind, considerate master thoughtful not only for his estate workers but also for those dearest to him. John worships you, he will model himself on your example."

Edward sighed, signalling surrender. "As you wish. I trust that in due course you will not also insist on squalling infants joining us at table?"

A toss of her head. "You presume too far sir." Then relenting as Edward made as if to protest: "But I promise you, no squalling infants at the table."

"Thank you. The teaching post is of course a temporary one..."

Caroline showed no mercy. "There again I beg to differ. If as you assume my status is to alter I shall still wish to teach...though not neglecting my other duties. I shall appoint an assistant."

Edward took her in his arms. "I see I have caught myself a tartar! What an exciting partnership we shall have!"

Caroline returned his embrace. "Your sensibilities are still unstirred, sir?"

"Very much to the contrary." Edward hastily released her. "Come, we must summon the courage to inform your parents of our plans."

"I am to be a gallant Captain's wife, I fear not the furious winter's rages of my dearest Mama."

Edward replied in kind. "She shall not bring us like chimney sweepers to dust." Chimney sweep, he pondered. But for Caroline's family... and yes, admit it, Lady Georgina's imperious dismissal of Billings' claim that John was his apprentice, his child would have suffered Tad's fate. Weep, weep indeed.

. . .

Edward and Caroline weathered Lady Georgina's wintry rages.
Even Sir Edwin Forester expressed some surprise at the uncon-
ventional plan, taking Edward aside for his assurance as a
gentleman of his honourable intentions. Edward gave the assurance, privately relieved his future father-in-law had not sought
the same from Caroline. Did the learned judge truly believe
women incapable of seduction? Surely his vast reading had not
overlooked the many temptresses throughout the ages... Delilah,
Jezebel, Helen whose face had launched a thousand war ships,
Anne Boleyn who by her refusal to grant Henry her favours
outside marriage had changed a nation's religious faith. And the
mythical Eve, her tempting of weak-willed Adam doomed
humankind to suffering and death. As had the equally mythical
Pandora's box? Edward thought it best not to remind Sir
Edwin.

It was agreed that he should accompany his daughter to
Maltravers Hall after Edward sent word the house was ready for
occupation. Edward planned a letter would be sent within the
next two days.

Sir Edwin then had the unenviable task of pacifying his lady.
The young couple were affianced. A splendid match, one to raise
envy in all the unmarried daughter ridden mamas of their
acquaintance. He then found sanctuary in his study, leaving his
dear lady to brood alone, to accept she would have a wealthy
highly respected son-in-law – and a ready-made grandson albeit
one who detested her. A very percipient child, decided Sir Edwin.
No more taunts from George and Rebecca, John an honoured
family member with awe-inspiring protectors in his father and no-
nonsense Tom Hart.

Edward and Caroline found sanctuary in John's room. Now
out of bed, still somewhat wan and not too steady on his feet he
was on the mend and eager to return home. He had been gently
informed of, and had deeply grieved for Tad's death, vowing to
visit and talk to him every day in the chapel grounds. Now he

snuggled between Papa and Mrs Caroline on the window seat, hearing their news with wide-eyed delight.

"You will be my new Mama?" he whispered to Caroline.

Caroline hugged him close to her. "Soon, my love. Would you like that?"

"Vastly much." John's face screwed up as if in painful thought. "Lady Georgina is your Mama. Does that mean she will be my Grand Mama?"

"Why yes...your step-Grandmama."

"Step? Like the wicked stepmother in stories? And George and Rebecca, are they steps too?"

Caroline laughed. "Yes, your step-uncle and aunt."

John closed his eyes against visions of taunting faces, blows, threats, lies. "Oh if you please I do not wish step uncles and aunts. They hate me and say bad things that are not true."

"You will rarely see them," Edward assured him. "I shall not invite them to our home, only Sir Edwin, you like him, do you not?"

John smiled, he much liked the kindly quiet spoken judge. And his guinea had helped him survive those dreadful days. "Oh yes, another Grandpapa. Anxiety entered his voice. "Will Nurse Hunt be at our home, Papa?"

"No indeed. What, a great fellow like you with a nurse? As I promised, you shall have your own room and attendant."

"Tildy if you please Papa?" Another thought. "And...and if I may please, Will? He is my friend and we clasped hands on it."

"It pleases me greatly," Edward assured him. "I could not have chosen better. When you are stronger I will arrange a tutor, Mrs Caroline will help with your lessons until such time."

John smiled up at Caroline. "As did my other Mama. And... and," again the fear. "Will Uncle Robert and Aunt Sophie be there? They forbade me my friends."

"No, I assure you, they will never trouble you again." Edward spoke with controlled anger. He could never forget or forgive their vile treachery, betrayal. Sophie no doubt the instigator, Robert had not the wits. She would drift from one wealthy lover to another until her beauty faded. Then what would be her fate? He cared not. But Robert, weak hopeless Robert. When first hearing of the pact with Billings, now with his oafish son awaiting transportation - heaven protect the heathens - Edward wanted to kill him, willing to bear the mark of Cain. Now he wished never to see him again. But though detesting him he could not leave him destitute. The annuity would continue once he knew Robert's Clerkenwell address. Lancaster Buildings, Sophie had disclosed. Have lawyers Harlow and Stanford sniff him out there, arrange for an increased annuity then dismiss Robert from his life ...if possible. Am I my brother's keeper? Unfortunately yes. Edward was no Cain.

The following morning found Edward and his party prepared to leave Forester Lodge. Tears, kisses and hugs between John and Caroline, she and Edward having made their temporary farewells more privately. Sir Edwin wished them God speed, Lady Georgina retired to her room with a headache. Confined to her room Rebecca watched the departure from her window. Putting her fingers to her nose she stuck out her tongue, unaware her governess had entered the room until she felt the cane across her legs.

Well wrapped, John sat in the chaise, Papa's arm round him, Will driving. Tom as outrider on Major. Tom was well content leaving stiffly formal Forester Lodge for the informality of Maltravers Hall. All boded well; the Captain would have his Mrs Caroline, the boy mending fast though he would never forget his experience as a climbing boy, his days as street urchin among the squalor of London's worst rookery; in a vermin-ridden cellar tending a dying boy, his first lesson in the obligations of friendship.

Amazingly well he had acquitted himself, a true son of the Captain. A likeable brat but a sight too precocious. Agreed, book learning he must have, but equally he needed the Captain's guidance – and his if the Captain permitted – into normal boyhood. His friend Tad never had that, poor little wretch. Now in his coffin, sent from the undertaker to the Hall chapel to await burial. A permanent reminder to the Maltravers of the dire poverty they had witnessed in London. The Captain was determined to remedy that. Good luck to him and other crusaders trying to stem the tide of industrialism soon to engulf London and other cities. Vast wealth for a few, misery for the many they exploited for miserly wages. Tom knew he and Mrs Caroline would have to work hard to keep a bridle on the Captain's idealistic schemes. A true innocent for all his courage and learning, open to exploitation by those taking advantage of his good heart and generous nature.

There would be plenty of sparks in that marriage, both strong-willed but they would rub along better than most. Happily ever after? Damnably dull that would be, but the deep affection between those three…and himself, God willing, would ensure joys outweighed sorrows. What more could one hope for in an imperfect world?

ACKNOWLEDGEMENTS

To Katharine Smith of Heddon Publishing who, despite a burden of work, took on the publication of a novel by an unknown author. To Simon Hatchard-Parr for his evocatively haunting cover design, Esther Harris of Bookollective for her Marketing and PR skills, Mark James of Author Sales Ltd for Amazon publicity and Andrew Ross for attending to finance.

And a special thank you to my editor, Logan Lewis-Proudlock, without whose unstinting work in arranging the aid of the aforementioned, 'Innocents' would still be floundering after its disastrous encounter with a previous publisher.

To my friend Christiana Horrocks for her encouragement and support.

To Lyn, Juliet and other staff members of Kathleen Chambers House for their help and encouragement during very difficult months.

ALSO BY SHEILA RAINEY